POTTER'S STAND

Charles Sage

D1521882

Special thanks to my editing team: Greg Vokoun Trent, Julie Ward, Dave Buick, Mrs. Sage and Mom

CHAPTER 1

With the temperature change, the fog grew and clung to the base of the terrain. The peaks rising above them and passing at just over 100 knots corresponded with the red of the iPad a terrain warning. Nosing down to the highway, he pointed toward the snow squall and stole a quick glance off each flank…

They were still there.

The two Little Birds had held fast to their formation just past the rotor disk through the last squall. He inhaled, his heart rate and breathing had slowed since they first formed up on him and since his first fruitless efforts to shake them.

The old Gazelle helicopter's ancient instrument cluster wasn't certified for flight into the reduced visibility, but he was well past being concerned about such legalities. The iPad and the Foreflight program and the synthetic vision gave him all the information he needed to be safe, if not legal.

The old man had considered, if only for a moment, diving into the base of the fog and continuing past the terrain warning into the red of the display and into the sudden, explosive crump of metal and plexiglass. That maybe then he could take one, or both, of the bastards with him.

But he had passengers and he had people who cared about him and he had responsibilities, so this wouldn't be so dramatic. Besides, he assumed they had some kind of high cover calling out obstacles ahead, the way they dropped back to a still tight trail when he ducked below the high-tension lines and weaved the pylons.

The best he could think to do, was put down on the beach at the city park and make it as public an event as possible. Someone would get video on a phone, someone would get it out to the world what happened next.

"I can't shake'em, guys," Bob said, crisp and stolid into the headset and through the intercom. "Like I said, I'll put it on the lake shore right next to all those new ritzy condos and at least there'll be witnesses. I'm too old to run, but if you're so inclined I'd recommend you each go different directions and make it as tough on 'em as you can."

There was only a murmured response from the three men as they watched the small egg shaped AH-6 helicopters glued in such close formation off either flank. The men were kitted up for a fight, but they would be terribly outnumbered if there were troop carrying helicopters nearby.

The highway veered more directly south as Bob picked up the railroad tracks and then the shoreline. They flew into more light snow that grew in intensity until, soon, one could only see the surface of the lake directly below and only milky white and grey and streaks of snow glancing across the plexiglass bubble. Bob followed the moving map and the artificial horizon on the Foreflight display and broke out of the squall as he intersected the beach shoreline. The ugly blockiness of the new condominiums grew darker and darker out of the murk, until the snow was finally gone and the details of cheap architecture was fully revealed.

"Get ready!" He couldn't help but yell into the intercom as he pulled into the flare, but really, yelling didn't help.

The grey and green camouflaged helicopter flared as aggressively as Bob could in one last hope of getting the Nightstalker helicopters to overshoot. It was no good, the Little Birds settled, seemingly effortlessly beside him. A large flock of Canada Geese flushed off the beach toward the condos and Bob noted that two MH-60 helicopters were landing outboard of Little Birds with troops dismounting before the doors on the Gazelle were even open.

The Little Birds were airborne again quickly, giving the troops room to safely maneuver toward the Gazelle and the AH-6s took up opposing orbits low overhead.

Just as his passengers finally opened the unfamiliar door latches of the Gazelle and stepped out past the skids, they realized they were surrounded by operators with weapons pointed in. It was an L shaped containment with Gazelle's occupants backs to the lake, where, of course, the concentration of the operators' fire would converge.

No cross fire, just a kill zone.

The men carefully placed their hands on their heads as they ducked beneath the rotor disc as the turbines wound down. Bob cut the fuel and electric before slumping a little as he took off his helmet.

It was over for him now, all of it. But he'd done it, done his part. Lured the advanced Army helicopters away with his decoy, so the Sheriff and the real Tom Potter could get away.

*   *   *

In the first week, Tom had taken stock of the cache. It was deep enough that it was much warmer than the outside, and as the snow continued to accumulate, there seemed to be additional insulation. But the snowfall brought its own concerns. First, he realized, if he didn't periodically keep the door cleared, it would be difficult, or worse, impossible to open with snow weight. Of course, Tom's father had thought to ventilate this northern cache, but how did that work?

One morning, Tom looked at the two opposing ventilation shafts and paced them off outside. On each side of the cache he came to snow covered hollowed out stumps that, when cleared of snow, he could lift.

Inside he found a ventilation pipe with a chimney cap on it. Upon further inspection of the hollowed-out stump, he realized his father had *modified* it. There was a series of baffles screwed inside and holes drilled around the stump. Tom could only figure that it was to disperse the heat signature from the ventilation system to thermal surveillance, like a suppressor on a rifle using baffles to disperse the sound. That would be something his father would think of.

His father had thought of everything, really.

Tom remembered what his father said, too. The quote from General Patton; *Fixed fortifications are monuments to the stupidity of man.* Or something like that.

So, despite all the shelter, all the provisions, all the... *comfort*, that it provided, his father never meant for it to be a long-term shelter.

Tom would use it as designed, but he had to play the weather. He knew they were still out there, watching, waiting to find some sign, some track. He would rest his sprained ankle for a while until it felt comfortable to move, then, he would move during snow falls. He had a good pack he could provision for weeks at a time, more with the snares and occasional hunting with the suppressed HK-416. But he had to always consider ways to hide his tracks, and in winter, snowfall and weather were his best bet.

When he did range out, he would live in a series of quinzhees and snow caves for a few nights at a time, always mobile. What was the word his father always used? *Agile.*

Yes, he would have to master that.

For now, as his ankle healed, the cache was his home. When his father stocked it, it was for three people. Now it was just him. Thirty cases of MREs alone, if he could get by on one a day that would last him a year. But that wouldn't be healthy. There was a fair amount of canned food, and dehydrated stuff. All kinds of different vegetables and fruit.

There were spare clothes, a couple of winter ponchos, extra BDUs and polypropylene long underwear. Spare packs and mountain bags. Glow sticks and batteries of several varieties. There was even a spare set of snowshoes, which was good, because the binding on his left one had broken. He had re-laced it in a fashion that would work but was not really efficient.

Three sets of woodland camouflaged Gore-Tex rain gear, and plenty of long thermal underwear.

His father had left a little collection of books, too. A comprehensive Air Force survival manual. A book titled "Never Say Die", which was apparently the Canadian Air Force survival manual. A well-worn Ranger's Handbook. Another digiflage copy of the Bible. Homer's "Iliad" and "Odyssey". A couple of combat medicine books he was eager to crack into. He knew the books were left mainly for him, like the ammunition was left mainly for Jane.

He tried to lose himself in this inventory and in the little library and in the Bible. Then he wasn't dwelling on thoughts of Jane, or his father, or the Sheriff or all the men who he'd seen that had rallied to help him and then he wasn't thinking about how very alone he felt.

*   *   *

Sheriff Grant Taylor pulled the sleeve on his sweater back to look at his watch, just as the prosecutor walked in the glass doors on the other side of the fountain. He looked harried, which in itself wasn't particularly unusual.

"Get caught up in something, Joe?"

"No, I, ah… didn't want to come directly here."

"What do you mean? Your office is a street over."

"This is the second time we've met here." Joe looked past the fountain and around at all the offices and the big bank on the east entrance. He looked unsettled.

"It's been a couple months now, Joe. I think we're OK." The Sheriff sipped at his coffee with a reassuring smile, but that didn't help Joe.

He laid his parka across the back of his chair and motioned toward the café.

"Sorry, Grant. I gotta get a hazelnut latte."

The Sheriff laughed a little and sipped his coffee again.

"Take your time, Joe. I'm actually off today. Had an orthopedic appointment this morning."

Joe hurried anyway, waited restlessly for his order and returned as fast as he could without spilling the nearly over filled mug.

"They always fill it too full, that's why I get it to go and put a lid on it. And if I get fancy stuff like that it helps keep the foam out of my mustache." The Sheriff offered.

Joe tried to smile as he set down his mug, then rearranged his parka behind the chair so the thick coyote ruff wasn't bunched up behind him. Sitting down, he spoke immediately.

"All of my suits regarding the War Powers Act have been denied, all my Freedom Of Information Act requests have gone unanswered. Any federal contacts I have, don't have time to talk to me and don't return my calls."

The Sheriff nodded.

"What have you heard about the disposition of Bob and the guys on his helicopter?"

"Nothing, they aren't showing in the system. No one will talk to me about any of it."

Joe paused and looked down at the decorative swirl in the foam on top of his latte.

"They're coming for us, Grant. They're coming for all of us. Everyone who participated in getting that kid lost."

The Sheriff didn't even bother trying to smile. He just leaned in a little across the table.

"You are part of the legal system, you did everything up and up. You're safe. The posse all took precautions. No cell phones, no license plates, no loose lips. Markdale and I are at the greatest risk, I could see the FBI trying something on us, but that's about it."

"It won't just be two of you that pay for this, Grant. It will be all of us. It may take time, but they have that and funding on their side. That's how they always win. They wear down the little guys."

The Sheriff inhaled and looked at the fountain.

"Grant, last week I got a call from a buddy who's with a JAG reserve unit in Maryland. Went to law school together. Told me he'd be out my way taking part in an exercise, said we should get together. Have you heard about this, this big exercise they're doing in Montana, Idaho, Wyoming and Utah?"

"'CRYSTAL HELM', I think they're calling it? Yeah, I've had some generic bulletins come across my desk. I guess JADE HELM was already taken." Taylor laughed and sipped his coffee.

"This is really serious, Grant. When I talked to my buddy he was telling me there were like seven or eight battalions involved. Guard and Reserve units all from the east and west coast. That's like seven or eight thousand troops. He said most were MP units and something he called Seaburn or something."

"That would be C-B-R-N, Joe. In my day it was called NBC, Nuclear Biological Chemical. These days we just have to over complicate everything including acronyms. I think its Chemical Biological Radiological and Nuclear... or something like it. And exercises and deployments like this don't mobilize a whole unit, Joe. It won't be seven or eight thousand people."

"Yeah, my buddy was pretty cavalier about it, too. Said it had to do with pandemic response and *community support*. Said we'd have to get together because he thought he might wind up in town. I tried calling him back a couple of times and now he's not returning my calls either."

The Sheriff shifted in his chair and leaned back.

"I imagine he's pretty busy."

"Oh, undoubtedly. This wasn't a scheduled exercise, this wasn't anything he had been prepared for in advance. And this is like the inverse of what the Chinese did in Tiananmen Square. But there they brought troops in from the country side to suppress rebellion in the urban area. All these units are coming from big urban areas, none of our local units are involved, in fact some are being deployed to some token operation on the Southern border."

"People went all kinds of sideways in Texas over that one JADE HELM exercise, Joe. Military conducts large scale exercises all the time."

"It was an acronym, you know."

"What was?"

"JADE HELM, the military came out and said so a few years later. I forget the JADE part, but HELM stood for Homeland Eradication of Local Militants."

"Oh, bull." Grant smirked. "Where did you see that?"

"I found it online on my burner laptop, I'll get you the link, it's a reliable source. And I've been reading all about PERSEC and tradecraft like you told me, Grant."

The Sheriff sighed and leaned his elbows on the table.

"Joe, I always told my kids: Reading books makes you smarter, reading the internet makes you dumber. I think the feds will be back, but it will be low key and they'll make an example out of a few of us. They aren't coming to take over the county."

"You know what I think, Grant?" Joe was suddenly more agitated. "I think a lot of these things start out as *exercises*."

Sheriff Taylor leaned back in his chair and crossed his arms across his chest, suddenly feeling a little unsettled himself.

*   *   *

Alone.

The aloneness was starting to creep into him and that surprised him most. All his life he was alone. His father had tried so hard to be there for him when he could that it really seemed to have the effect of pushing him more distant. And Tom couldn't really connect with people his age, and he'd never had a girlfriend.

So, being alone should be something to which he was accustomed. And back before everything came apart, back in the world the way it was, really, he had come to relish being alone.

Why would it start to creep in to bother him now? How long had it been? Weeks for certain, many weeks. Months? When had they gone on the run? Sometime before Thanksgiving, but he wasn't sure of the date. He had thought about looking at the GPS, it had a date on it. And he could count the MREs that were missing from the cases here in the cache to know how long he had been here, one a day.

But it was better to bury such thoughts as they didn't matter. It was better to keep busy with the routine.

There was waste of which to dispose.

The avalanche shovel that was next to the entrenching tool on the shelf was good for removing the snow to get down to the earth, and then he could use the E-tool adjusted, pick like, to break the first inches of frozen soil, then fight with the persnickety nut on the tool to reset it to a shovel configuration to bury his MRE wrappers and cans and biological waste that he collected in a large bucket with a lid that he assumed his father had placed there for such a purpose.

He had found numerous elk and deer trails nearby that seemed to be used regularly and he reasoned that the heat signature of something buried there would be mitigated by the normal travel of the animals. And he stayed close to the cache and used a pine branch he had cut to try to roughly cover his tracks as best he could, but he didn't know if that really helped in the snow or if he was just making it more obvious.

One of the first nights he had been there he had been startled by the crunching snow of the approach of many foot prints. He had steeled himself behind the .45 he had taken from the FBI man and had his HK strapped across his chest. His plan was to empty the pistol and transition to carbine, just as he'd been taught by his father and the bastards wouldn't take him, not after all this.

With his head he had raised the hatch on the cache and he leveled the pistol. Activating the weapon mounted light he saw a sea of glowing eyes bobbing and looking at him.

His finger had slid to the trigger as his thumb clicked the safety off and he lined up on the eyes closest to him.

And he remembered.

Men's eyes don't glow.

Switching off the light, the eyes all simultaneously disappeared. Thumbing the safety back on he laughed to himself and proceeded to talk to the herd of mule deer that had paid him a visit. Their eyes glowed in the light and their heads shifted as they took him in from different angles, cautiously, curiously trying to assess what this bright light was that suddenly appeared before them. They or the elk or both passed through nearly every night. He stamped the sound of their crunching hooves deep into his consciousness and imprinted it on the subconscious telling himself to awaken if it ever sounded different.

And every time he heard it, he knew there was something out there he could see that he could talk to, just to talk.

Today's special task was to zero the FBI HK-416 he had taken. He'd paced off a young jack pine that was just about 25 meters from the mouth of the cache. Breaking a low branch and jabbing an empty MRE bag through its stump, the label made a decent target and would let him see where it was shooting.

It was a low overcast with a misty ground fog coming off the snow as it melted in the little warm spell. Overhead ISR shouldn't be a problem, but just in case he would shoot from inside the cache, with the muzzle well back from the opening to reduce the thermal signature.

His father taught him that a 25 meter zero was the same as a 250 meter zero and he figured that was about the farthest he could really shoot. Long distance shooting was Jane's thing, not his.

But wait, was that zero just for iron sights or would it work on the Eotech equipped 416? There was no one to ask and it wasn't covered in the Ranger Handbook. Well, he knew if he was on at 25, he'd be close at 100. He wasn't in this for a fight, he would be avoiding contact at all costs, especially now.

Stacking up cases of MRE's to provide a stable shooting platform, he rolled up his jacket on top to rest the carbine. Taking time to properly insert foam earplugs, and let them slowly expand in the cold, he knew even suppressed it would probably be loud, and there would be overpressure in the relative confines of the cache.

He snuggled in behind the stock.

Lining the ringed red dot on the center of the MRE label, Tom thumbed the safety off and his finger went gently to the trigger. Pressing it slowly, the carbine cracked and bucked lightly. Holding the trigger for the follow through, he released to the reset and realigned the sight without looking for the first hole.

He put three rounds into the tree, then looked out cautiously. The suppressed weapon seemed loud to him and he'd been so careful about noise for so many weeks, he imagined someone, somewhere must have heard it.

Satisfied this must just be his imagination, he emerged from the cache with the 416 at a low ready. He smiled when he saw his target. Three holes, almost touching. The carbine shot well, it was just up to him to do the rest.

Tom's ears suddenly caught something on the wind, his senses heighted, like those of any hunted animal. He crouched. Cupping his left hand behind his ear, he heard it a little better. A distant, sorrowful wailing. Not human, he thought, but he couldn't quite place it.

Thinking a moment, he assigned it the far-off caterwauling of a mountain lion. Another being, sometimes hunter, sometimes hunted, alone in the wilderness.

*　　*　　*

The abatis had long been blasted to splinters, but the smell of fresh pine hung even over the fresh snow cover. As Sheriff Taylor entered the perimeter of the cabin, he stepped over the crime scene tape that drooped under the weight of snow. The wrecked DHS helicopter was gone, but the blood stains in the doorway were still there. The FBI had just abandoned the scene. Inside it smelled damp and musty and was void of the life an active home maintains.

He didn't know what he had hoped to find here, he just hoped he'd know it when he saw it and he did.

Under the big chair in front of the wood stove he saw the corner of a book.

Reaching down and picking it up, Taylor instantly realized it was Jeff Potter's cherished Bible, the one the FBI used to label him an extremist.

Tom was still out there, as far as he knew, somewhere, and he deserved this. Maybe even needed it.

Bound in calfskin, it was well worn without dog-eared pages but with many, many book marks and verses underlined in pen or highlighted, some both.

Breaking the ethereal silence of the place, his phone seemed to explode with its ring, enough to startle him.

It was the prosecutor.

"Hey, Joe."

"Grant, I think I'm being followed. Two different pickup trucks and a Suburban, I keep seeing them."

"There's lots of pickup trucks and Suburbans in town, Joe."

"Yeah, but these are clean… Like someone is taking time to wash them at the end of the day. Only the FBI would do something like that."

The sheriff laughed at what Joe hadn't really meant as a joke.

"Joe, the kind of people who are that obvious about a tail *aren't* the ones you need to worry about."

"This isn't funny, Grant. They have my apartment staked out and they show up around me all over town."

"Alright, where are you now?"

"At my office. There's a red Chevy crew cab, late model, parked across the street with a guy just sitting in it. You can't miss it, it's the only one in sight that's clean."

"Alright, Joe. I'll come by and see if I can't talk with him. I'm about forty minutes out, you want me to send a deputy that's closer?"

"No, I'm not leaving my office and he won't leave until I do."

*   *   *

Tom's ankle was feeling better, but now felt stiff from inaction. His short jaunts outside the cache were not enough. If he moved things around inside the cache, he could do limited exercises. Push-ups, crunches, different isometrics. Even different stretches from the different yoga poses he had seen Jane doing.

Any activity was better than just sitting staring at the shelves of the cache. He was thankful for all that it was, for all the thought and effort his father had put into it, but it seemed to be closing in on him.

He cracked the hatch to see only a partially cloudy morning, but still shrouded in ground fog from the relatively warm temperatures. Weeks ago, he wouldn't have considered going outside on such a day. And he was afraid he was getting careless in his restlessness.

The night before he had cried himself to sleep from prayer. He had just come across and committed to memory a few verses from Psalm 25;

My eyes are always on the Lord, for he rescues me from the traps of my enemies. Turn to me and have mercy, for I am alone and in deep distress…

It was like the Bible was speaking to him, or through it, God was… He humbly feared this was presumptuous. But giving it too much thought, this early in the day would make for a long day. He would pray later, he had to get out of this hole.

Like a timid rabbit, peering out of his warren, Tom lifted the hatch again. Each movement of his body preceded by a careful survey of his surroundings, near and far for threats. The immediate area for new disturbances, the distant tree lines for reflections off optics, high overhead for silhouettes of the seemingly omniscient drones.

Creeping out to the nearest pines to stretch his hamstrings under the cover of their bows, he feared his complacency would catch him. Tom leaned the 416 against the tree behind him. He sighed as he reached down for his toes and inhaled the cool fresh mountain air.

A handful of small wrens flitted about the branches and their songs seemed to offer some company, then;

Tom froze when he heard the roar.

At first, he feared it was a jet or something they had yet to unleash on him. He smiled at the realization that it was a far-off avalanche washing down a mountainside somewhere out of sight.

As it trailed off, back toward the silence of the snow, broken only by the wrens' calls, he heard the other sound again. Standing up straight, he cupped both ears as he sought the source, bouncing off mountainsides and down the valley. Not so much a caterwauling this time, it still didn't seem quite human, but now seemed… *melodic?*

*　　*　　*

"You don't think they're going to let it go?"

"Not a chance, Craig. Joe is concerned he's under surveillance. All of his filings have gone nowhere, he's being shut down by all his contacts above county and state level."

"You think he might be cracking, Sheriff?"

Sheriff Grant Taylor leaned back in his chair and inhaled. He had Jeff Potter's Bible in his hands on his lap. The calfskin cover was soft and comforting. He'd had it on his desk for nearly a week now trying to figure out if he should try to get it out to the area where he'd last seen Tom Potter. The young man should have it, he had determined. But the threat of avalanche with the warmer temperatures made going out that way by horse or sled inadvisable until conditions changed.

He spoke as he ran his fingers across the binding.

"I don't think so. I think it's really happening. I've tried to get out there when he calls me to tell them they're parked outside his office or condo. They're always gone by the time I get there. Sometimes he says he sees them on a cell phone right after we talk."

"Like they're getting warned?"

The Sheriff just nodded as his finger found an incongruent bump in the binding. His fingers felt for the outline of it as Deputy Craig Markdale continued talking.

"Well, I guess I wouldn't doubt it. But lots of people are getting nervous right now. This big military exercise, people are tying it with the border closure. You saw that notice from the RCMP?"

"Yeah, Craig, construction or something…" Taylor said absently as he put on his bifocals and looked closer at the binding of the Bible.

"So, what's our next…"

"Oh, no…" The Sheriff nearly shouted under his breath as he jumped up from his chair.

He hurried inexplicably out of his office with Markdale struggling to keep in close trail. The Sheriff stormed into the break room, opened the microwave door and placed the Bible inside. He harshly punched in five minutes and for just a moment his finger hovered over the start button.

"Whoa, Sheriff. I'm not as religious as you, but I'm pretty sure nuking the Bible is *not* cool. I think it's an Old Testament thing or something…"

Taylor's index finger froze. He thought a moment and nodded to himself as much as acknowledging Markdale. Opening the door, he pulled the Bible out with one hand and reached into his pocket for his old Buck knife with his other.

Markdale's eyes went wide as the Sheriff carefully cut into the binding of the Bible.

From beneath the leather, looking through the bottom of his bifocals, the Sheriff carefully pulled out something looking like an electronic chip.

"You've been tagged, Sheriff."

"They didn't accidentally leave this at the Cabin, they put it back after they did this to it. They knew I'd try to get it to Tom. Do you think it transmits audio?"

Markdale shook his head.

"What little I know about that stuff, I'd say that's passive. They have something that pings it to find its location."

The Sheriff tried to push down the edges of the binding he had cut and tucked the Bible under his arm as he examined the device closer.

"We're going to need to get some people together for some contingencies, Craig. But let's not talk here."

*   *   *

The hatch took a little more effort and he hoped that meant fresh snowfall. When it finally broke free, the darkness of the cache was relinquished to a dull brightness under a milky grey sky.

Hoarfrost had frozen over the hatch and glistened off every tree and surface in sight as a thin ice fog layer dissipated in retreat from a warming day.

It wasn't ongoing snowfall as Tom had hoped, but with a surface frozen hard, he might not leave many noticeable fresh tracks and aerial surveillance would be hampered by the multiple cloud layers. He was going to range out further today, start working on his conditioning again and stretching the stiff, still healing, ankle through its range of motion.

He travelled as light as he dared. Thermals, fleece, Gore-Tex and finally a snow camo poncho. The snow on the elk trails was compacted and frozen enough he didn't need snowshoes, but it was difficult. He moved slowly to be sure of his footing so as not to re-injure the destabilized ankle. He carried the 416 and a spare magazine. He'd oiled the bolt carrier before departing.

Moving with the greatest caution and awareness he could muster, he was so happy to be out of what he now just referred to as his 'hole'. The elk trail was difficult and its own kind of treacherous with all the unevenness created by the big hooves that had melted and refrozen many times. But the freedom of being out filled his being just as sure as the cold winter air filled his lungs and he smiled despite all the hardships.

The sky seemed to brighten with his smile and for a moment so did his mood. Layers of cloud slid past one another and a schism of blue penetrated the otherwise gloomy sky. Rays of sun broke through and his smile blended with a forced squint and suddenly he shuddered.

Gulping at the cold air, he was much farther from the hatch than he realized and worst of all, out from under tree cover. The sky was opening and *they* would be able to *see him*…

Turning a full three sixty looking for the nearest trees, in near panic, he then scanned the sky, squinting and holding his hand up to shade his eyes. First, he looked in the patch of blue, but then to beneath the highest cloud layer where the silhouette would stand out best. The ice fog was burning off fast now and the lowest layers of cloud dissolving quickly.

They had to be out there, still looking for him, still hunting him.

Slowly now, and deliberate. Tom was trying to suppress the urge to run to the hatch. That would be the kind of quick movement that would catch a drone operator's eye, or set him up for a fall that would re-injure the ankle.

The panic seemed to melt away when he heard the caterwauling again. He looked at the hands on his watch, getting on mid-morning. About the same time every day. He stopped and turned to face it. Cupping his hands behind his ears he turned his head, direction finding. The wind and the temperature were just right today and he was finally confident of its general direction of origin. It was out the valley west, and now it sounded something like music.

*   *   *

The Sheriff looked at the little tag in his fingers, flipping it over, trying to figure out what to do with it, how to use it to his advantage. Looking up to his coffee, like he expected an answer from it, he saw Joe approaching from the other side of the fountain.

Taylor was deliberately carrying the tag with him everywhere now, developing what he knew would be recorded as an established routine, a pattern of life they would count on. And he'd maintain that until he needed to do otherwise and he decided how he could make the little tag work for him.

Joe was smiling and carrying himself in a more relaxed manner. His comb over was more intact and he was wearing a lighter jacket in the warm spell.

"Hey, Grant."

"Joe. Gonna grab a coffee?"

"No, don't have time, got an appointment I have to head out to in a few minutes. They seem to have backed off of me. I think you coming out was just enough heat to keep them away. I think they've lost interest."

Stuffing the tag quietly in his front pocket, Sheriff Taylor didn't tell Joe his lack of a visible tail probably meant no such thing. He was glad to see Joe unwound a little.

Instead he gave a warm smile and lifted his coffee.

"What's the latest with you, Grant? Are you getting *anything* through your channels?"

Taylor shook his head.

"Like it never happened. My one contact at the Marshals called me a few days later. Said he was in big trouble for not actually taking Aubrey Harries into custody at the old rail tunnel. Said he was anticipating a forced transfer over it. I haven't heard from him since. The news media didn't pick it up beyond the local level; they managed to quash everything about it. I guess it's showing up in the conspiracy theory and prepper type parts of the internet, but no one else wants to touch it."

"Well, I'm re-evaluating how I'm going out to the senators and congressmen and the press. They won't let me get an investigation started through normal channels, I'll pass the ball to someone who can. I'm sending copies of all the filings and all the info I've collected on this to them and some contacts I have in the mainstream media that might have the guts to bring this to light on a national level. I'm feeling good about this, Grant."

"Why?"

"I don't know, maybe just because I'm not being followed 24-7 now. That's kind of a big relief.

The Sheriff sighed a little but managed a smile.

"I'm glad you've relaxed a little, Joe. And I hate to do anything that might bring you down again, but we do have to remember to be paying attention. The longer this goes on without any apparent action by the feds, the greater the risk complacency becomes. There's no way they just let this go."

The prosecutor nodded, but continued to smile.

"I get it, Grant... You gotta relax a little though. We've got one or two more days of warm weather before this big storm hits, might as well enjoy the sunshine. You can't go around living your whole life looking over your shoulder, what kind of quality of life would that be?"

The Sheriff raised his coffee to his lips and paused before sipping as Joe finished.

"Well, Joe, I guess you'd have to ask Tom Potter that."

*   *   *

The man in the chef's apron turned the sign on the door to 'CLOSED'. He paused and noticed the first of the snowflakes falling past the street light outside. He returned to the only two men in his restaurant, seated together at the table.

"Pizza sound good? On the house, I've got a couple left over and you can take the rest home. Stan is out of town this week and Bill said he'd be a few minutes late, to get started without him."

"Ah, pizza would be great, thanks, Doug." The older man had a pot belly on what was once an obviously athletic frame and his grey beard and hair were ill kempt and unruly.

"Thank you, so much, Doug. I'll take whatever you've got." The younger man said.

"And I can do free soda."

"Could I just get a glass of water, Doug?" The thin younger man asked.

"Sure thing, Roger. I'll go grab all that."

"Can I help?" Offered Roger.

"No, you leave it to the professional."

The man in the apron returned first with a tray of pitchers and glasses that the two men situated around the table, then with pans of two pizzas on serving stands with various toppings.

At that point, a tall man in Carhart overalls and a fur bomber hat stood outside the door with the 'CLOSED' sign.

Doug waved him in and yelled;

"It's still open, come on in, Bill."

Bill smiled beneath his reddish beard as he stepped through the door.

"Food... Pizza, great. It's starting out there already. I imagine I'll be plowing all night if it goes the way they say it will. Is the Sheriff coming?"

"No, he very specifically isn't coming." Doug said as he pulled up a chair and sat in it backwards. "The Sheriff and I are in the same cowboy action shooting club together. I saw him at the range a few days ago and he pulled me aside..."

"Cowboy action shooting?" The older man said skeptically.

"Yeah, Ski... Hey, Sammy Davis Jr was one of the fastest guns in Hollywood, not jokin'." Doug smiled and continued. "He said we needed to get together sometime because we were all there to help the Potter kid and he thinks we know most the other people who were there. And we have some kind of, well, I guess he said 'leadership' value in that posse he put together. He's concerned what's going to happen next and he wants us to start preparing."

"No chance they just let it go?" Bill asked as he took a big bite of pepperoni and mushroom.

Everyone else laughed nervously.

"Not a chance, Bill." Doug smiled, but it came out seriously. "Anyway, we need to stay on top of things like our operational security and communications security. That's why he isn't here, that's why I dropped notes in your mail boxes and specified no cell phones for this meeting. We need to set up networks among the posse members we know and circulate with. We need to do things like establish dead drops and one-time pads and get folks who don't know about things like that quietly up to speed on them. We need to get all this in place before it's needed so we're not playing catch up later."

"You flew helicopters, right Doug?" Ski leaned into the table as he asked.

"Yeah, flew helicopters for the Navy, Ski. That's why we're gonna need guys with your background for stuff like this, setting up indigenous forces in a hostile environment was your bread and butter. We'll need your lead on this stuff, I'm just the messenger."

Ski laughed a cloud of alcohol breath.

"Navy?" he said through the laughter. "Wasn't that a little dangerous for you?"

"What do you mean, Ski?"

"I mean like on ships surrounded by water?" Ski looked Doug up and down, then at the others who weren't getting the joke.

"Oh, you mean like, because I'm black, I can't swim or something?

Ski laughed harder and curled up a little waiting for others to laugh.

"Not cool, Ski." Doug said flatly. "First of all, because your delivery was horrible, second because I grew up in Texas, we had a pool in our backyard like everyone else in the neighborhood, I think it's a state law. Third we don't have time for that and we're going to really be relying on you. Now might be a good time to cut back on the booze."

Ski held up his hands.

"Sorry, sorry. Back when I was in we used to be able to joke with each other about stuff… I mean, I'm a Polak, that's why I go by Ski. My name has more syllables in it than any normal man should be expected to be able to pronounce."

"Jokes should be funny and pertinent, Ski. Try to keep up."

Roger spoke up to try to defuse things a little.

"My sister sent me a link with pictures of a National Guard convoy somewhere in Illinois and I saw a Youtube video of a train full of armor, M-1s and Bradleys, westbound out of Ohio."

"Roger," Ski smirked and shook his head. "You were a Ranger, right? People have been posting that kind of stuff on Youtube and Facebook for years. You know the military is always having big training exercises. They move the big stuff by rail, could be headed to Fort Irwin, a whole unit headed out for training, nothing unusual."

Roger just raised his eyebrows and half shook his head, not buying it.

"We prepare for the worst, hope for the best." Doug nodded. "All that JADE HELM hysteria a few years ago didn't do anyone any good…"

Ski crossed his arms over his chest and cleared his throat.

"Of course, conditioning is a tool of the psychological warrior." Ski said. "You fill the air with enough signals, people start to tune out. Doesn't matter if the signal is good or bad, they just won't hear it anymore."

"Well, you think about it Ski, I'll yield to your expertise on this. Personally, I don't think they have resources with the food riots going on. They have whole cities that are out of control, they can't come to our podunk little county and enforce martial law. They've got millions of people in Seattle, Portland, New York eating rats."

"And each other." Ski added.

Doug shrugged, he'd heard the rumors. More of those signals filling the air, he didn't know if it was true or not. He tried to continue on a more positive note;

"Well, we're doing pretty well here, and we need to keep it that way and we need to be prepared for an increased federal presence. Maybe that's going to be a couple of FBI agents assigned here, maybe it's full blown, troops in the streets martial law. My bet is something in the middle. We have to try to be prepared for anything. First step is making sure people keep quiet. We all need to be operating under the radar, everyone on that posse needs to forget about what they did that day."

"None of them will talk." Bill offered.

"Everyone has their price in this world. How many were vaccinated?" Ski asked.

"What does being vaccinated have to do with anything, Ski?" Bill smiled and shook his head.

"Why did they get vaccinated, Bill?"

"Maybe they were worried about their health, it was a pretty hard push for a long time there."

"What else, Bill? Most people your age weren't at risk, why would they do it?"

Bill shrugged as he finished another bite of pizza.

"I don't know, Ski… Worried about their job, I suppose."

"Right, so they got the shot because they were worried about their pay check. That was their price, whatever their paycheck was."

Bill swallowed his pizza and gave a rather blank stare.

"Ok, let me put it this way. I'm FBI and I pull one of those guys I think was on the posse in off the street and he's not talking. I tell him under the War Powers Act I can hold him indefinitely. Ask him if he minds a long stay in jail. He's a tough guy, a lot of guys on the posse were. So, he doesn't care. Then I ask him, will your wife's salary alone pay the mortgage and feed your kids?"

Bill looked down at his pizza, but suddenly didn't look hungry.

"If everyone had put their integrity before their paycheck the government could have never sustained the push." Doug said. "But they got away with it through coercion and fear. I don't blame people, but I don't trust them either. All the NRA guys and their 'from my cold dead fingers' crap. At least ninety percent of them go flaccid when their paycheck is threatened, that's now been proven. Maybe that's part of the conditioning Ski was talking about. The more I think about it, the more I think they're gonna roll heavy on us and only a few will do anything about it. When I was TDY in Souda Bay a few years ago, I hung out with a buddy whose grandfather was in the Greek resistance, he gave me a real interesting tour of Crete. The thing that stuck with me most was, he said; *After* the war was over, *everyone said* they had been resistance. And culturally, on the whole, we're not as tough as they were."

*   *   *

With the palm pusher, the needle pierced the pre-punched holes in the leather and the Sheriff leaned back in his chair with a smile of satisfaction as he drew the heavy waxed thread through to where the knot stopped it. Mary had just buzzed Craig Markdale in and the deputy opened the door himself.

The Sheriff sat behind his desk, which was stacked uncharacteristically with reports and other assorted paperwork he was falling behind on. The Deputy looked bemused at the strap of buckled leather in the Sheriff's hands.

"I thought you swore off dogs after you lost the last one, Sheriff."

"This?" He was looking at it through the bottom of his bifocals as he continued stitching around the little square. "Just a little diversion, Craig. Everyone needs a little diversion."

Craig got the distinct impression there was more to it than that, but also got the impression the Sheriff didn't want to say more.

"I just stopped in to see if you got to that B & E report we did over on the unoccupied place on Long Ridge."

The Sheriff nodded at the pile.

"I'm running a little behind there, Craig. I'll have it reviewed this afternoon, what questions did you have on it?"

The direct line from dispatch rang on his desk just as Craig was about to respond.
The Sheriff nodded to Craig, pulled the palm pusher off his hand and picked up the phone.

"Go ahead."

Craig heard the female dispatchers voice mumbled from across the room, still he heard a certain seriousness there and that was confirmed by the smile rapidly melting from the Sheriff's face.

"OK, I'm responding immediately from my office, I'll have Deputy Markdale with me, separate unit, as back up. Notify the coroner and mark me and Craig 10-6 on this." The Sheriff hung up the phone and looked up to his Deputy, visibly shaken.

"What is it?" Craig hadn't seen the Sheriff like this for a long time.

"This is bad, Craig... Really bad, come with me."

*   *   *

It was a very light snowfall, but it was enough for Tom. He could feel the moisture in the air and he was confident more was coming, hopefully enough to cover his tracks. He worked his way west with the valley following the sorrowful, lonesome sound. His pack was full to be out for as long as a week and his snowshoes strapped to it, knowing that he'd likely need them.

He was certain it was music now even after it stopped as he neared it through the valley. And he hoped he wasn't following a desperate wish. He hoped he wasn't making the caterwauling of a mountain lion to be the sound of something more inviting or just plain human. Tom desperately trod over the difficult elk path wanting to see a person and not the cacophony of a hungry pack of coyotes. It would be devastating to his sanity if his ears had tricked him.

Either way he would need to be careful of his approach. For hours he traveled and a little after noon, the snow had increased and he found a spot under good cover to set up camp for the night. With the avalanche shovel he began piling snow after taking off his fleece layer, it would be easy to start sweating with the exertion of building a quinzhee.

With the snow piled as high as he was tall he paused and held his hand out to the horizon. Each finger was fifteen minutes and there were three hands between the sun and the mountain crest. He had three hours. Tom knew he had to wait an hour to let the snow settle and sinter and then he would begin digging out the hollow. The next task at hand was to cut branches about the length of his forearm and place them porcupine like all over the pile of snow.

These would be his depth gauges and would assure he didn't make the structure too thin. It didn't take long and he was satisfied he had the quinzhee adequately porcupined. Looking at the snowfall and the stormy skies, he pulled the hexamine cooker from his pack along with a metal cup. Cracking open an MRE he went straight for the M&Ms and the drink mix that turned out to be an apple flavored concoction. He just wanted some warmth and calories as he waited for the snow to bind together properly before he could begin carving it out.

It gave him just enough time to snack and let the little folding metal cooker and cup cool and repack it before it was time to start digging. Soon he'd be getting his body temperature up again under the Gore-Tex shell.

The digging with the little shovel was somehow inspiring and he felt himself in a race against the descending sun and it's diminishing light in the ever-increasing snowfall. At first it was slow and ponderous, but the deeper he got into the structure, the more of a rhythm he developed to move the snow out. At a certain point he developed a whole-body technique that was like swimming in the snow to move it back out the entrance.

As darkness settled in over the mountains, he had carved just enough head room. Cracking a glow stick and tossing it inside, he followed with his pack. Inside, he unrolled his Thermarest pad and pulled the big mountain bag out of his pack. He'd thought about cutting a proper bed of pine boughs, but it was so near dark and the snow was falling wet and heavy now and he was done for the day. He didn't even have the energy to put together the MRE heater and entrée. And it was mac and cheese, his favorite. Instead he broke out the crackers at the entrance of the snow shelter. He hadn't thought to pocket the accompanying cheese spread, so it was frozen solid. Tom ate the crackers plain and cold and lit a candle just for the added warmth in the shelter. A candle, it was said, was the equivalent warmth of another body in the shelter. Tom didn't know about that, but the little dancing flame did feel like a kind of company.

He didn't consider the austerity of his circumstance. Inside the slightly warming quinzhee, he would crawl into the heavy sleeping bag and pray to God for success the next day. He would fall asleep a little hungry and a little cold, but full of faith that tomorrow, he would find the source of what he knew had to be music. And for the first time in a long time, he would at least just see another person.

*   *   *

The Sheriff shook his head as he crossed the freshly hung crime scene tape. Snow was falling and they were putting up a kind of tent over the body as his Deputies continued to photograph the scene and collect evidence.

The balding head and crumpled neck had taken most of the impact of the two story fall and the face was now barely recognizable, covered in freezing and still congealing blood. The body of County Prosecutor Joe Braunstrup lay amid the broken glass of the window through which he had crashed. The Prosecutor had landed long of the bushes and a snow bank that might have softened his fall. Instead he'd landed on the sidewalk head first.

The Sheriff looked up at the back bedroom window. Snow fell in through the jagged, broken glass and a drape hung awkwardly out and blew a little in the breeze. He resisted the temptation to get close to and crouch down and touch the body of the man he considered such a good friend. Instead, he barked to the Sergeant on scene;

"Canvas the area for anyone with video that might cover this condo, especially out front."

"Yes, sir. We're working that. We've got one witness, the complainant. They heard the glass break and found the body. That's all we've got so far."

The Sheriff nodded and withdrew a little, confident his men would do their jobs better without his looming directly over them. Car doors closed and he saw his detectives already arriving on scene. He physically stepped back and Markdale stepped in close to him, knowing the man needed support.

"You OK, Sheriff?"

The Sheriff shook his head.

"…Just talked to him yesterday."

"Still in a bathrobe, that seems kind of unusual for him, this time of day."

The Sheriff just nodded. Steam still rose from the blood attesting to the freshness of it. The paramedics were still standing by, but it had been called before the Sheriff had arrived. They waited, mostly helpless until they could assist the coroner when he arrived.

"Last week he'd been really worried about people following him, this week he thought they had backed off and…" The Sheriff couldn't finish, thinking maybe if he'd done more than just chasing the ghosts of a tail the prosecutor had reported, this would be different.

"What's that they say about flak, Sheriff?"

"Thickest when you're over the target." He finished.

A heavy car door closed behind him and the Sheriff turned expecting to see the coroner's wagon. Instead it was a dark, clean Suburban and a man in a nice wool overcoat and suit was walking toward him from it. He didn't recognize the man as quickly as he might have.

"'Morning, Sheriff." The man was flipping open his badge wallet but assuming a certain level of familiarity.

That was when it dawned on the Sheriff.

"What the hell are you doing here, Booth?"

The Special Agent smiled and put his credentials away.

"Happened to be in the neighborhood, got the call."

"Bull." The Sheriff squared up to the man as he approached.

"Thanks for getting this started for us, Sheriff. We've got it from here. You can have your men clear the scene, I'll have a team here within the hour."

"Get out of here, Booth. Right now." The Sheriff stepped closer to the FBI agent.

"Try it, Sheriff. Gonna go a lot differently when I don't have a concussion."

Markdale stepped between the two men.

"Now's not really a good time." He said to Booth.

"Well, that's too bad. This is a federal crime scene."

"Craig, I need your radio."

The Deputy unclipped the remote mic and swiveled the radio out of its holder on his belt.

The Sheriff keyed the microphone.

"All units, November One requesting all available to the scene at Lakeview Condos, we're establishing an expanded perimeter. I don't want anyone but our county people inside that perimeter, I don't care what badge they show. Break. Dispatch I want all SWAT qualified called out to this scene immediately. November One out."

Without removing his glare from the FBI agent, the Sheriff handed the radio back to Markdale.

Multiple units chimed in en route over the radio

"You are making a big mistake, Sheriff." Booth said.

"Wouldn't be the first time." The Sheriff called over his shoulder. "Sergeant, I want at least two deputies assigned to help convey this body to the coroner following all normal procedures all the way up to the release to next of kin."

"Yes, Sir."

"I'll be taking that body, Sheriff." Insisted Booth.

"Not a chance."

*   *   *

Tom had broken camp and struck out before it started. Now he followed the sound to a rise and he was certain, cresting it he would see the source of the music.

The snowfall had diminished, but it was still coming down. Visibility had gone down and was even less than the day before. Approaching the crest, Tom took off his pack and crouched low to prevent skylining.

Now, he could even recognize the specific song. It struck deep to his very core.

The first time he'd heard it was at a memorial on the compound at Fort Bragg for one of his father's fallen team mates when they came back from a deployment. It was the first time he'd seen a strong man cry.

Tom had dropped to his elbows and carefully crawled up the rise, peering over the crest and mouthing the words he knew as the pipes played.

Amazing grace, how sweet the sound, that saved a wretch like me, I once was lost, but now I'm found, was blind, but now I see...

CHAPTER 2

Doug was just about to lock the door behind the last customer leaving, when the Sheriff arrived. Instead he flipped the sign closed and locked it after he came in.

The older man in uniform wasn't smiling and had a package under his arm.

"Did the meeting go well the other day, Doug?"

Doug nodded and untied his apron.

"Did you want your usual, Sheriff?"

"Please, Doug." The Sheriff laid a ten-dollar bill on the counter and Doug had long ago given up protesting. He stepped in back and grabbed two slices of peperoni and put them in a small box. Sheriff Taylor was unusually grim and Doug knew it had to be because of the death of the county prosecutor.

Laying the pizza box on the counter, he took the ten, punched in the register and gave the Sheriff his change. Not knowing what else to say, Doug folded his arms across his chest and leaned back against the prep table.

"What do you think, Sheriff?"

The Sheriff leaned heavy on the counter and sighed, like he was straining against the weight of all he was carrying now. He stared at the pizza box and spoke slowly and thoughtfully.

"I think it was murder."

"Defenestration." Doug said.

"Huh?"

"In Europe, Italy and Russia especially, it's such a common form of political assassination it has its own name. Defenestration. The Italian word for window is finestra, the Latin is probably about the same. Death by being thrown out a window, defenestration."

"This wasn't Russians and it wasn't Mafia, Doug."

"Who?"

The Sheriff shook his head.

"Joe was rattling the cage. He kept pushing the legal channels, he was contacting press and all the government reps. He was pushing Freedom Of Information Act requests. I think he was getting too close."

"Lots of people are getting nervous, Sheriff. People are feeling it. Something isn't right; something is about to happen. You know old man Willard?"

The Sheriff nodded and smiled.

"Beneath all the animal skins and the occasional delusions, that old hippie has it goin' on more than a lot give him credit for. He's worth listening to."

The Sheriff's smile went acquiescent.

"I'll give you that, Doug. He has some occasional wisdom and moments of enlightenment or at least clarity."

"He was in this morning, talking about how he could feel something in the air. That the vibe was off or something. He attributed it to 5G, then he brought up the troop movements and this CRYSTAL HELM exercise the internet is ablaze with. A few weeks ago, I was laughing that off just like the JADE HELM hysteria a few years back. But that's how they do it sometimes, isn't it, Sheriff? I don't doubt they stage stuff to make people look like crazy conspiracy theorists, then when the crazy stuff happens, everyone blows it off. I think it's a psyop technique called poisoning the well."

The Sheriff sighed and shook his head, then pulled the package from under his arm, handing it to Doug.

"This is very important, Doug. It's Jeff Potter's personal Bible. Tom Potter deserves to have it. Don't jeopardize opsec or anyone's personal safety or freedom, but that young man deserves to have his father's Bible. If you or any of the cadre make contact with Tom, you get that to him."

"Why don't you do it, Sheriff?"

"Ol' Willard ain't the only one catchin' a bad vibe right now, Doug."

The Sheriff's cell phone rang, he saw the number and shook his head.

"Sorry, Doug. I need to go."

*   *   *

Tom wasn't sure why the emotion was welling up inside him, or why he was crawling closer. It was as if the falling tears and lump in his throat was making him stupid. Or maybe it was some magical lure of the pipes.

The man on the other side of the crest with the bagpipes under his arm was adorned in a kilt and old British commando sweater. He wore some kind of fur hat that seemed to be coyote, because of the tail that hung down the man's back. The piper wore unlaced Sorel boots in the well-trodden deep snow. The man was facing away from Tom looking down on an enormous cabin.

No, Tom thought. Rather, a mansion of logs with three different chimneys, all smoking and a couple of significant log out buildings. There was a large south facing solar array and only the immediate area of the structures had been plowed of snow. Just north of the buildings was a large flat area clear of trees that had to be a frozen alpine lake.

Maybe it was just the need for human contact that drew Tom over the top of the rise. He moved cautiously, the sound of the crunching snow masked by the sound of the pipes. Tom was careful not to look directly at the back of the man. His father had taught him that, while they didn't understand the mechanism yet, a man would sense in a primal way that he was being watched if stared at directly for too long.

The piper had finished Amazing Grace. Tom didn't know what new the song was, but he knew he'd heard it before and the man played it well. Just beyond the rise, Tom sat cross-legged with the 416 across his lap and he became so entranced that he allowed himself a smile through the tears and what felt like, for the first time in so long, a sense of joy, lost in the melody. He was entranced and watched the man until…

The piper turned around unexpectedly and seeing Tom there, the pipes squawked off key and stopped.

The man visibly collected himself, seemed to take a moment to inhale and reset his breathing, then, spoke with a deep and commanding voice.

"Can I... *help you?*"

Tom was caught off guard and froze a moment.

"Are you Scottish?" was oddly the only thing he could get past his lips.

The man smiled and paused, then spoke without a discernable accent.

"I am a little bit of a lot of things, but mostly... I'm a whole lot of nothing."

"I'm sorry, Sir..." Tom stammered, more than embarrassed. "Just, the sound... the music... it..."

The man's smile broadened as he saw the streaks of Tom's tears.

"I will take your presence and show of emotion as an indication that I am improving, rather than the possibility that I have absolutely crushed your soul with my incessant off note honking."

Tom cocked his head.

"I ah... no... I liked it, very much. It reminded me of..."

The man's smile flattened a bit, like he'd encountered a sudden reality.

"I know who you are..." As he said it and nodded, the smile returned.

Tom shrugged.

"I mean, I've heard about you."

"What have you heard?" Tom asked.

"Well..." The man paused a moment, considerately. "They say your father was trying to start some kind of right-wing white supremacist cult. That he'd roped you kids into it, brainwashed you and that you were destined to die in the winter wilderness."

Tom stood up, his smile evaporating in the fog of his breath, his hand instinctively slipping to the grip of the 416, thumb staged on the safety.

"No!" Tom yelled, "No, that's all a lie! None of that is true!"

The man held his hand up and spoke calmingly.

"Oh, believe me... I know. You asked what I'd heard, I'm just telling you what I'd heard, not what I believe. You need to get warm; you need some proper nourishment. Come with me."

*   *   *

The Sheriff slammed the door of the Tahoe and rushed into little wing of the hospital. Don Wagner, the county coroner was there and trying to talk to the Sheriff on the run. He spoke quickly but it was lost amid the chaos of the scene. Sheriff Taylor was most worried about his two men.

Horn and DiPasquale were both big, fit, hard chargers. Both were SWAT qualified. Both were military veterans, both with combat experience.

Both were laid out on the floor receiving medical attention in a dissipating haze of nostril burning smoke and next to the burn marks of some kind of concussive diversionary device. Sirens of other responding units added to the confusion and the Sheriff keyed his radio.

"All units responding to the hospital, slow your response and kill the sirens."

Kneeling next to Horn first, he could see the man was mumbling his way back to consciousness while being attended to by one of the hospital's doctors and a nurse. Turning to DiPasquale, he saw the man was conscious and propping himself up on his elbows, talking to two paramedics about his injuries.

Sirens from responding fire engines wound down and knowing his men were alive, the Sheriff jumped up and ran to the cold chamber of the morgue. The door had been blown off its hinges, the stainless drawer was pulled out and empty and the body of County Prosecutor Joe Braunstrup was gone.

His right thumb slipped behind his Sam Browne, the Sheriff rubbed his beard and swore quietly. They didn't do this because they needed to, they did this to prove a point.

With less urgency, the Sheriff returned to DiPasquale. Horn was up on his elbows and talking now and Deputy DiPasquale was saying he couldn't hear anything. They both had a buzz of people around them that the Sheriff didn't feel the need to further complicate.

Craig Markdale and Sergeant Cole had arrived and Cole was kneeling beside DiPasquale with his notebook in hand.

"They hit us with some kind of flashbang and tasers. They were fast, they were really good, I didn't even have time to clear leather. I want to say it was like twenty guys, but I don't know, all I remember seeing was boots and legs, they were wearing dark green... No, it might have been black." The Deputy shook his head, frustrated with the holes in his recall. "There may not have been twenty... I don't know."

"I would guess there were twelve to fifteen of them," Stated Wagner. The coroner rubbed his chin and thought a moment before continuing. "Probably more like a dozen; they came in two white sprinter vans. There were more men left in the vans, but I don't know how many and I don't think I saw any license plates, but I'm not sure. Like the Deputy said, they were very fast, they knew exactly what they were doing."

Sergeant Cole stood up and reached for the microphone on his shoulder.

"OK, I'll go out with vehicle description." He said.

"No, Sergeant. That stays in house for now." The Sheriff said.

"We have a good chance of catching them with how fresh this is, Sheriff."

Sheriff Grant Taylor shook his head sternly and the Sergeant dropped it.

"I'm sorry I don't have more." DiPasquale struggled and shook his head. "It was just so fast."

"It's not the deputy's fault." The coroner said. "I saw it from the outside. I couldn't move that fast in the building and they were shooting things, blowing things up and coming out with a dead body. It was shocking, I think I froze."

"Did you get the autopsy done?" Asked the Sheriff.

"No, Grant." Wagner looked at his watch. "I was just coming over to prep for it, make sure paper work was in order, get the body moved. Got a Medical Examiner friend from Spokane coming in to assist in an hour."

The Sheriff shook his head and said nothing. He was running the calculus in his head of having a couple of deputies pull over whoever was in those Sprinter vans and no matter how he ran the math, it still added up to some number of dead deputies and zero number of returned corpses of dead friends. He had resigned himself to marking this a grisly check in the win column for *Them*. Whoever *They* might be.

*   *   *

The stone floor was deceptively warm when Tom reluctantly took his boots off. The inside of the home reflected an opulence in size that gave the magnificent log construction the feel of something much more than a cabin. Perhaps the logs were just supposed to give the large home a rustic touch.

Despite all the neat, orderly appearance, the warmth of the geo-thermally heated floor and the coziness of well stocked, multiple fireplaces, it had a palpable emptiness to it.

"You're alone here?"

"Yes… I have no family and I prefer to keep to myself."

Tom smiled.

"It's like your fortress of solitude?" Tom smiled as he looked around. Despite what appeared to be great wealth behind it, the place was very modestly decorated. No real art work or pictures or anything that gave any insight to the man in the sweater and kilt.

The man had taken off his boots in the mud room, placed the bag pipes on the couch in the great room and walked to the kitchen without comment. Tom followed suit and left his boots and pack there, his 416 still slung across his chest. He sensed the expectation that he was to follow, but there was no formal invitation.

Tom was amazed by the size of the big house.

"What do you do for a living?"

"Nothing anymore, I'm retired. I used to work for a rich uncle." The man seemed to want to change the subject.

"You look like you need proper nutrients and smell like you need a good shower. There is a bathroom with a shower down that hall. There are towels, I'll scrounge up some clean clothes you can borrow while we wash those and leave them just outside the door for you. For the sake of my battery bank, please limit your shower to twenty minutes. You can get it as hot as you want, but if you run it longer than that I'll need to fire up my generator with the sunlight the way it's been. I need to save diesel.

"You can leave your rifle in the corner there if you wish; I have no use for it. Or you can keep it handy, I understand."

Tom looked at the man curiously, the idea of a shower was appealing, but not leaving his carbine. As it was he found himself looking nervously down hallways and clearing corners of every room he entered.

"My name is Max, you're Tom, right?"

Tom nodded and expected the man to extend his hand for a handshake, but he didn't.

"What else have you heard about me, Max?"

"Not much, just that most people expect you to be dead out there."

"Have they stopped looking for me?"

"Not a chance, Tom. They don't work like that... go take a shower, relax a little, wash off that awful smell. We'll talk as you eat."

Tom sniffed discretely, he didn't smell anything. He nodded and pointed toward the bathroom with the look of a question mark.

"Yes, Tom, first door on the right, you can't miss it. There are towels and soap and shampoo. Twenty minutes though, no more than that or I'll be knocking. I'll leave a clean sweat suit or something for you just outside the door."

Tom smiled and nodded a little bit.

Entering the bathroom, he locked the door behind him and inhaled the clean perfume smell of the place. The floor was warm in here too. It was unlike any other off-grid solar home he had been in before. There seemed to be little of the consideration of the limitations of the solar power system, other than the time limit placed on the shower. All the appliances looked normal and high end. He took a moment to look in the mirror but he didn't really recognize the dirty, bearded face he saw there. Reflection did him no good. Shaking his head, he stripped off the slung HK 416 and leaned it against the sink counter.

He took the 1911 out from his belt and laid it on the toilet near the shower where he could get to it quickly.

Tom took off the Gore-Tex shell, and when he slinked out of the fleece top, the smell suddenly struck him against the perfumed soapy smell of the clean bathroom.

"Agh." He cringed at his own filth. Tom had tried to keep up with his own hygiene with the baby wipes in the cache. He took what his father had interchangeably called 'Ranger Showers' or 'Whore's Baths' depending on the company at the time.

Sniffing selectively at himself, he realized now how horribly all of him really smelled and wondered how he had become so accustomed to such stench. Stripping down all the layers, he walked to the big shower. It had two heads and two sets of controls. He now thought that it might take more than the allotted twenty minutes to scrub months of grunge off. He reasoned that perhaps if he was only using one head, he could stretch the water a little more than 20 minutes.

It didn't take long for the hot water to scald from the shower head and Tom adjusted the temperature to a reasonable level to sear the dirt off. Starting with a bar of soap, he stepped in and lathered every part of his body, never having paid quite so much attention in a shower before.

Certain that that wasn't enough, he used the expensive looking bottle of shampoo as a liberal follow up, again, making sure the finest details were covered then washing it off. Leaning his forehead against the wall, inhaling the hot steam that comforted his nasal passages and relaxed his suddenly tired muscles.

The rap at the door startled him, had it really been twenty minutes already?

"Tom, that was twenty minutes."

Tom dutifully shut off the shower, grabbed his towel and dried off. He looked at his pile of filthy, smelly clothes as he wrapped the towel around his waist. The bathroom was filled with a dense fog of steam. Picking up the 1911 and holding it behind his leg he opened the door slowly, not sure what he would find. Steam roiled out before his eyes.

In front of him was a chair with a neatly folded sweat suit sitting on it, with what he took to be a folded laundry bag. Like everything else in the house, the sweat suit was warm and he realized this must be some kind of artifact of just being so cold for so long.

Stuffing his dirty clothes in the laundry bag, it was so bad he washed his hands again when he was done.

Tom looked at the 1911 laid on the sink counter and the HK leaning there. Slinging the carbine, he carried the 1911 in his right hand and laundry bag in his left. Opening the bathroom door released a full cloud of steam and Tom padded barefoot toward the kitchen. The perfume smell of the bathroom replaced rapidly by the delicious smell of something being cooked and it took a moment to register…

Steak.

He walked faster and heard the sizzle of the ribeye before he rounded the corner and saw it. His eyes were locked on the center island gas stove and the meat being cooked there, a pot of green vegetables steaming next to it.

"Sorry about the shower, Tom." Max said as he flipped the steak. "Diesel can be hard to come by and this time of year the sun doesn't always cooperate."

"No, I'm sorry. I lost track of time."

The man looked at the carbine strapped across his chest and the pistol in the young man's hand. Hammer back, thumb safety on, Tom kept his index finger well clear of the trigger.

"You've been on the run for a long time, Tom. You have certain, honed instincts at this point."

Tom followed the man's gaze down to the pistol.

"It's a 1911, it's cocked and locked, it's meant to be carried like that."

"Yes, I'm aware… A holster would be good though." The man smiled.

"Oh, well… I took it from an FBI man. I didn't get the holster. I've been doing Mexican Carry… ah. Jane said I shouldn't call it that, it's racist or something."

Max just kind of squinted at Tom.

"I just carried it tucked in my waistband." Tom clarified.

"Well, Tom. I can honestly say, I understand some of your feelings and instincts right now. I assure you, I have no need for your guns. Feel free to keep them however you need to, but understand, I won't take them from you or use them in any way. I'm going to dish this food up for you then I'm putting that laundry directly in the wash, it will be done in a few hours and you will be welcome to stay, or re-provision and move on, whatever you feel you need to do. I'll try to provide you with all the assistance I can. I may even have a holster that will work for you, well, not with the light, and maybe not a railed 1911. I'll see what I can scrounge.

Max lifted the skillet, tilted it toward Tom and lifted the steak a little with the spatula. "It's about medium now, would you like me to cook it a little more?"

"No, that's…" Tom was certain he had never seen food look so good and he inhaled deeply and savored the aroma. "That's fine, I'm… very hungry."

Max gave a smile of sympathy, turned off the burner, set the skillet down and quickly slid the steak on to a pre-staged plate. From the steaming pot he produced a spoon full of broccoli and took the plate to the little table where a place setting waited.

Tom set the pistol down on the table, dropped the laundry bag and jumped in the chair behind the steak with a voracious savagery that made Max chuckle. Wordlessly he grabbed the laundry bag and walked off to leave Tom, still strapped with his carbine, tearing into the steak.

Tom was certain this was the best meal he had ever eaten and he didn't notice the quality of the well-crafted steak knife. He only noticed every juicy piece of every morsel until it was gone just as Max was returning and then Tom was shoveling broccoli into his mouth.

"That was a 16 ounce ribeye, Tom… I have another thawed. Would you like me to cook it up?"

Tom paused a moment, realizing any notion of manners had abandoned him. Then he cast that concern aside and nodded vigorously as he finished the broccoli.

"I'm sorry about the vegetables being frozen, Tom. All I have this time of year."

"Thank you, sir. I think this is the best meal I've ever had."

Max just smiled and shook his head as he walked to the refrigerator.

"What would you like to drink?"

"Water is fine."

Max walked back to the stove top, firing up a burner as he opened the steak packaging. Dropping it in the skillet, he walked back to the sink to pour Tom a large glass of water.

"What else could you use, Tom?"

"News."

"Of what?"

"Start with the war. Is it over yet?"

Max laughed and shook his head. His smile faded and he inhaled.

"It's really just getting started, Tom." Max flipped the steak.

"You don't need to cook that one as much…"

"Ok, what was the last you heard?"

"That a couple nukes went off in Ukraine and the Chinese Navy had set a blockade around Taiwan. When the nukes went off, Dad knew we'd be going to war. When the blockade happened, Dad said it would be two fronts and we weren't prepared."

"It turned out to be one nuke in Ukraine. At the head of a major Russian offensive. Still not clear who did it, blame being thrown about still, months later. By all accounts it killed an equal number of Russian and Ukrainian troops, but more non-combatants than anything. There was another detonated by the Chinese, on the border of China and India. That one didn't get as much attention. And the PLAN, the Chinese Communist Navy has seen direct and bloody action with the US Navy. Two carriers sunk, one of ours, one of theirs."

Max presented the steak in the skillet and Tom nodded that it was done enough. Slipping the steak onto Tom's plate, the young man began cutting immediately. He had just processed the information Max had told him.

"A whole carrier, that's a lot of people."

"Early reports are that CVN-74 went down with all hands, Tom… That's the Stennis, that will be over 6000 crew members." Max leaned back against the kitchen island, folding his arms across his chest and his word trailed off reflectively. "I'm not sure of the crew compliment of the Shandong, or if it was sunk out right. The Chinese Communists have begun a missile bombardment of the island of Taiwan as well.

"The Chinese are saying the failure of the Three Gorges Dam was actually the result of some kind of mercenary air strike they're accusing the US of orchestrating. The death toll for that is estimated to be over one hundred million now, we'll never know the full extent I suspect."

"Sounds like Chinese propaganda to me." Tom said his mouth half full.

"Sounds like the plot to a cheap novel to me." Max smirked.

"What do you think will happen next?" Tom said between bites.

Max shook his head.

"It's hard to say and truth is surprisingly hard to come by right now. With all the access our modern technology gives us to information, there is so much of it. And the information is muddled with misinformation and disinformation. It's hard to know what to believe. And that is just one of the reasons I'm here."

Tom paused.

"You've given up on truth?"

Max smiled again.

"Maybe I have, unless you have some idea where one might find it these days, Tom."

Tom finished another bite.

"I find it in God."

"Really?"

Tom nodded with another mouthful.

"It's that easy and that obvious for you?"

"Yeah." He said with a shrug. "Prayer and reading the Bible."

Max nodded skeptically.

"I'm afraid I'm an agnostic with serious atheist leanings, Tom."

Tom accepted that with a nod and continued eating.

*   *   *

With the last stitch complete and tied, Sheriff Grant Taylor laid the heavy-duty leather collar on one side of his desk with a smile of satisfaction. Looking at the other side of the desk and the stack of reports accumulated there, his smile disappeared.

When Deputy Craig Markdale entered, he saw only the Sheriff's stern expression and the pile of reports.

"It's not like you, Sheriff. Things piling up. You OK?"

The Sheriff sighed and leaned back in his chair. It took a moment before he spoke.

"The other day I was talking to someone about old Willard."

"The old hippie or mountain man guy who wears the bobcat pelt hat thing? Still has the face on it?" Markdale gestured with his free hand where the bobcat face sat atop the old man's head and the Sheriff smiled.

"That's him. Ever talk with him much?"

"Try to avoid it really."

"Oh, he can get long winded, but if you get past the chemtrails and fake moon landing stuff, there's some wisdom buried in there. Some real insights too, it's good to listen to people we don't always agree with, Craig. Sometimes they're the ones we should be listening to the most.

"Anyway, he was telling someone about a strange vibe he was feeling. Of course, he was attributing it to 5G and this JADE HELM exercise…"

"This one is CRYSTAL HELM."

"Oh, yeah, whatever it is. Anyway, once someone mentioned that conversation, it got me wondering. I've been feeling off, too. With Joe's death, and them stealing the body, what else are they doing that we can't see. Have they backed off, or are they taking time to… prepare the battlespace."

Markdale handed the Sheriff the envelope he was carrying.

"I don't know if this will make you feel any better, Sheriff. I've been working with the detectives on Joe's death. I got the security tapes from the gas station on the corner. These are some stills from it; detectives are editing some other video together but I wanted you to see this right away."

Sliding the glossy prints out of the envelope, the Sheriff looked hardened.

"If you look at the time stamp, that's three and a half minutes after the complainant's call came in about Joe going through the window. They were moving at a pretty good clip to get out of there."

"A white Sprinter van and is that a 2004 Silverado?"

"Our car guys are saying a 2005, not brand new. And the Sprinter van is four wheel drive and all rigged out overland style."

"Nothing that would attract any attention here."

"Nope, somebody living the 'van life' and just your average pick-up."

"What about the plates, Craig."

"As they 'round the corner there on the video, we got a great view of the plates. They're in state, but they come back as never having been issued. They don't exist."

Setting the two prints down on his desk, the Sheriff looked at them.

"If they were in such a hurry to get out of there, I'm guessing it didn't go as planned."

"You don't think they threw him out the window?"

Leaning back with his arms crossed over his chest, he shook his head.

"Now, no. I don't think they meant to kill him. At least not kill him there. The only trauma we saw was associated with the fall. Maybe the autopsy would have revealed a small caliber gunshot wound under all that, but none of us saw evidence of that. And two stories are certainly enough to kill a person. But if that was your objective, would you trust a relatively short fall like that to do the trick? I'm starting to think that maybe Joe was trying to prevent being taken to a secondary location."

"You think he jumped?"

"I think there may be a good chance he was panicked and he was just trying to get away. That he thought his chances were better off with whatever was on the other side of the window than going along with what was happening inside."

*   *   *

"It's hard to say, Tom." Max pulled up a chair across from Tom at the table. The young man had slowed down significantly, but wasn't going to give up on the second steak. "The only thing for certain is that they won't have given up. They have to carefully realign assets and resources."

"But, if they think I'm dead…"

"They'll want a body to be sure of that."

"What about all the people who helped me?"

"What do you mean, Tom?"

"It seemed like there were hundreds helping me escape, horses, ATVs, helicopters everywhere, they sent the Night Stalkers after us."

Max seemed unconvinced.

"You didn't hear anything about that? It was huge. Did they cover that up?"

Max thought for a moment. The young man had been through a lot. He didn't seem to be the kind to make up stories; it didn't seem he would need to.

"I'm fairly isolated here. I allow myself an hour on the Starlink everyday to keep up on news, but I don't dig or dwell on it much. I could have missed it." He paused, trying to continue without questioning Tom's veracity. "Tom, that many people involved in something like that… It's very hard to keep something like that quiet. Are you saying the 160th, the Night Stalkers, were there and flying in an effort to capture you?"

"Yes, Little Birds and Blackhawks, and we even had a helicopter on our side, I don't know what it was, it looked military, but the camo was different. The Sheriff even outran one of the Little Birds with me on the back of his horse. Everyone cheered when we got to the tunnel, it was pretty awesome. I mean, now it was, then it was pretty scary."

Max smiled.

"You're saying the Sheriff outran an MH-6 helicopter with a horse?" Max's skepticism showed through.

"Well, I talked about that with the Sheriff when we left during the snowstorm. His theory was that the Little Bird pilot's heart wasn't in it. That it was about the thrill of the hunt and that was the only reason he even put on the show, that and his bosses were watching on the drone feeds."

"Tom, all those people involved in this, especially the Sheriff are in grave danger."

"But we all vanished in the snowstorm."

Max shook his head.

"The US government has nearly inexhaustible resources. They will hunt you and all involved in this and they will imprison, kill or financially ruin whoever they can catch."

"Well, they won't catch the Sheriff, he's really smart. And they won't catch me either."

"I guess you're pretty smart, eh, Tom?"

"Oh, I don't know about that… I'm just trying to do what God wants me to."

"That's what you get from prayer and the Bible?"

Tom nodded with his mouth full.

"So, has your time in the wilderness been like Jesus in the wilderness?"

"I'm not sure. I kind of skipped ahead and read through that part. I don't feel like the devil tempted me out here, I felt more like I was at home. In order, I'm at the Psalms; I really like that part."

"Could your feeling at home in a barren wilderness, be the result of the devil's temptation?"

"But it's not barren. God has provided me with everything I need. Well, and my father too, but God provided me with him, I figure."

"Does God speak to you, Tom?"

"You mean like a voice in my head?"

Max shrugged a little, then shook his head.

"No, nothing like that. But I'm trying to learn how he guides me, it's not easy."

"So, Tom, you're putting your faith in a book written by men and in a God that hasn't told you anything directly?"

Tom put his steak knife and fork down and grinned a little.

"Are you the devil, Max?"

Max showed no emotion.

"Most definitely not, I don't think I believe in him either. But you need to be very careful who you trust and if I were a person like you, I wouldn't trust a person like me."

*　　　*　　　*

Bill was never late and Sheriff Taylor was tired of sitting in his truck. He had stepped out
and now looked down at the Marlin he cradled as he leaned back against the old Ford. It was a classic 336. His father's favorite rifle. The rifle was a few years older than he was, in a caliber most would consider obsolete, or at least out of fashion. But the rifle was solid with a respectable trigger and a tight lock up. It was from a time before safeties and WARNING: READ SAFETY MANUAL had to be roll marked on everything and before a JM stamp mattered because Marlin said enough about quality, just like WINCHESTER or SAVAGE did. He brought it because it would look less threatening than an AR if they were under surveillance. The old lever gun would be expected on a trapline, really.

Its old bluing was aged to a fine patina that he was careful to keep well oiled. He'd refinished the stock set when his father had died. The last twenty years with his father, it had seen some neglect. If Grant had seen it, that would have been an early indicator of the beginning of his father's descent into dementia.

The .35 caliber Remington cartridge was hard to find now, and it was expensive when you could, but it was no slouch. He figured he could take anything in the area including the grizzlies, if he had a steady hand and he did his part. This time of year, that shouldn't be a problem, but the mountain lions might. Then there were the predators of the two-legged, four wheeled variety.

The heft and the reliability of the old lever action felt reassuring in his arms though most would see it as an anachronism. Fact was, the Sheriff knew he could be armed with the very latest in tactical firearms and it wouldn't be enough against what they were up against. Being armed had little to do with the fight they were facing. He would have to be smart, and ultimately that might not be enough.

Bill's Dodge was coming down the highway to the pull off with the trailer in a blur of snow blown off the road. He pulled in behind the Sheriff's personally owned vehicle and hopped out with a smile.

"The stuff you talk me into, Sheriff."

"Me? If it weren't for the deep snow and me wanting to take it easy on old Betsy, we'd be doing this on horseback. You sure we can't just snow shoe in?"

"No way, Sheriff. That would take all day, embrace some technology for a change."
Bill was untying the tarp covering the machines on his trailer.

"I'm not necessarily averse to technology, Bill. These things are just noisy and I find myself spending more time digging them out of snow or pulling them out of the water than riding them every time I use them."

"You just have to read the snow and manage your energy, Sheriff. Just stay in my track, you'll be fine."

"Alright, Iron Dog."

"Hey, I'm gonna win it one of these times."

"You goin' this year, Bill? It's comin' up isn't it?"

"In a few weeks, Sheriff. Naw… Hopin' I have enough saved or line up some sponsors for next year. Lost all my sponsors during the covid stuff."

The Sheriff had slung his rifle and was helping wrestle the snow and ice coated tarp from the snow machines. One was a drab old Polaris utility machine with an ample rack on the back, the other a high-performance Yamaha with colorful struts and springs. It looked new and sleek and had a big paddled belt that the Sheriff was certain would get him killed.

Bill rocked the trailer back and rolled the machines off one at a time.

The well-tuned and maintained garage-kept machines each started with a single pull. The Sheriff went back to his old 250 and pulled his helmet, the heavy-duty leather bag and catch pole from the back seat. Without having to ask, he secured his gear to the modest Polaris as it idled.

"You're sure we'll find one?"

"Yes, Sir, always do on these sets. And they've been soaking a couple days now waiting for the overcast you wanted. This is actually pretty short and easy terrain for as far as we're going, and it's good snow, but stay in my track and you'll be fine."

Bill and the Sheriff both donned their helmets. The Sheriff waited a moment to make sure he didn't catch a face shield full of snowy rooster tail, but Bill was a pro and gentle on the throttle. The Sheriff thumbed his throttle to keep up and they followed the tree line across what was farm field in the summer time.

70

Approaching a small, mostly frozen creek, Bill slowed his machine and stood up as he rode by. It must have been one of his sets, but it was empty. A few miles later, he slowed and stood again but the results were the same.

When he stood the third time, the Sheriff saw they had what they were looking for. They both stopped near the wary animal.

"Sheriff, I've known you what? Six, seven years?" Bill hadn't dismounted his machine and he had to yell over it, even at idle.

"Bout that." The Sheriff yelled back, stepping off his snow mobile with the catch pole, pulling the heavy gloves out of the thick leather bag.

Bill reluctantly shutdown his high-performance Yamaha sled.

"I've known you to be a man to come up with some great ideas in that time, Sheriff." He said without having to yell over the running engine.

"Why thank you, Bill." The Sheriff was genuinely flattered, but Bill cut off his thought.

"I don't believe this will prove to be one of them."

They both looked at the hapless animal before them as it paced nervously, anchored in place by the leg hold trap.

"Ah, this'll work fine, Bill. I snag the dangerous end with the catch pole, you wear these animal handling gloves and put this bag over its head. That's 10 ounce leather I triple stitched myself. You get him under control, I get the collar on. Then you can back up and release the trap when I tell you, I let the catch pole loose and the bag falls off... Easy."

"First off, I'm not sure there is an end of an animal like this that isn't dangerous when it's in a trap. Second, the only way I've ever got control of an animal to get him out of a trap is with a plywood screen or put a .22 behind his ear, third... well... this is just all kinds of messed up, Sheriff."

"Surely you've released by-catch safely."

"Well, then I use a screen, but that won't work for what you're tryin' to do and coyotes are by no measure any kind of by-catch. They all get a .22 behind the ear."

"Not this one, Bill. He looks strong and healthy and he's of much more use to us alive."

Bill sighed as he took the gloves and bag.

The coyote began a low growl on their approach. The Sheriff led with the catch pole and the coyote dodged it as best he could, then barked and bit at it a few times, but was finally snared by the neck. The Sheriff drew it tight, giving him some measure of directional control then finally pinned it to the ground.

"There ya' go, Bill, now get that hood on and keep hold of it."

The animal snarled and Bill awkwardly slipped the hood on as it began to fight harder. Holding the bag and the scruff of the coyote with authority, Bill made sure it was secure before announcing;

"OK, Sheriff... got it, get that collar on quick."

The Sheriff let go of his end of the pole and moved in, slipping the collar around its neck. The two men were a tangle of arms in each other's way for a moment until they had things sorted out and the Sheriff finally had the collar buckled securely.

He stepped back and resumed control of the catch pole and Bill moved in to step on the spring levers to release the jaws. As he did the coyote shook a bit and the hood came off, the Sheriff pinned it back to the ground. Bill frowned but moved quickly to the spring levers and the coyote pulled its leg out as the pressure from the jaws was released.

"Alright, Bill, stand back."

Bill back pedaled and the Sheriff let the noose of the catch pole go slack. Shaking it a bit, the coyote found its way out. It paused a moment, looking at the men, then taking off at a sprint with a barely noticeable limp.

Bill moved in and reset the trap.

"What are you doing, Bill?"

"I'm gonna remake this one then we can head back."

"I don't know if that's a good idea, Bill... we don't want him trapped again."

"That's one educated 'yote now, Sheriff. He won't fall for it again."

*   *   *

Tom wasn't sure what to make of Max's warning. Afterward he'd accepted the hospitality of a spare bedroom. The bed was large and warm, warmer than he'd felt for a long time. He'd included in his prayer before sleep a little something about Max and he hoped Max could find the kind of peace that Tom sensed he lacked, despite the abundance of the man's home.

He also prayed for guidance and the discernment to know if he was being led astray by some kind of temptation, but the comfortable bed and the warm covers seemed to come without obligation. In some way that Tom didn't understand, Max seemed sympathetic. Tom drifted quickly in to a hard and deep sleep.

When he woke, he wasn't sure how much time had passed, but he thought it was the next day. It was light still, or again and Max was up and about.

Max was in the kitchen; Tom's clothes were neatly folded on a chair there.

"Sleep well, Tom?"

"Yes. How long was I out?"

"I think that was over twelve hours. Get yourself some water, make sure you're hydrated."

Tom nodded, grabbed a glass from the cabinet and filled it from the faucet.

"Would you like some eggs? That's one thing I have fresh year-round, I keep chickens."

"Yes, please." Tom looked out the window over the sink to see it was snowing again. "You don't keep a driveway plowed, I noticed. Are you stuck here all winter?"

After a pause, Max spoke. He seemed a little reluctant.

"Stuck would be a relative term." Max looked at the basket of eggs on the counter. "Would you like to eat or see something interesting first."

After all the steak the previous meal, his curiosity reigned.

"Well, I'm not very hungry right now."

"Wait here a moment."

Max disappeared around a corner and Tom heard something that sounded like the sliding of a door.

"Alright, Tom. Come this way."

Tom rounded the corner and found a wall panel opened in the hallway. Max was standing at the top of a hidden set of stairs that Tom initially thought would descend to a basement, but it didn't.

"I keep things plowed between the out buildings, but this is easier than grabbing a coat."

"You have secret passages?"

"It wouldn't be a proper fortress of solitude without them, would it?"

It was dimly lit, but warmer than going outside, and it came out to stairs and a door concealed behind some kind of aluminum cabinet inside the large log barn. At first, Tom was taken by the mechanism of the cabinet and how it slid out of the way to access the steep steps, but then he turned to see the large shop area lit by sky lights. There was a side by side UTV and a John Deere tractor in front of him lined up in the first bay. The next bay was huge with some kind of towering single engine airplane on amphibious floats and tucked half under its wings was a large rubber tracked Sno-cat with a large plow.

"Whoa."

Tom had seen plenty of side by sides and tractors, but the Sno-cat looked brand new and was painted white with swirls of grey, like a stylish winter camouflage. And that and the big airplane drew his attention.

"Do you fly the airplane?"

"No." Max laughed. "They were moving that from Alaska to fight some fires down south. A fuel pump or gear or something, I don't know, but the engine failed. The pilot managed to land it in my lake back in the summer. They thought they'd have it out in weeks, just waiting for the part. Waiting for parts these days, that turned to months. They flew some mechanics in and we dragged it into the barn. Even sent me money for the barn space the first few months. With everything going on I don't know if that thing will ever get out of here. The Sno-cat is my latest toy, we'll take it out some time if you like. If need be, I can get out of the property anytime. I haven't seen any conditions it couldn't handle."

"What did you do for your rich uncle?"

"Hmm?" Max thought for a moment and laughed a little. "Nothing of consequence really. I'm just a spoiled nephew I suppose."

Tom turned his attention to the Sno-cat.

"So, I guess you're as stuck here as you choose to be."

"Exactly, Tom."

"My dad would have loved all this. If he'd had more money, I imagine he would have wanted to do something like this. Nobody messes with you here, I bet."

"Given the right impetus, someone can mess with you anywhere, Tom."

"Fixed fortifications are monuments to the stupidity of man." Tom stood up a little straighter as he recited the quote.

"General Patton?"

Tom nodded;

"My Dad used to say it."

"Your father was a wise man, Tom."

"I think you guys would have liked each other."

"I suspect we may have chewed some of the same dirt."

Tom looked him questioning, but Max looked away like he'd said too much. Tom looked down from the machine to the painted concrete floor. He hadn't talked about his father in the past tense with anyone but Jane and it struck him suddenly how easy it came.

"I would have liked to have met your father, Tom. I knew the things I heard about him were untrue, I know how these things go."

"I wish I'd heard what they're saying about him myself." Tom brooded. "I've been listening for any kind of news I can about it, but it's like it never even happened out in the rest of the world."

"What do you mean you've been listening, Tom?"

"On my radio, I have a little AM/FM with shortwave."

"You what?" Max's expression went suddenly flat. "Do you have that radio with you?"

"Yeah, it's in my pack."

"You need to get your clothes, get your gear and you need to get out of here immediately, Tom. It's snowing, they won't be able to acquire you visually. Get far away from here, ditch that radio. You are welcome to come back anytime, but never bring a radio or cell phone here."

"It's just a receiver, it doesn't transmit."

Max was ushering Tom back to the passage.

"It doesn't matter, Tom."

*   *   *

Markdale pulled his marked unit up to the Sheriff's unmarked Tahoe in the parking lot of the big gas station.

"Hey, Sheriff. Sorry to bug you on your way home. I just got a text from a buddy who came through state line. He said the rest area is packed with Army vehicles. He's an Army vet, said a bunch of Hemmets, ASVs, five tons and lots of troops. Said he estimates it at a couple of companies to reduced battalion. I'm not sure what all that means but figured you might. I'm working that side of the county so I thought I'd swing by and take a look."

"Well, the Hemmets are the big eight wheeled trucks, ASVs are Armored Security Vehicles, I think. He's talking several hundred guys at least if he thinks it's a reduced battalion. Give me a call when you get there; tell me what you see. I've got to get back home and get the animals fed, wife has a meeting tonight."

"Right, I'll let you know what I find. Have a good night."

"You too, Craig. Be safe."

After Markdale drove away, the Sheriff wheeled his unmarked Tahoe out of the parking lot full of tractor trailers. Turning northbound onto the highway he looked to the mountains looming dark to the west. The sun was beginning to set beneath the dark grey overcast that spit the occasional snow flurries. Turning east on his quiet country road, Grant Taylor was thinking about how much feed he had left and if he could make it to the end of the week before going to the co-op.

Maybe it was the sun angle in the mirror, maybe it was his old eyes, old everything really. He didn't notice the old Chevy and the Sprinter vans turning off the highway, didn't notice them at all until it was clear they were accelerating fast toward him amid the open farm fields surrounding the road.

It all came together as the Chevy went into the oncoming lane as if to pass. The Sheriff was accelerating and hit the switch for the electro-lock to release his AR. His first thought was they were going to box him in, so he veered toward the center to hog as much road as he could.

The acceleration and the turn into the pursuing vehicle played right into what was actually a deftly executed PIT maneuver and the Sheriff's Tahoe spun across the oncoming lane winding up going backward along the shoulder. Taylor stomped on the brake until the ABS was kicking back at him and he held it. The Mercedes grill ornament of the lead sprinter van loomed large in front of him. Dust and gravel rose into the setting sun and as things ground to a halt, the Chevy had nosed into his rear bumper.

Before he could move his hands from the steering wheel, the side window shattered and a flash-bang went off. The Mercedes emblem and the top of his dashboard danced in the after image of his sight. There was a yelling of imperceptible commands and he knew someone was cutting his seatbelt and it felt as though a dozen hands were on him pulling him out of his truck.

Thrown roughly to the ground, he clenched his eyes closed trying to restore his sight and he tried to hear all the muffled voices that were yelling, maybe at him. Flex cuffs closed tight around his wrists and ankles. As his vision came back he saw at least five men all over him, one coming at him with trauma shears, somewhere in the mix he saw a syringe. Things grew quiet as they secured more complete control over him. They were cutting the sleeve off his right arm and when he felt the pinch of the needle he knew his real problems were only just beginning.

A warmth flooded his body and as it did, he felt a panic and sense of detachment as it seemed everything was shutting down. He couldn't breathe, he couldn't move, he couldn't scream.

"Succinylcholine chloride, Sheriff." A voice called out to him from the blur of his vision. A voice he had heard before but he couldn't place now as he fought the terror of the shutdown of his vital systems. "Nasty stuff. They'll have to intubate you now. That's never pleasant either."

The Sheriff heard the men directly over him saying something that he couldn't follow and he heard the ripping of Velcro and they had something in his mouth to pry it open and then they were shoving the tube down his airway.

"It shuts down everything but your heart and brain activity, you have no control over anything, but you are conscious the whole time unless they give you something else. I told them not to.

"You shouldn't have taken advantage of me when I had that concussion and you should have let me just take your prosecutor's body from the get go… Yeah, it's me, Special Agent Booth, well, I've been promoted now, kind of. It's now Regional Public Safety Administrator Booth. But that won't matter to you, where you're going. You still get to play a big part in all this. Thank goodness we got to you so soon so we can get you treatment and hopefully contain this terrible outbreak before it can spread."

He heard the mechanical clacking of the machine breathing for him. Trapped in the constraints of a paralyzed body, kept alive at the whims of a machine they had shoved down his throat, it had all happened faster and gone farther than he ever could have imagined.

Sheriff Grant Taylor tried to subdue his panic and reached out to God from a mind that was tormented by a government out of control. He sought peace and solace from God because no man could help him now.

CHAPTER 3

Both the west and eastbound lanes of the highway had a rest stop at the state line. Both were crowded with what seemed to be exclusively military vehicles, a blend of green but many still painted desert tan. There was a mass of activity, men and vehicles in motion and "civilian" traffic was bottlenecking as barriers were being put in place. He saw a military caterpillar cutting a turnaround in the snow. MPs and some kind of armored vehicle had just blocked incoming traffic and were rerouting it to the rough U turn the engineers had just created.

"Dispatch, Mike forty-nine. Highway rest stops at state line, be advised we have some kind of military road block being put in place, I've been trying to contact November One but I'm no joy with him. Where's the Lieutenant?"

"November four is out on a fatal at the fish hook. We are getting other reports of unusual activity around the county."

"Ok, mark me out here, I'm going to talk to someone and see if I can find out what's going on."

"Roger, Forty-nine. We show you out at westbound state line rest area, 1722."

They had had a couple of the armored car things blocking the off ramp and a couple of soldiers with prominent MP shoulder bands motioning for him to stop. The armored vehicles were desert tan and had turrets with some kind of machine guns pointing at him. He reckoned these to be the ASVs but couldn't remember what the Sheriff said that stood for. All he could think about was how angry and unnerved he was all at the same time.

He rolled down the window as the one soldier approached.

"Sorry, Sir. We can't let anyone through."

"OK, I see that's what you're going for. I'm obviously with the Sheriff's department and we haven't been informed about this. I need to talk to whoever is in charge here."

"Your name, Sir?"

"Deputy Craig Markdale."

The soldier took a step back, spoke into his radio and held it close to his ear for the answer.

"Becker!" The soldier shouted to one of the others. "Take my position, I'm going to escort to the CP." He turned to Markdale. "I can take you to the Command Post, but I'll have to ride with you."

"How far is that?"

The soldier pointed past the ASVs toward the center of the crowded parking lot.

"Just up there, Sir. The five-ton expandable with all the antennas."

Markdale sighed and nodded. The soldier made a hand motion before getting in and one of the ASVs backed up just enough to let the Deputy drive his Tahoe through.

Markdale tried to take in everything he was seeing. Antenna masts going up, satellite dishes being erected, men stacking sandbags at approach points and a general hustle and bustle that was hard to follow.

"What's going on?"

"I'll have to let the Captain talk to you about that, Sir. Honestly I'm not really sure myself."

He was able to park reasonably close and his passenger hopped out and stayed dutifully close as they walked to the big 5-ton. A large generator next to the vehicle would make talking outside challenging and a man with two bars on a tab at the center of his uniform was waving to him to come up the little stairs and enter the back of the truck.

When he closed the door behind himself, it was still loud and now there was the breaking of static and a dizzying amount of radio traffic being passed. There were half a dozen stations inside with multiple computer monitors set up and soldiers with headphones on behind the keyboards.

"Deputy Markdale, I'm in charge of this location. We have a lot of work to do."

"What are you doing?"

"Shutting everything down, some kind of new pathogen."

"Is this real life or some kind of exercise?"

The Captain looked at his watch anxiously then paused awkwardly, looking at his watch again. There was a knock on the door.

"Ah, that's for you, Deputy."

Confused, Craig opened the door. A man in full kit, in a dark uniform unlike that of the other soldiers greeted him with a smile.

"Deputy Markdale, if you'll come with us, we can take you to someone authorized to fully brief you."

Reluctantly, Craig descended the steps into the mass of similarly equipped men. As soon as his first foot reached the ground, his right arm was grabbed and fully controlled and kept far away from his pistol. His left arm was taken on the other side and an arm like steel wrapped around his neck as he was taken backwards to the ground.

"Relax and the needle won't hurt as bad." someone yelled. But it didn't matter, he met irresistible force with an instinctive, futile resistance.

The needle burned going in and as a rush of warmth and panic flooded his existence, he heard someone say; "We're gonna have our top ten by the weekend at this rate, boys."

Markdale realized he couldn't move and he couldn't breathe.

*   *   *

Tom was shivering almost uncontrollably by the time he got dry clothes on and into his sleeping bag. It was the coldest he had been and it scared him, because he knew what could come next.

He knew that cognitive decline could sneak up on him, cloud his judgment and make him indecisive. He could relent to an overwhelming desire for sleep from which he would never awake.

Max had imparted on him such a sense of urgency that he had set off at a run with the snow shoes in the freshly fallen snow and he'd set out with full layers and the old Gore-Tex wasn't breathable enough. By the time he had arrived at the stream and broken the ice enough to deposit the radio, he realized he was sweating.

Even now he was shaking his head at himself and his folly. Shaking his head beyond the shivering in the big sleeping bag. When he found the snow bank, he dug with a fury and the sweat continued because he didn't want to stop to take off a layer, and as he dug, the snow fell down his back and further soaked and chilled him.

Tom cursed himself, he knew better. But something about Max had so unsettled him. He didn't understand why Max had such a problem with the little radio receiver. But Tom realized he didn't really understand Max.

Was the man really the devil in Tom's wilderness? Had that little temptation of comfort so quickly softened him?

Tom unzipped the sleeping bag to try to capture the heat coming off the orange flame of the candle glowing in the rough-hewn snow cave. Being warm enough to be alive, and warm enough to be comfortable were two very different things and Tom savored the warmth of the little flame in the small snow cave… or was he already into the paradoxical undressing stage? That point where the mind was so affected by hypothermia, that the body thought it was too warm and started shedding the very clothes it needed for survival…

Was his mind playing tricks on him because of the cold, or because of the sudden uncertain return to isolation, or because of temptation by the devil?

Steady Tom, steady.

He inhaled for a four count and held it for a second, then forced his exhalation to a five count, then repeated until he felt centered.

"God, I really need you now… please help me. Please be my warmth, please help me know I'm OK here."

Inhale, 1… 2… 3… 4… hold one. Exhale 1… 2… 3… 4…. 5…. Just like Jane taught him when the world started closing in…

"Oh, Jesus, please be with me now." The shivering was beginning to slow. He didn't feel the need to strip out of his polypropylene long underwear, that was a good sign, right? *"God, I'm feeling warmth from within, is that you with me?"* Something embraced Tom, warm and reassuring. The self-doubt, self-pity and self-loathing was pushed aside, he suddenly knew he was going to be alright. He watched the dance of the little flame and drew the now warm sleeping bag around himself with great comfort, wrapped in the embrace of something greater than he had ever known.

*   *   *

The blonde woman had a natural beauty that went beyond aesthetics and went to the very kinesthetic. Her every movement was blessed with a grace that everyone noticed. A lineage of sensuality from a region of northern Italy and a sense of class and decorum that everyone admired. Her accent was barely noticeable, but tonight, she didn't speak much.

Bianca was Doug's wife and she was the beautiful face of their Italian restaurant.

She almost seemed to dance as she delivered the food and drinks to the table but there was nothing superfluous or pretentious in her movements. It was all natural and on a normal evening, most men's eyes would be drawn to her and Doug would feel nothing but flattery. There was nothing normal about this evening, and all the men's eyes were on the television mounted high on the wall of the restaurant.

The news channel kept replaying the scene of the Sheriff and his Deputy being wheeled, unrecognizable in the gurneys from the ambulance to the big grey Gulfstream jet with the cargo door opened wide.

It was clearly footage from the airport.

"There's no way of telling that's even them." Said Roger with a dismissive wave of his hand.

"Doesn't really even matter if it is or not." Ski offered.

None of the men bothered with the pizza, beer and soda Bianca had placed before them.

"I heard it has some kind of... I think neurologic component, I think they said. That it can affect behavior. Maybe that's why the prosecutor jumped through the window, sounds like he was patient zero." Bill innocently parroted the expected narrative. Doug and Ski looked at him, obviously disappointed.

"What? That's what I heard."

"That's what they want you to believe, Bill." Doug offered gently.

"What the hell, Bill? Ski was less comforting.

"Yeah, but... well, I don't know, I'm no doctor..."

Doug inhaled, crossed his arms and leaned back in the constriction of the booth.

"I heard they've closed off the whole county." Roger said.

Doug motioned to the TV and the crawler that said as much.

"Yeah, full quarantine, no one in or out... They got the Sheriff and Markdale and Joe is dead. Anyone else they don't want, anyone else they know was involved in getting the Potter kid free, off to the *treatment center in Seattle* as they put it. But we all know that's not what they're doing." Doug finished his sentence with a disgusted shake of his head.

"Sheriff got us spooled up just in time." Ski said.

"What do you mean?" Bill asked.

"We all started getting contact with our guys, right? We're starting our networks."

Doug nodded solemnly, Roger looked down at his untouched beer, and Bill just looked a little confused.

"Sheriff knew this was coming, on some level, Bill. We are all in touch with at least ten to twenty guys." Ski played with his unused straw. His tired puppy dog eyes suddenly had a certain fire to them. "We are the foundation of the resistance to this." He pointed at the TV with his straw.

"They have to lock down all the roads, all the trails. One county, but that's three states and the Canadian border. How many men would that take?"

"There's no way..." Roger was astonished. "Obviously they have control of the airport, we did airfield seizures... all the roads, trails, logging access, the border... it would take hundreds of thousands of men. They can't do this, there is no way."

"First…" Ski held up his finger and it was like a sudden exclamation point. "It doesn't have to seem possible to us, it has to seem possible to whoever is conducting the op, right or wrong. Second, we're assuming manpower is limited because of the bigger picture of the war going on. What if, for whatever reason, this is a priority?"

"What if it's like a big experiment, like proof of concept?" Doug suggested.

"Like how they could enforce martial law nationwide? Impossible." Roger said with a laugh.

"Or," Doug said. "Proof that they don't need to, just one locale at a time. Come down hard in one place and everyone else falls in line."

*   *   *

Tom woke up shivering, but he said a quick prayer, thankful to have woken up at all. Shivering was a good sign. He pulled the MRE he had been sleeping with out of the sleeping bag and didn't bother trying to peel it open with his shaking fingers. He unsheathed the big Junglas knife from its home on his pack and sliced into the bag. The knife was comically large for the task, but he needed calories quickly.

He had a glow stick still providing illumination so when he spilled the body-warmed contents out on the snow cave floor, he quickly grabbed the tube of peanut butter. Tearing it open with his teeth, he clenched it in his shivering fist and chewed a little and swallowed it. He tried to get the crackers open, but they were harder to open, and he went back to squeezing the little brown tube-like package of peanut butter he held in his mouth.

Calories were all that mattered. Stoke the internal furnace.

Tom pulled the glow stick into the warmth of the sleeping bag and tore open the meal heater. He had a water bottle in the sleeping bag with him as well and he poured a little water in to the heater bag to the line indicated on the instructions. He crammed the entrée pouch into the heater and held it close, welcoming the warmth the chemical reaction of the heater and the water would soon provide.

Tom knew he needed to get moving, he didn't know how long he had slept, but he woke up cold and his body wasn't keeping up. He needed to get on the move again.

Where should he go?

Back to the northern cache? What if Max's allusion was right, what if *They* could somehow track his radio receiver? They would know about the cache.

But now they would know about Max's place too… And what about Max? The man himself had said he shouldn't be trusted and that whole weird devil in the wilderness conversation…

Tom dreaded getting out of the warmth of the sleeping bag. The MRE heater was getting warm and he wrapped himself around it and pulled the sleeping bag a little tighter. He would eat whatever the entrée was and then get dressed in his only change of clothes. He would pack up and move out of here.

Was the northern cache compromised? He could, under normal circumstances, live out of his pack for a week.

But now he was cold, so cold.

Maybe he could get somewhere, cut some hanging dead wood and get a good fire going, but that would be a huge infrared signature.

Max seemed as concerned about being caught as he was. And if he had wanted to, he could have turned Tom in. Or was that all part of the temptation?

Tom tried to wrap his arms around himself and put the MRE chemical heater at the core of his body. It was so cold now.

Maybe one last run to the cache, secure things he might need if he couldn't get back to Max's. Tom finally pulled the fleece pants from the warmth of the foot of the sleeping bag. He squirmed into them quickly, then he donned the fleece jacket he had used as a pillow. Under his pillow was the 1911. Releasing the safety, he performed a quick press check to make sure the action was free of ice. He thumbed the safety back on and he stuck it in the front of his waist band. The Gore-Tex shell was dry, but chilled from hanging in the cold over the backpack.

Pulling his wool knit cap a little further over his ears, he slithered out of the cave. It was still dark, very dark, pre-dawn. A solid overcast prevented starlight and hopefully overhead surveillance. Pulling back into the cave, he assembled the night vision goggles and helmet and staged them by the entry.

With his sleeping bag and mat packed, he stowed the green glowing light stick in his pocket and proceeded to push the pack and 416 out the narrow cave entrance. Grabbing the NVGs, he unstrapped his snowshoes from his pack and rested the helmet on the pack. Taking a risk using the glowstick held in his mouth, Tom sorted out his bindings and cinched them down on his boots.

The shivering had stopped, but the cold striking so deep to his core had not. Snowshoes on, helmet on and strapped, heaving the pack on one shoulder then the next. Fastening the waist belt, adjusting shoulder straps, sternum strap. The world went green as he lowered the goggles with a positive click. He fine-tuned the focus, adjusting inner-outer-inner.

Then the wool gloves, and the arctic mittens hung over his neck, worn when he needed them.

It was all so routine, it was all smooth and instinctual. This was his existence now, would he forever be a man hunted?

Questions like that didn't help and he buried them and concerned himself with the task at hand, the routine was good in that way. Pulling his GPS from his pocket, he strapped it on his wrist over the Gore-Tex sleeve.

Straight line, the northern cache was 8.9 miles away. He was glad that in his haste to depart from Max's place, he had somehow managed to run roughly toward the cache rather than away from it. There was a very light snowfall that flickered occasionally across the NVGs. He estimated a fresh two to three inches on the established snow pack. Tom hoped there would be more snow to cover his tracks. It would be a long haul to the cache and he knew it would take him most of the day.

Chancing the IR illuminator, he switched it on for a moment to survey the animal trail he had walked in on, and that would carry him in the general direction of the cache. Invisible to the human eye, anyone with NVGs or properly filtered thermals could see the IR illuminator, but it gave him a better view of details on nights like this when the ambient light was reduced by overcast.

Setting off generally east, the horizon over the mountains soon began to glow bright where the rising sun was creeping, undetected yet by the limits of the human eye. He estimated that he would have to travel aided by the goggles for an hour give or take.

He had hoped for increased snowfall and felt it a realistic expectation. He could feel the moisture heavy in the air. That was another thing Tom had developed, beyond all the weather indicators his father had taught him, so much time in it, dependent on it for his survival, he now had a feel for the weather.

The cold, he suddenly realized, wasn't just some kind of psychological impingement. It wasn't just from being spoiled at Max's or whatever temptation he feared might come with it.

The already cold weather was turning further. He estimated it to be well below freezing. Tom would learn from the previous day. Manage his calories in and out, manage his layers to keep sweat to a minimum.

As the snowfall increased there was an increased sound of silence around him. Even the sound of the footfalls of his snow shoes was dampened in the soft snow. As the ambient glow from the eastern horizon brightened and grew, it was easier to follow the trail and he could find off shoots of the trail to follow. He cut a more direct route to the cache whenever he saw the opportunity, but progress was slow. Tom was patient with himself and deliberately rationing his sweat.

Before the sun was up over the horizon, it was light out enough to stow the goggles. As he was doing it, he took the time to rearrange his knit hat that didn't really fit comfortably under his helmet, drink water and finally eat those dry MRE crackers. So dry they demanded even more water.

Setting off again, the glow of the sun tried, but failed to burn through the clouds and ever-increasing snow. And it still felt colder.

Glancing at the GPS he had to take a second look. The distance had somehow increased, had he read it wrong earlier?

Tom continued on the animal trail and it was carrying him up a rise. It appeared from the elevation lines on the GPS, after a few miles of this, the rest would be downhill to the cache.

The silence of the snow was broken by a sudden sound that startled Tom. He froze and listened. Smiling as he recognized the sound, it was actually a pleasant thing. Like the sound of pulling his sleeping bag out of its compression bag. It was the cascade of snow falling from the tree tops, gathering a little avalanche as it collected snow and momentum through the lower branches.

It was caused, he knew, by the weight of accumulation at the top. As it grew too great for the tree to bear, the tree would either break or shed it. A healthy tree would shed it and this was nothing unusual. Of course, it could also be triggered by the distant, still unheard, vibration of rotor blades, maybe? Or was it a man at the base of the tree, clumsily bracing against it to steady his shot.

A wave of anxiety suddenly washed over him and he looked quickly to the GPS. He had to be within five miles now.

His lips parted in disbelief as he read the display, 20.7 miles. How was that even possible? And the direction indicated he was heading west. Tom looked up at the bright spot in the sky where the sun was hiding. Then he looked around himself as his mind tried to reconcile the difference between what his eyes and mind were telling him. Tom struggled to get his lensatic compass out of the breast pocket of his fleece coat.

The dial swung around and quickly confirmed he was headed east.

Looking back at the GPS, and Tom was, for a moment, beguiled by the reassuring read out. 3.8 miles, and the direction was better.

Something was wrong, that was too close.

Inhale 1…2…3…4, hold 1, exhale 1…2…3…4…5.

Tom looked around, he listened carefully, then looked back at the GPS. The displays were all zeroes and across the middle it read ACQUIRING SATELLITES.

Something was terribly wrong, he had had good coverage all around the area of the cache and Max's.

Earlier the movement and the sense of hope he had felt as he'd fallen asleep had helped sustain him, burned in him like an inextinguishable flame of faith. Now he felt suddenly cold … and lost.

Looking at the GPS quickly, it was still offline. Was this some kind of jamming?

Unconsciously he gripped the 416. Was this it then, would he hear the helicopters soon? He imagined them emerging shark like from the snow laden skies. A catastrophic cacophony of rotors and mini-guns ripping the silence to finally take him down.

1…2…3…4, hold, 1…2…3…4…5…

Steady, Tom.

Looking east, could he find the cache without the GPS at least getting him within a mile in this snowfall? Turning in his tracks and looking west the snowfall was too heavy and he knew he would lose his way in the snow if he tried to work his way back to Max's.

Maybe both those options should be off the table now, maybe both should be considered compromised and he should just vanish in his wilderness.

He'd stood still long enough the cold stabbed at him.

Tom bowed his head and pulled his hands out of his mittens to hold them together.

God, I'm cold and lost. I don't want to die here but I don't know where to go, please, please help me find my way …

As he looked up and turned his head, he heard it. It was a distant and haunting playing of pipes.

*   *   *

"Two days in a row may be pushing it." Ski said looking up at the blank TV screen. It was on, but there was nothing on any signal.

"I get that," Doug said. "But we have to meet somewhere to coordinate. This is as good a place as any, getting lost in the crowd in town."

Bill ate his slice of pizza and Roger looked at his ginger ale as he spoke.

"So, they're jamming everything then. No cable or network TV, no satellite coms or internet of any kind. Cell phones are apparently working for calls but no data."

"They've notched out cell phones for tracking and surveillance purposes." Ski said, leaning his elbows heavy on the table. "We need to rally our teams and get people out looking around. We need information, solid intel from reliable sources."

"What are you thinking, Ski?"

"Range out, find our boundaries, not test limits yet, just get an idea where they are. We each take a side of the county. I can go east, send my guys out to see what the manning is at each checkpoint, see if there's anything they've missed... Back road, logging trail, any kind of access that we can get in or out. Bill's crew has the least people, I'd suggest he take the northern border because we already know the Canadians had shut down the crossing for, uh, construction. Then with the mountains up there, him and all his high marking buddies are more suited for probing some kind of access on their snow mobiles."

"I can take south." Roger offered. "I've got relatives across the county line that way."

"Sounds good, my guys will go west." Doug said. "Excuse me a second."

Doug stood up and walked to the kitchen. When he returned he had a small pizza box in his hand.

He opened the lid revealing what had to be a book wrapped in heavy shipping paper.

"What's that, Doug?"

"This, gentlemen, is something we need to discuss." He sat down in the booth, looking down at the book on the table in front of him. "I was given this by the Sheriff the last time I saw him. It's Jeff Potter's Bible. Sheriff thought we should get this to Tom."

Ski laughed with a smirk that seemed out of place.

"Uh... That's not really something we can make a priority right now, Doug. You know that, right?"

Doug leaned back, crossed his arms and shrugged.

"Yeah, I get that, but... This whole thing started with the Potter family. Tom Potter is still out there because of us."

"Maybe, Doug. If he's still alive. It goes below zero again tonight. There's no telling if he lasted this long out there."

Doug nodded and continued.

"You knew Jeff Potter in the Army, right Ski?"

"We crossed paths, did some schools together. I wouldn't say I knew the guy."

"He used to come in here fairly regularly before his wife died. Jeff was good people, as an Army guy, you get him though, right, Ski?"

"Oh, I know the type, know what he was capable of."

"You know how he would have raised those kids, how he would have trained them."

"Kids aren't always receptive to the ways of their parents."

"Tell me about it..." Doug looked out to the kitchen where Bianca was working on cleaning up. "But, those kids held off the FBI for over a month. And even after his sister died he kept running through all that. I'm inclined to believe he'd survive this, that Jeff would have set him up to survive it. Jeff was a man with a plan. I think we have to assume Tom's still alive."

"So?" Ski said bluntly. "We have our own problems, we bought him time. I don't regret what we did for him at all, but I don't think we owe him anything further."

"Wait, Ski." Roger interrupted softly. "Maybe we do owe him. Did he cause this, or did he reveal it?"

Ski leaned back and looked at Roger contemplatively as Roger continued.

"The federal government went off the rails a long time before anyone knew about Jeff Potter. And the fact that they've worked so hard to bury this story about him and his family and now we're seeing this bogus new pandemic so they can crack down on us. Tom Potter is the real victim of this; he's out there trying to survive and stay free. We're in here warm trying to stay free. Do we owe him more? I don't know, but at the very least, shouldn't we try to live up to his example?"

Ski smiled and nodded.

"Not priority one." Doug said. "but we can't forget about Tom, and as we start to getting things sorted out, we are going to move from a reaction and collection phase to an action phase, right, Ski?"

Ski nodded, smile turning solemn.

"And really," Doug continued. "he could be a critical component in all this, because at some point, truth is going to have to matter again."

*   *   *

The boats were pushed to the back of the bay and every folding chair that could be scrounged was arrayed in front of the lectern. Booth leaned on it, reviewing his notes. He had a fresh haircut and wore a comfy red sweater with a tie and pressed khaki slacks. Ted Zites stood behind him, at a kind of parade rest looking position wearing black 5.11 cargo pants and sweater.

A few people were still filing in and there was an excited hum of quiet speculation going on. Roll call was not a normal event, but clearly these were not normal times. The very deliberate staging of Booth in comfortable, relatable attire, backed by Zites in a formal, structured uniform had been engineered for a very specific message. Indeed, everything they were about to present to the day shift of the Sheriff's Department had been carefully scripted for a very specific desired effect.

There weren't enough seats. The large number of administrators, on-coming dispatchers, supervisory staff, and the usual deputies wouldn't all fit in any one room so it was decided to use the large open bay corrugated metal building of the Marine Division to host the Federal Brief, as it was being called. That, of course, added to the not so hushed discussion as well as the appearance of the sand-colored military five-ton expandable truck with all its antenna and satellite dishes in the parking lot. Only Deputy Boggs challenged the soldier standing at the steps to the truck. His obstinance was quietly noted and Booth talked him into the Marine Division building with a smile and promise of complete information.

Boggs wasn't as busy rumor-mongering or speculating as the others at their seats were. He sat quietly now on the cold metal chair.

"Everyone, if I could please have your attention now... Please everyone, quiet down. I'm going to give you as complete a picture as we have at this time." Booth was smiling and the room settled down.

"I am Regional Public Safety Administrator Booth," He motioned behind himself. "this is Public Safety Magistrate Ted Zites. Those are titles new to everyone, even us." Even his laugh seemed scripted. "We'll have more on that in a little bit. First, I'm sure everyone is as concerned as we are about the condition of Sheriff Taylor and Deputy Markdale. They are both in medically induced comas at this time. That move has apparently arrested their respiratory distress and they are considered stable.

"Sheriff Taylor and Deputy Markdale are suffering from Pandemic Enterovirus Respiratory Syndrome. You may have seen this originally called the Maroa Virus from the small town in Venezuela where it was first categorized a few months ago, if you watched the news closely. Of course, we are trying to get away from naming viruses after places after the confusion that caused during the last pandemic." The way he said it made it sound like some kind of ancient history and Deputy Boggs wasn't the only one who squirmed a little in his seat.

Booth went on, almost jovial;

"We are officially going with the World Health Organization designation PERS 24. Everyone is well aware of what we went through with Covid and this is another respiratory virus, but something different has emerged with this and we are unsure right now if there is a chance this is a mutation of something. Currently, this seems to be a stand-alone virus and it has a few chilling differences. First there is a neurological component. This virus may actually affect behavior which may explain County Prosecutor Joe Braunstrup's strange death. That is still being investigated. Of further concern with this virus is the 30 to 40 % mortality rate. That is why we are seeing such significant response here. Initial studies show, if we can lock this down hard, there will be a minimum spread and we'll drastically reduce loss of life because this virus seems to burn itself out fairly quickly.

"That is why the county has been sealed off, nothing in, nothing out. The Federal Government will provide for the needs of all county citizens. When necessary, we will be distributing food and we will control resources such as fuel and heating. Propane and even fire- wood will be provided by the federal government, that is why we are stepping in. And of course, we will step back as the emergency subsides. As soon as the Sheriff is feeling better, he will be reinstalled. Until that time, we ask for your critical cooperation.

"For the time being, all patrol units will be accompanied by a federal deputy. No more riding solo, now you deputies will benefit from an immediate back-up in the form of a federal ride-along partner. These will be a mix of federally deputized military and law enforcement partners. While some of you may be used to riding alone, I think everyone is aware of the nationally recognized statistic that a second officer on scene reduces the probability of violence by over seventy percent, so clearly, this benefits everyone, even the community.

"I'm ready to open the floor to questions now."

Boggs's hand shot up.

"Yes, Sir." Booth smiled.

"So, now, ah… we are under federal control? The Sheriff has always been an elected position, at the service of the people, not politicians. You've been appointed, not elected. So, now I have to listen to you, and whoever you're putting in the car with me?"

"Great question, I'm so glad you asked that." Booth looked down at his notes before responding further and it took him a moment.

"Yes, the federal government has taken control in these extreme circumstances and we ask for your patience and cooperation as we work through this together. Together we can save lives and restore a normal order."

"Incidentally, we understand this may be uncomfortable for many. We will make sure your pay and benefits remain in place throughout this trying time. If for whatever reason you wish to submit your resignation, we understand that these are difficult times."

Boggs raised his hand again.

"Yes?"

"So, you're saying the Sheriff and Markdale were exposed because they were on the scene of Joe's death."

Booth looked at his notes, then paused further.

"Yes,"

"Well, I showed up on scene there a little after you showed up. Were we exposed? How would we know?"

Booth gave an artificial laugh as he shuffled through his notes.

"You know, ah... Deputy ah..."

"Frank Boggs."

"Yes, of course, you were outside by the military command post... I think... well we believe we are safe. We would have been symptomatic by now; this thing moves fast. I'm not exhibiting symptoms, are you?"

"Ah, what symptoms should I be expecting."

"Well, ah..." Booth looked down at his notes. "Fever, chills, cough, sore throat, muscle or body aches, fatigue."

"So, the flu."

Booth looked down a moment.

"Well, yes, *and* unusual thoughts or behavior."

Deputy Boggs folded his arms across his chest skeptically.

"You guys know, we don't do a formal roll call here, right? This is a rural department and guys go into service from home."

"Well, deputy, some things will be changing as we move forward and we look forward to your co-operation. We'll turn this over to the Sergeant now. We'll do another briefing next week and you will be seeing broadcast news sometime today. Thank you, everyone." The two men departed as the Sergeant stood up. Booth closed the door behind them as he headed for the parking lot.

"I'm heading over to brief the county commissioners now, I'll stop by to see how you're settling into your new office and I'll update you then, Ted."

*   *   *

"This would have started about the same time you noticed your GPS going sideways, Tom. I guess it's what passes for news. There are two 'channels' that are the only things that come up on my internet browser. I've tried resetting my Starlink, this is all that comes up. I listen to the radio, there are two stations. They are all saying the same thing. For hours it's been a kind of reassuring public service announcement, dressed up like network news."

"Propaganda?" Tom said as he hovered over the steaming hot chocolate.

"More sophisticated than that. Information Operations. They are exerting full spectrum control over the county. Restricting freedom of movement, controlling information. Disappearing people like the Sheriff…"

"Do you think he's going to be OK?"

"Are you asking if I think he's really sick?"

"That too."

"I don't believe he's sick, Tom. I don't know if he's going to be OK."

"They'll interrogate him, won't they?"

Max just nodded.

"This is all because of me." Tom said as he set the hot chocolate down on the table.

"No, Tom. This is because of a government that is desperate to exert control. They are doing this. They have a war to fight and they need bodies. And as things progress, they need to crush resistance in any form it takes."

"Should I turn myself in?"

"It won't change anything, Tom."

Tom looked around at the big, well-furnished kitchen, enjoying the warmth and shelter again.

"I can't stay here, Max."

"It would be unwise. We are going to need to move you as far away as possible from the signature you established in this area. They are going to detect that, they are going to start searching here. Preferably we need to move you out of the county or country."

"I've put you in danger because I came here with that radio."

"I'll manage, I know how to talk my way out of things like that. I'm going to go into town and see what's going on, see what our options are. Do you know any other people that helped you get away?"

Tom thought for a long time and started to shake his head.

"There were so many people and so much going on... wait a minute, the guy who owns that real good Italian restaurant in town, the black guy. I remember seeing him. We used to go in there pretty often. My Mom really liked the place, and my Dad really liked the guy. Doug, I think his name was. I guess it turned out my Dad was TDY in Sigonella at a time Doug was stationed there."

"Alright," Max thought a moment. "what about clothes, what do you have for clothes?"

"Just that winter gear, a spare set of thermal underwear and a set of BDUs."

"Hmm. That won't do." Max grabbed a pad of sticky notes from the kitchen drawer and slid it with a pen to Tom. "Write down all your sizes, I'll pick up some things for you."

"I... I don't have any money."

"Don't worry about it. The way you eat it will be cheaper to buy you clothes and get you out of here than to keep feeding you."

Max smiled and Tom grinned back. Max started walking away for a moment, headed down the hallway.

"Are you going to drive your Sno-cat all the way into town?"

"No, I have a little place down by the highway that I keep a truck in. I'll swap out the cat for the truck, much lower profile. Hold on a moment."

He came back with a small box that took Tom a moment to recognize.

"Is that a Polaroid?"

"Yes, Tom. Turn the computer around to show the news broadcast for a date stamp. This is going to be your proof of life picture…" Max snapped the picture, the flash went off and the picture came out. He pulled it from the camera and looked at it for a moment before showing it to Tom.

"That'll do, Tom. I'm going to start checking around with some contacts that might be able to take care of you and I'm going to very carefully see if any networks may already be in place. And get you some clothes that will help you blend in and allow you to come in from the cold."

*   *   *

Booth smiled as he presented his ID to the soldier at the desk. The soldier picked up his phone and spoke professionally.

"Sir, Regional Administrator Booth is here to see you." The soldier listened to the response and reached for the door button. Hitting the button, the door buzzed and the soldier jumped up and opened it for Booth.

"He'll see you immediately, Sir."

Still smiling as he walked through the door, Booth spoke warmly.

"Got rid of a… oh what was her name?"

"Mary, yes. Firing her was one of the first things I did." There was a soldier taking down the Sheriff's sparse decorations and replacing them with what appeared to be several boxes of framed certificates and diplomas. "Specialist, go take a coffee break, we'll be meeting here for about the next hour."

"Yes, Sir, Mr. Zites."

The soldier left with some haste.

"Yes, all a big improvement Ted. How are you liking your new office?"

"A little small, but we're all having to make some sacrifices right now. How was the meeting with the Commissioners?"

"About as I expected, Ted. I mean, they don't really have much choice. They go along and keep their jobs, or they quit and if they give us any real problems, they just go away."

"That was part of the brief?"

"Not directly, they'll get the picture soon enough. All kinds of people will be going away for 'treatment.'"

"Are the camps ready?"

"Just about, Ted. The grocery stores are already just about out of food. The first C-130s will start running tomorrow. Inbound with food, outbound with patients and conscripts as we start finding them."

"The Sheriff and Markdale? Have they provided any info?"

"They haven't started working on them, I don't think. Won't really matter, just be patient. They've soaked this county for the last two months with an incredible array of assets.

Wide Area Motion, IR, Day TV, LIDAR, Synthetic Aperture Radar, Hyperspectral Imagery, Radio Direction Finding, digital tracking. Mapping out every incongruity in every part of the county. I've even got a man inside. If Tom Potter is alive, we'll have him in good time. If he's dead, we'll find his body in the last hole he crawled into. And along the way, we'll gather up all the people who would be a problem for us. Like that Deputy Boggs, I'd watch him close…"

"Oh, he's already on my list, he gave me a hard time when I was on Field Training here, I could tell then what kind of person he was."

"We'll get this county straightened out. It will be a template moving forward. That's why they're doing this. This is the test bed for real change. They know we can't crack down on a national level all at once. But we can isolate, root out and destroy centers of resistance in backwaters like this. The surplus, unproductive parts of the cities will burn themselves down. Out here is where we will get people in line. Eventually, we'll get this whole country under control. And you and I will be in very good position."

"You mentioned a man inside, who?"

"Long time informant. Hasn't done any work for us in a while, but I'm sure he'll play ball. Old navy man, got himself in a bind, had to work off some charges, then went pro."

*   *   *

His throat was raw and sore from the intubation. He sat shivering in the dim light on the little mattress, wrapped in the scratchy wool blanket. It was cold, but a furnace of some kind would fire off periodically somewhere that he could hear.

All of it was artificially controlled, they didn't want him dead, yet. They wanted him uncomfortable, they wanted him… malleable.

The air was heavy with the smell of seawater and Sheriff Grant Taylor knew he was a long way from home.

The room was all concrete, the small window had been covered over and the big steel door had only a small hatch in the bottom that he had received a meal and water through earlier. There was a bucket in the corner.

There was a vague recollection of a doctor and someone else, maybe a guard, in the room with him as he regained consciousness. There had been no human contact after that. It must have been 24 hours, but he couldn't be sure.

His mind was still fogged as he was coming down off of whatever they had given him. He couldn't focus, couldn't really complete a thought.

Grant clasped his hands together. He needed a prayer. For Tom, wherever he was. For his wife, he wondered what they told her. He needed a prayer for himself.

So, he would start.

God…

But he couldn't put it together, his brain wasn't working like that yet. He knew he needed help, he knew Tom would need help.

God…Please… I can't let them come between me and you… Please…

Grant shook his head. The right words just wouldn't come to him. He sighed with frustration. The cold wasn't helping. He needed something, and he knew it was in prayer but his thoughts were fragmented. He needed something, something to allow him focus, something that was like instinct.

"I know." He said quietly to himself.

Our Father, who art in Heaven, hallowed be thy Name, thy Kingdom come, thy will be done, on earth as it is in heaven...

CHAPTER 4

When the tall guy walked in, he scanned his four corners, checked behind him and took his place in line behind the customers Doug was ringing out. The couple ahead of him took their change and left with strained smiles, tense with the times. The tall man stepped forward and said nothing for a moment.

"Could I see a menu, please?"

"Yes, Sir." Doug said handing him a menu. "First time here?"

"Yes, came on the recommendation of a friend." The man was watching the couple leave. When the door closed behind them, he continued. "A mutual friend actually."

"Oh, who is that?"

"Young man, named Tom."

Doug looked out the glass door a moment, then shook his head.

"Doesn't ring a bell, sorry."

"I would think this young man would be hard to forget. Especially for you. Last time you saw him would have involved helicopters chasing men on horseback, led by our Sheriff who has apparently fallen terribly ill."

"Well, that sure doesn't seem like something I would forget."

"No, it all seems very dramatic and very dangerous for all involved, especially for you… and very especially for me. I'm trying to help him, but he will be in danger at my place and with all these new developments in town, I suspect the noose will be tightening soon. We need to bring Tom in from the cold. I'd like your help and I understand your concerns, Doug."

"Well, you have me at a great disadvantage. Who and what are you?"

"My name is Max Valencour. I'm retired."

"Well Max," Doug extended his hand. "Nice to meet you, wish I could help you but I really have no idea what you're talking about… would you like to place an order? No telling how long I'll have food or how long they'll allow us to stay open with everything that's going on."

"Doug, you are right to be suspicious. I know a thing or two about this game, I played it a long time ago. The technology is a lot more sophisticated now and they will find him soon if I don't get him some place safe. You and your men must have good security protocols if you haven't been swept up in the first wave. Presumably you have a network, you can get Tom underground. I have contacts here, for all kinds of reasons, but I'd prefer not to use them. You know they are working on the Sheriff and his Deputy now. It's only a matter of time before someone talks, before they come knocking on all our doors."

Doug sighed. The tall man had spook written all over him; this had to be a trap. He shrugged.

"Sorry, Sir. I have no idea what you're talking about."

Max's expression was unchanged, he looked very cold and calculating and Doug instantly felt that not trusting him was the right course of action.

Max looked out the glass front of the restaurant, then pulled the Polaroid picture of Tom from his jacket pocket.

"It's very dangerous for either of us to be caught with this picture. I've been carrying it around all day, I'm leaving it here with you. Burn it when you're done with it."

Doug took the picture reluctantly, like something he really didn't want to touch. He didn't really know Tom well, and he looked different from when he did know him. But the long hair and the scruff of beard looked like the glimpse of the young man he'd seen ride past him on the back of the Sheriff's horse amid the chaos of that day.

"Can you come back tomorrow, same time?" Doug stepped back to the kitchen and came back with a small pizza box.

"I can be back in two days." Max said taking the box he was being handed. "What is this?"

"It's for Tom, and you shouldn't be walking out of here empty handed." Doug sighed and shook his head.

*   *   *

The driver's window rolled down as Boggs approached the vehicle. The driver had pulled off into the big gas station, just outside of town. He'd slowed immediately and put on his flashers as he was stopping. Boggs called the stop in and gave the vehicle description as they were coming to a halt. Not the cleanest of traffic stops, but that's how it goes sometimes.

"License, registration and proof of insurance, please."

The young man had tears down his cheeks and a harried look about him. His information was quick at hand.

"I'm sorry, Deputy… I know I shouldn't have done that. My baby ran out of formula and he's not latching onto my wife… They're about out of everything at the store now and I just wanted to get there fast to try to get formula if they have any left."

"Passing two cars on the double yellow on that curve is a risky proposition…" Boggs looked at the license, the picture matched and he looked at the name. "Dave… Doesn't do anyone any good if you go out for an emergency like this and have a head on collision with someone, OK? You guys have some food at home?"

"A little bit."

"Wait here a minute, calm down. I know it seems like a big emergency but everyone has to be cool right now. You need to be really calm for your wife and kids, right?"

Dave nodded, his hands gripping the wheel.

"I'm going to just write you a quick warning, they want everything documented now, but you need to promise me you're going to hold it together, right? I got kids, I get it, just relax. I'll be right back."

Boggs sat back behind the wheel and keyed his mic as he looked at Dave's paper work.

"Dispatch, November Twelve needs 28, 29 on my stopped vehicle and Dave Smith, common spelling, one-five- ninety-eight."

"November Twelve, he comes back as the registered owner of that vehicle and is negative for wants and warrants, but we are showing a WPA hold."

Boggs keyed the mic, then released it, not sure what to say. Instead he looked at the young MP in the seat beside him. The young guy seemed insulted because after his first traffic stop with the guy he'd told the young Specialist to stay in the car. Boggs further advised the soldier that drawing his weapon for someone rolling through a stop sign was unwarranted.

"WPA Hold is part of the War Powers Act. You're obligated to hold him until the arrival of a federal arrest team."

"November Twelve, Dispatch, we're looking at our instructions here, a WPA Hold is new to us too. It just says you have to hold him until the arrival of Federal authorities."

"Yeah, roger. Discussing this with my Federal ah, partner."

The specialist smiled smugly.

"Alright, well how long am I supposed to hold him here? I can only hold him a *reasonable* amount of time."

"Forget all that stuff, Boggs."

"*Forget all that stuff?* Like the Fourth Amendment, the Constitution?"

The Specialist nodded with that big smug smile and pointed down the road a ways.

"None of that matters right now, Boggs." The soldier was pointing to a pair of ASVs and a Humvee. The little column pulled quickly into the gas station and surrounded the scene of Boggs' stop.

"What the hell..." Boggs opened the door to step out but the Specialist grabbed his arm.

"Just let it happen, Boggs."

The Deputy looked down at the soldier's hand, then up to him with disgust.

"I was going to just write this guy a warning, he's got a kid to feed, he's young and scared." The ASVs were positioned to block Dave's vehicle in, but still allow for the depression of the turreted machine guns.

"Write your paper work, Boggs. He won't need a copy, not where he's going, but you'll need to document your part."

Boggs looked at the warning book on the dash and out to the two soldiers in full gear rushing to pull Dave roughly out of the car.

"This is insane, what did he do?"

The Specialist shrugged, indifferent.

"Insurgent ties maybe. Ours is not to reason why, Boggs."

Boggs watched helplessly as the man was thrown to the ground and flex cuffed. He was lifted up and thrown in the back seat of the Humvee, all the while the machine gun turrets of the ASVs tracking his every move.

The little column took off with as much haste as it had arrived and Boggs keyed his mic.

"Dispatch, November Twelve, I guess I'm clear my stop, federal team took the man I stopped into custody."

"November Twelve, Dispatch, roger."

Boggs put the Tahoe in gear and followed the military vehicles as they weaved through the small town. The ASVs towered over other vehicles and seemed very foreign.

"What are you doing, Boggs?" The Specialist asked.

"I just want to see where they are taking him. I'm sure you won't tell me."

"I don't know and I don't care. I'm just following orders."

"You need to read your history, that doesn't always fly."

On the north side of the airport, a military encampment had sprung up, it was hard to see what all it comprised of as it was surrounded by a wall of stacked Hesco barriers topped with razor wire and cameras at every corner. Suddenly there were cameras all over town, all over the county, really.

The little column entered the front gate, manned by soldiers in a darker uniform and out side there was an illuminated, but hastily constructed ply wood sign that read "FOB Prather." The gate was quickly shut after the last ASV. The soldier manning the gate gave Boggs aggressive hand signals that clearly meant he just needed to go away.

The Specialist waved from the seat beside him.

"We need to get out of here, Boggs. If you don't like the rules you and I are operating under now, you don't want to know about these guys' rules of engagement."

"Alright, I've got his address, I'm going to his house to let his wife know what happened."

The Specialist laughed mockingly.

"You want her rolled up too?"

"What do you mean, she deserves to know what happened."

"Yeah, then she comes down here to protest... She gets disappeared too, Boggs."

Boggs drove away, trying to look at anything other than the Specialist and anything that was symbolic of the occupation. There were no easy choices now, not even any good ones.

*   *   *

Booth slumped in the chair opposite Zites' desk. He inhaled deeply before speaking.

"If I have to do one more initial brief on all this... just got done with state employees. They're all panicked because they are out of contact with their chain of command. Talked with all the different state services, administrators. The State Patrol guys were particularly worked up and not thrilled with having our federal deputies with them. Take it or leave it, if you want a pay check, you gotta play ball." Booth laughed.

"Oh, and the game wardens... they're already getting reports of poaching."

"It's only been a week since things have shut down, the stores only just ran out of everything. I thought people in this place were all about preparedness and independent living."

Booth shrugged with a smile.

"I suppose some more than others. And we're going to see a lot of different behavior. I don't think most of those cases are of people who are already hungry and desperate. I think most of them are just people who think they can get away with it now, probably think they can sell the meat on some emerging black market. They don't understand the blanket of surveillance they're operating under. Idiots. This one was classic, we're getting the reports correlated with Gorgon Stare, so we go back at the time of the incident, look at the imagery in the rough grid and bingo. Best part was one of them was a 20 year old kid... Unregistered..."

"No way..."

Booth laughed again.

"Absolutely, conscription incident to arrest. Only question going through that kid's mind right now is whether he's going to fight the Russians or Chinese."

Zites grimaced without sympathy, then looked at his encrypted console.

"Are you trackin' these charter flights we have to facilitate tonight?"

"The VIPs? Yeah, there's several families getting out that were able to prove primary residency elsewhere and no connection to insurgent activity or political misalignment."

Zites nodded and commented.

"Good for them, it's going to start getting real uncomfortable for some folks here with another storm rolling in. Are they going to be able to get to Potter before this next storm?

Booth shrugged.

"Doesn't matter, we'll get him eventually. We have all the time in the world now. We own this place. We've got good leads, pattern of life signature and even a beacon they're following. They're in two different places, but we've got the resources to follow up each now. Analysts believe the kid has survived so far. They want to catch him alive to see who has been helping him. We'll probably get more involved in that in the next week or so, once basic public administration is stabilized. Right now it's a contractor show; these guys they have that are doing the man hunting. They could have that part wrapped up in a few days, we'll see."

*　　*　　*

"Valencour, you gave that Bible to Max Valencour?" Ski was incredulous.

"He showed me this."

Doug said as he threw the Polaroid of Tom to the center of the table.

"Who is Max Valencour?" Roger asked.

"I don't know." Doug said.

"I hope you don't know who he is." Ski said, suddenly suspicious.

"Well?" Doug's hands went up a little. "Enlighten us already, Ski."

Ski sat back and looked at Doug, Bill and Roger.

"You guys don't travel in the circles I do here. You're all clean, well established, family types. The underbelly, that's where I live. The seedy bars, the bikers, the outlaws. The people that would surprise you that they even exist in this county, I know them. And they all know Max Valencour. Some believe he's here on some kind of witness protection program, most believe him to be a very well-paid federal snitch."

"What?" Doug exclaimed.

"That's right, Doug. If we still had internet I'd tell you to look it up. There are websites devoted to that guy. A few are sympathetic, some claim he got in trouble in the Philippines when he was in the Navy. The general story is that he got mixed up with drugs or something, he was intel or crypto or something, I don't remember. He went informant to work off the charges. Infiltrated some drug outfits, then some terror groups. A lot of it overseas and they say it paid really well. It's rumored he worked stateside stuff as a deep cover snitch for the FBI after that."

Doug sank his face into his hands.

"What did you tell him, Doug? We need to know everything. Did you tell him about our meetings?"

"I told him to meet here today, he said he could come tomorrow."

Ski shook his head.

"That's all I told him, I didn't tell him anything except to give him that Bible."

"Well, gentlemen, this is our last meeting here. Just as well, I suppose. Let's finish up this meeting and start thinking of where we can meet next. I'll report first;

"I've had guys probing the whole eastern border it's locked down tighter than a…

Ski looked around at his rather wholesome company. Roger laughed in speculation of where Ski was going with it, but he had caught himself and continued.

"East side is locked down tight. Highway, state roads, county roads, private roads, logging roads, hiking trails. If it's not a manned checkpoint, they have remote cameras and drones if the weather isn't too bad. There's no getting in or out. One of my guys went past the remote cameras and got rolled up half mile down the road. They chewed him out, told him he was lucky, if the other crew was working, he'd be *off to the camp*. What did your crew turn up on the north border, Bill?"

"Same. One of my guys even took his sled up Whiskey Run Pass, said they came at him with a Blackhawk and he could see them pointing the machine gun at him. Now this guy, he's prone to telling stories. But he's one of those that's always the hero in his stories, right? Not this time. He was scared when he told it. He said he's not going out there again. The border crossing itself is sealed tight by our military on this side and Canadian military on their side."

"I thought I might be able to get through to my relatives," Roger said. "I know a lot of the backroads to the south there, when there's an accident on the highway I use 'em a lot. Nothing, everything sealed up."

"Same out west," Doug said. "I can't imagine the massive number of troops they put into this. And all the C-130s at our little airport, FOBs going up, stateside... in our home."

"I'm guessing at least 150,000 maybe 200,000 troops for this." Ski estimated. "To seal that kind of border and staff as many checkpoints as we see around the county. I hear they're bringing food in on the 130s. The grocery stores have been a mess and are about out of food."

"I heard they're going to close down all businesses except the grocery store and that's where they'll hand out government food. They're saying rations are based on census results." Bill looked at Doug. "Have you heard that?"

Doug shook his head.

"Customers come in with all kinds of worried rumors, I don't know what to believe, but that would follow the Covid template wouldn't it? I'm about out of cheeses. Plenty of prepped dough and flour and yeast. Lots of tomato sauce and paste and I got a huge shipment of fresh vegetables the day they closed it all down. That's gonna go to waste. I've seen a big drop in business. People are afraid to be out other than to the grocery store."

"Afraid of the virus?" Ski asked.

Doug shook his head.

"Not what they're saying, they're afraid of the troops. Afraid of rioting and looting, but I don't think that's happened at all yet."

"An armed society is a polite society." Roger quoted.

"What about the virus?" Ski pressed. "Is that seen as bogus?"

"People are getting sick, I know a bunch." Bill offered. "Everyone's afraid to go get checked out or they get disappeared like the Sheriff and Markdale. I've heard of others disappearing."

"Well, that all jibes with what I've seen." Ski said. "It's flu season, there isn't any virus at all. They made this one up as an expedient control measure. Covid was the proof of concept."

"Where is the local Command and Control on all this, Ski?"

"At the most basic level, that looks like it is at the Sheriff's Department. They've taken it over. Apparently, this guy Booth, who used to be an FBI agent is now in charge of the county. He's got some long-winded title. He was associated with the initial raid on Potter's Cabin. My contact at the Sheriff's Department isn't really clear on that. I guess the Sheriff was managing the Potter situation with just him and Markdale. Kept it pretty compartmentalized. Oh, and the guy who has 'taken over' the Sheriff's role is a Deputy that the Sheriff had fired during that whole thing. He's called the 'Public Safety Magistrate'."

"Judge, jury and executioner?" Doug asked.

"Sounds like it to me. His name is Ted Zites and he made himself right at home in Sheriff Taylor's office. He has no friends in that department, that's for sure."

"They called me in for a meeting, all county employees mandatory attendance, that guy Booth was running it. Basically, some kind of cheerleading session that the county is going to continue to function…" Bill paused. "Seamless transition is what he called it. We'll continue to get paid, we'll be getting food. I guess the grocery stores will be food distribution sites. I'll be runnin' the plow when this storm hits just like usual. But folks are real nervous. He wouldn't answer when people were asking him about lockdowns and private sector folks being put out of work. And someone brought up the fact that people are just going missing. He wouldn't address that other than to say that people who are coming down with PERs are being flown out to get immediate care in some hospital in Seattle. I do know they had me runnin' a dump truck to fill these Hesco barrier things up by the airport. I don't know what they put in that, there were a bunch of portable buildings going in, and we had to be accompanied at all times. There were some serious looking dudes in dark uniforms running around there. Looks like they got whatever it is operational; it's got a sign out front that says FOB Prather. What does that mean?"

"FOB is a Forward Operating Base, I don't know what a Prather is." Doug said. "We had FOBs all over Iraq and Afghanistan. I can't believe we have them here now."

"You remember what they were named after, right?" Ski asked.

"Our guys killed in action." Roger said as Doug nodded.

"Might have been one of the FBI agents killed early on. The one on the helicopter with the Sheriff or one of the ones the girl shot." Ski was sipping at his coke.

"What do we do now, Ski?"

"We exhibit extreme tactical patience. Keep building the intel picture. Figure out who is who in the zoo. Look for targets of opportunity, but make sure we don't go out in a blaze of stupid."

"This meeting spot is burned, we have to meet somewhere else from now on, maybe identify a couple of different ones we can use randomly. And, Doug, you haven't given Max anything but that Bible. Your story is that the Sheriff gave it to you with instructions to get it to Tom if you heard anyone talking about his location. If you don't mind, I'll meet with Max alone tomorrow."

*　　　*　　　*

"You will never be Sheriff again." The man in the big parka sat in a folding chair and consulted his tablet. "Your department no longer exists as a Sheriff's department. It is a Federal Public Safety Department. Your county no longer exists. It is now a Federal Cooperative Enclave. As far as the people of your county know, you are being treated for the PERS virus in Seattle and you are still in a coma."

The man was older and balding; he had a thick white mustache that didn't conceal his smirk.

"But you don't have PERS and this ain't Seattle. You are here because we need two things. The location of the fugitive Tom Potter and a list of all those who assisted in his escape."

Grant said nothing.

"Mr. Markdale isn't being particularly helpful either. That's OK, we have lots of time. We have the entire enclave locked down. Food has run out at the grocery stores, we have been flying in pallets full of MREs and famine rations. Another big storm is about to hit. It's going to be really rough for the people of the enclave. If you provide us with the information we seek, things can go a lot easier on people, restrictions can be lifted, freedoms restored. We just need you to work with us. The people of your community need you to work with us."

The man looked down at his tablet, tapped around with his stylus, gave a curt smile, then stood up, taking his folding chair with him. He stood at the door a moment and it was opened for him. That meant there was a camera somewhere in the room. The Sheriff had looked for cameras and microphones a few times but came up empty handed.

What little food they were giving him had just enough nutritive value to keep him alive, but not enough calories to keep him warm, or to let him think straight. He had two anchor points.

One, he couldn't let Tom Potter or the men of his posse down.

Two, he couldn't let God down.

*   *   *

Tom had loaded his pack and the little duffle bag full of street clothes into the back of the Sno-cat. He'd broken his HK-416 into its upper and lower halves and placed them in his pack. He carried his 1911 on his hip in a strap holster that wasn't made specifically to carry that particular piece and its mounted light, but it was more secure than simply tucked in his waistband.

He was sitting in the passenger seat as Max drove the big beast in the driving snow. Its panel and exterior lighting gave it the appearance of some kind of interstellar exploration vehicle. The seat was comfortable and the ride was far smoother than Tom imagined such a machine would be.

When he first sat down, he saw the small pizza box between the seats.

"Pizza!" He had exclaimed.

"No," Max responded, "A surprise, but you'll have to wait a minute."

Now that the diesel was humming and the four tracks were churning along reliably in the snow, Tom asked again.

"So, about the surprise."

Max stopped the machine and smiled, handing him the box. Opening the box, Tom found the brown wrapped book

"Go ahead. Open it."

He didn't need to open it all the way to realize what it was. He'd seen his father reading it for years.

"Well, that's the biggest smile I've seen on you, Tom." Max returned his attention to the snow blown trail ahead of them and got the beast rolling again.

"How… where did you get it?"

"Your friend, Doug. The Italian restaurant guy. The Sheriff found it and passed it along to him to make sure you got it."

"Wow…"

"You sure put a lot of stock in that book, Tom. I envy you in a way."

Tom tilted his head a little, unsure of how to respond. He thumbed through the well-read and annotated Bible. When he was alone, he would find it proved to be an important connection to his father and to God.

"It's got bigger print, it'll be easier to read in low light." Tom paused and thought there was something more important to say and it took him a moment to put it together for Max.

"Do you put no stock in the Bible at all, Max?"

"Oh, well… I mean…" That was a more difficult question than he was expecting. "Do you believe it's the word of God, Tom?"

Tom nodded.

"But it's written and printed by men. Do you think old King James there didn't have something to say about what tone it should take? And the Council of Nicaea, how did that work? A bunch of men deciding which word of God to accept?"

"Council of what?"

"Nicaea. It was a meeting very early on by Christian church officials to try to standardize things. People decided what was in the Bible, Tom. When you think about that, does it change how you see it?"

Tom thought quietly as the Cummins diesel purred behind them. He continued to leaf through the Bible, but he wasn't sure that was where he'd actually find the answer to such a question.

"Lots of people have different interpretations of what they read in here, Max. Lots of people are sure that their interpretation is the only one."

Max nodded knowingly.

"Does that make the value of anyone's interpretation any less? Does that mean what I get from the Bible isn't important?"

"Well, I didn't mean…"

"Not to me, Max. That's between me and God. I don't understand everything I read here, but if it brings me closer to God and makes me want to be a better person, isn't that a good thing?"

"Well…"

"I've come a long way, I've gone through a lot."

"You were well prepared and your father taught you well."

Tom nodded.

"But there was more to it than that. I didn't pay attention to all the things my Dad tried to teach us, and I'm not even that smart."

"Don't sell yourself short, Tom. What you have done has been amazing."

"I've had help all along the way."

"Present company excluded, you've had some good people helping you."

"Maybe God guided them to me, or me to them."

"You'll never know."

"But I do, Max. I have faith, I believe. I just want to be left alone and He's helping me with that."

"You may not always have that luxury, Tom. They can never just leave us alone, they hate that more than anything. At a certain point, you can't run anymore and you'll have to make a stand. What will you do then?"

"I'll have faith."

*   *   *

The pilot turned the big Sikorsky into the wind, glancing at the second S-92 in orbit over him watching the Area Of Interest. He had planned his approach on a line into the wind to maintain enough forward motion to stay just ahead of the whiteout he knew his downwash would create in the fresh snow.

As the lowered ramp settled on the fresh snow, the five men and a dog were out of the helo and he lifted off to take up the lower orbit and allow the team to maintain easier coms.

The beating of the rotor downwash and noise of the departing helicopter abated and the team leader was looking at the little tablet flipped out from its spot on his plate carrier.

"Yeah, about thirty meters, straight ahead."

Post holing through the fresh ankle deep snow, they occasionally broke through the older layer, going to their knees. They were traveling light and were fit, but it was still frustrating and they were glad to have immediate helicopter support as they checked this, the third surveyed Area Of Interest, or AOI, of the day.

As they approached, the tracker, the K-9 handler and the team leader all saw it about the same time. This could be different. Different from the old car chassis, or the old mine tailing pit that had shown up as a possible structure to the analysts in their study of different overhead imagery that had saturated the county.

This, they could see, was a difference in snow depth in what was shaped as a very uniform rectangle. The team all stopped at once. Orbiting overhead, the helicopters were far enough out to allow easy conversation, but close enough their pulsing rotors were reassuring in that the team knew that each helo had a door mounted minigun trained on the AOI.

"Goin' out…" The team leader keyed up his microphone to talk to the helicopters. "We may have something here, watch us close."

Paulsen was looking over the team leader's shoulder, distracted a little from his area of responsibility.

"Frag first, then dog, Gary?"

"Ah, no."

"Banger, then dog?"

"No, Paulsen." Though new to the company, Paulsen had enough training, background and combat deployments that the team leader expected more. But Paulsen was young and the maturity just wasn't there yet. "No, Paulsen. We start detonating things in there and we could spoil a good scent for the dog and blow evidence Chambers could use. You're going to go up there and figure out how it opens, then you're going to hold it open for the dog. We'll go from there."

"Why me? Why always me?"

"Because my tracker and K-9 handler have special skills, Paulsen. You're just another young shooter."

A little laughter went out from the other members of the team as Paulsen crept forward, carbine muzzle up on the unknown rectangle and whatever might lay beneath it. The younger man had cleared enough holes in enough forgotten, forsaken places, he was all business as he approached.

Quietly probing the edge through the snow, he found a partially frozen paracord loop that had to be a handle. Grasping it carefully to take the slack out, he held his other hand up over his head in a fist. Spreading his thumb, then trigger finger, then middle finger in for a predictable five count. The handler saw this and went for the dog's quick release. Paulsen's hand went to his carbine as the hatch was pulled open and it was well-timed as Rocket, the K-9 brushed passed his leg, blasting eagerly into the hole.

The dog emerged quickly and Paulsen had the light on his carbine on.

"Clear, it's small, but this is it, this is a big deal I think, guys."

The handler and Chambers, the tracker, approached.

"A fully stocked cache, Gary. Everything a guy on the run could want or need. If he just used this alone he could resupply for a long time." Chambers looked around, holding the hatch open, while Paulsen took a knee and covered to the west. The handler took his dog down in the cache and let the dog smell everything.

"There's a couple pretty good tracks under this fresh snow, I'll go in after the dog here and see what I can find, let him come out and see if he picks up the scent. Then I'll see what I can do with those tracks. Right now, Gary I'd say he's at least 24 hours ahead of us the way the snow looks. I'll give you a better estimate in a minute."

Gary was approaching.

"Alright, good job guys, going out on command…" He keyed his mic. "Command, Charlie Four with a jackpot. This is a recently active cache, developing track from here."

"Alright, Chambers, we're comin' out, all yours. He sure has a bunch of stuff down here, some spare snowshoes you'll probably be interested in."

"Paulsen, could you hold this open again, please. I'm goin' in with Chambers."

The tracker was slow on his descent down the steps, holding his flashlight at different angles.

"Looks like a sleeping mat with a bag was on it for more than an overnight, see how that packed dirt looks different on that side? I think he was camped out here a while, Gary. Yeah, a waste bucket…" The tracker picked it up. "Empty. The MRE's and some of the stacks of canned food have been moved. The forensics guys are going to find that and his waste buried nearby."

Chambers came to the snowshoes. He shook his head with a grin.

"Not a spare, he took the spare. This was his original pair. The binding was broke so he swapped it out." The tracker pulled out his measuring tape and note book. "Yeah this matches what the other guys had."

Looking at the shelves with his flashlight, Chambers stopped and took a second look at something toward the back of the shelf, a familiar reflection had caught his eye.

Reaching back behind the canned food he came back with a piece of brass and he checked the headstamp.

"Five five six." Looking back on the shelf, he produced another shell. "He fired from here, no holes in the hatch."

Poking his head up out of the cache, he saw the old trail under the snow to the nearby pine.

"That's about twenty-five meters, Gary." Chambers looked to the last member of the team who was closest to the tree. "Smith, go look at that tree and tell me how many bullet holes it has in it."

The man trudged through the snow.

"Three, nice group."

"He was confirming zero on his rifle."

"Or," Gary suggested. "Confirming zero on a gun that wasn't his. Like the 416 he's reported to have snagged from the FBI agent."

The tracker nodded and climbed out of the cache. He started carefully digging the freshest snow out of the old tracks to assess them.

"Any word on that beacon and the suspicious skidoo that showed up?" Chambers said as he pulled out his measuring tape.

"No, they launched on it but nothing back yet." Gary said with a shake of his head.

"Gary, I'm very confident this is our guy. I believe these fresher tracks are no more than 72 hours old."

"Yeah," Gary said. "Let's develop this guy's trail and grab him. Less time we spend on this contract, the higher our daily rate."

*   *   *

"Doug, you got any more containers?" Roger asked.

"No, all out, they're gonna have to take it in the bulk container if they want the tomato sauce."

Roger handed the older lady the container and a head of lettuce and a few onions.

"Sorry, ma'am. You can hand it out to friends and family." He smiled back to Doug who was busy handing out wrapped bundles of dough. The line was out the door and Ski was sitting by himself at the table facing the door. Ski wasn't happy with the situation at all. He wanted to be alone in the uncrowded restaurant. With the unexpected crowd, Doug figured Roger could help while they could both watch Ski's back.

When the tall man entered, he squeezed by the people in line through the door and started to walk back to the counter where he saw Doug distributing food. Ski stood up blocking his path and motioned for Max to sit down.

Max balked and looked back to Doug.

"The man is busy, you talk to me today, Mr. Valencour."

Max turned to leave, Ski grabbed him by the sleeve and spun him just enough to put him off balance and shove him into the booth.

"Oh, Sir… I'm so sorry, I slipped." The line of people, preoccupied with the food distribution didn't notice what had really happened. Ski leaned into him, his right hand on his 1911 in a shoulder holster, revealed by his left hand opening his coat, just enough.

"I won't hesitate to drill a guy like you in times like these, Valencour." Ski said quietly. "Now sit tight and answer my questions."

Max leaned on the table as Ski sat across from him. With discretion for the benefit of the crowd, Ski slipped the .45 from the shoulder holster and was holding it under the table pointed on Max. A man like Max saw the movement and knew he wouldn't be able to get to the SIG on his waist.

"Who are you?"

"I'm the guy asking the questions, Valencour."

"Are you a Fed?"

"That was my question, Valencour. You're not real good at following directions are you?"

"What do you want?"

"Where is Tom Potter?"

"What do you care?"

"I'm one of the ones who got him out. I heard you were looking for me."

Max leaned back.

"I've already taken care of him."

"If you turned him over to the feds, we'll kill you."

Max looked unperturbed.

"What is going on here?" Max nodded toward the crowd.

"They just announced they're closing down all the restaurants. Doug is giving away what he's got on hand so the food doesn't go to waste and he can help people out."

"Restaurants too, huh? Gun stores are all closed down as well, no guns or ammo to be sold at the co-op or farm store either. I'm on your side, it would behoove both of us to work together."

"I know what you are, Valencour. Doug back there, family man, goes to church every Sunday, pillar of the community. Me, not so much. The circles I travel in know about snitches and federal informants."

Max leaned forward, looking at the table, shaking his head.

"I've been through this enough times to not even bother explaining. Your mind is made up. You have me all figured out, you win."

"How did you find Tom?"

"I didn't, he found me. Wandered onto my property. He was cold, hungry and tired. Took me a bit to figure out who he was. First time he showed up, all this was just starting. I fed him, let him get a hot shower and sleep in a real bed. I helped him."

"And now?"

"And now what? You get nothing from me. I came here to cooperate, to integrate into your network, to help however I could…"

"Yeah, sure, that's how you guys work, isn't it?"

"What do you need with Tom? What are you planning?"

Ski said nothing. Max leaned back.

"I think we're done here, may I leave now or are you that determined to shoot me?"

Ski just nodded with his head, his lip upturned a little.

Max stood up, straightened his jacket and walked out past the line of people. Roger and Doug were looking at Ski inquisitively. Ski walked back and asked to see Doug in the back office.

Doug closed the door but didn't bother to sit down. "Well, Ski?"

"He said he's already taken care of Tom."

"Well… good, right?"

"No, for all we know he turned Tom over to his fed buddies."

"So, you just let him go?"

"I know where he lives, big place way out past Placer Creek. Very remote, had all the construction materials brought in by helicopter, had a bunch of Quakers building the place."

"Quakers, we don't have Quakers around here, you mean Mennonites?"

"Whatever." Ski shrugged.

"What do we do now, Ski?"

"Think it over, talk about it at the new meeting place. We'll need to make sure Bill is there."

"He said he was gonna be checking a trap line or something, expected to be working nights for a few days plowing. Might be hard to get a hold of."

They heard some yelling out front and the sound of a disturbance. Doug turned to run to the front and Ski followed closely. The small line of people was being crowded out of the store by a couple of MPs in full battle gear. Their Sergeant was behind them yelling unnecessarily for people to hurry out into the street where the snow was falling.

"Whoa, what's going on?" Demanded Doug loudly.

The sergeant turned, gripping his M4.

"This is a violation of Area Administration Code 40-2 and also it's subsection b."

"What?"

"Local War Power Act maintenance of order and administration."

"Sergeant," Doug was trying to calm himself. "What are you saying I'm doing wrong here?"

"Basically, all food distribution is to be provided by the government. The distribution centers are the local groceries. Restaurants are closed."

"What a bunch of bull!" Ski snarled, he started to step toward the sergeant but Doug held him back. "This is ridiculous, Doug. You're just trying to get food to people and keep your stocks from going to waste."

"The order is to ensure the safety and integrity of the local food supply and fairness of the distribution."

"Do you believe that, Sergeant? Are you hearing yourself talk?" Ski continued to get heated.

"Alright, Sergeant." Doug stepped in front of Ski with his hands up. "Sorry, didn't know, won't happen again."

"Also, gentlemen, just so you know, enforcement of social distancing and limitations on gatherings to no more than four people outside the family unit begins tonight."

"WHAT?" Ski was pushing to get around Doug, but he turned to push Ski back. "That was all bogus the first time! Just like those damn masks you're wearing."

"Cool it, Ski." Doug had grabbed Ski by the collar, he half turned back to the sergeant. "I'm sorry, we're trying to follow the rules, of course, Sergeant. They just get a little hard to keep up with sometimes."

The last of the crowd of people was out the door; the Military Policemen followed without saying any more.

"Ski, you gotta take it easy. It does nobody any good this early in the game to go out in a blaze of stupid, remember?"

*   *   *

Bill thumbed the throttle and the sled picked up speed across the snow. He had a couple hundred dollars of traps to try to recover before the real snow hit. He'd only kept this trap line active to help the Sheriff and thought he'd let it go a little longer.

He was glad to be out on the snow. Away from work. Away from the insanity of what was happening to the county. Away from worrying about that insanity. The skies were a very dark grey and the clouds low and occasionally spitting snow. The clouds hugged the mountains and hid the peaks and Bill knew he'd be working the next few nights on the plow, more from what he saw and felt than what the meteorologists were saying.

Bill had collected a few traps already and was moving up to the one where he'd caught the coyote for the Sheriff. He saw the disturbance in the snow as he stopped his machine. He left it running and it looked like he'd caught something. Bill could see some fur sticking up above the snow as he approached. He looked at his rifle in the plastic scabbard on the Polaris, but he had his .22 magnum on his hip, that would be enough and less of a handful to lug back to the sled.

Bill smirked as he got closer, another coyote.

But his heart sank as he got up to it. It wasn't *another* coyote.

"Awe ya' dumb 'yote." Bill said out loud looking at the collar. It was the same coyote. "Of all the idiotic…"

Over the noise of his machine, he heard the blades of the approaching chopper. Spinning to look, he saw the Blackhawk sweeping in low under the grey overcast. It flared steeply and Bill started to run for his machine, but the door gunner opened up and the minigun rounds sent up a wall of snow and dirt between him and his sled.

As the Blackhawk settled to land, not far from his snowmobile, he saw another helicopter a little farther out, it was something different and painted more like a civilian helicopter, but it was even bigger than the Blackhawk.

What was the other helicopter? Did it have guns? A million calculations were running through Bill's brain. Should he vanish into the tree line behind him? Make them work for it?

Landing, the Blackhawk had created its own little whiteout cloud with Bill's snowmobile on the edge of it, this was his chance. A quick glance at the second helicopter and Bill was running with all his might to his trusty machine.

Jumping on, he gunned the throttle and the track spun up fast kicking up a fountain of white. His eyes teared as he didn't have time to put his goggles back on. He was climbing the mountainside, straight for the cloud deck that concealed the peaks. Looking over his shoulder, he didn't see the Blackhawk, but the bigger helicopter was on him now, getting close enough he could hear it over the scream of his own taxed engine.

The slope was steepening and a wall of white went up in front of him, the other helicopter had a gun too and was trying to get him to stop before he ran it up the still increasing slope. The throttle was wide open and he turned up higher, steeper, standing on the machine, balancing and feeling the snow now. He didn't take time to evaluate the snow conditions visually, there was no time for that, he had to get to base of the clouds where the helicopter would lose him.

He was so close when everything suddenly felt wrong, it felt as if the world had dropped out beneath him and now he was out of control. Lifted from the seat he held onto the handle bars and heard the pitch change of the engine, the blow off valve whining and track as it was now spinning free, as it started to go over, he finally caught up with what was happening.

Avalanche...

CHAPTER 5

Booth sat casually in the chair across from Zites' desk. He wore a conservative blue suit and tie and had a heavy overcoat draped across the back of the chair.

"The churches, huh? Better you than me." Zites said.

"All part of the programming. It all helps. That's why you're getting so many tips and leads. Convince people they're doing their part and they're glad to help. We haven't started the fugitive drive yet. Have to be patient, build up to it. We're providing them with everything. They'll be reliant on us for everything and they'll see it as their duty to turn in anyone who is against us."

"They have a saying around here, Booth. A fed bear is a dead bear. Theory is, if a bear gets too reliant on handouts, they start to get unpredictable and dangerous."

Booth smirked.

"I don't care about what happens to the bear in the end, as long as it performs as I need it to right now, Zites. As it is we have two teams out following significant leads for Potter. We may have him by the end of the day."

At that moment two helicopters roared overhead, one much lower than the other and it seemed to be right over the building.

"Oh, somebody is so grounded… that is totally uncalled for." Booth jumped to his feet and Zites followed him quickly out of the building.

An Army Blackhawk was proceeding the short distance to the airport while a gleaming white S-92 held a tight orbit beneath the leaden sky. It turned into the wind and flared in the small helipad in the back parking lot. The big helicopter narrowly fit and the beating rotors set off car alarms and blew up a cloud of snow, dust and debris.

A fit man wearing multicam black and a battle belt with pistol, magazines and all the accoutrements of the modern operator stepped down the airstair of the idling helicopter. The man ignored his bushy dark hair, windblown by the down wash and had an ominous saunter and an even more foreboding background. The man was carrying something furry in his left hand and part of whatever it was dragged on the ground.

Booth knew *of* this man and despite hierarchical positions, he knew he was someone to be reckoned with. The operator walked with much purpose directly toward the two administrators and Booth's attitude was suddenly tempered with caution.

What turned out to be the carcass of coyote was thrown at the feet of the two administrators.

"You need to start tightening things up right-quick, Booth." The man yelled loudly to be heard over the spinning rotors and turbines of the helicopter behind him. "If they are playing these kind of games now, it will only get worse fast if you don't put the squeeze on this county now. That's your tracking beacon, the one they planted for the Sheriff. We get outplayed now and this drags on and gets way dirtier than it needs to. Do something about it, Booth."

The man turned and walked back to the helicopter. The door closed after he boarded, the helicopter spun up immediately and blasted the two men with rotor wash as it turned in place and made the quick hop over to the airport ramp.

Booth squinted into the blown dust and snow and saw the hair on the neck of the coyote part from the down wash. Just below a large bloody gunshot wound on the base of the animal's skull was a homemade leather collar.

*   *   *

"Ahh, Taylor." The balding man in the big parka made a show of trying to subdue a laugh as he tapped his stylus at his tablet. "You really shouldn't have done this, man. You have no idea how this got people worked up. Personally, I thought it was funny, but you have to understand, the people we're dealing with here, the ones in charge now… they don't have the sense of humor you and I have."

The man turned the tablet around for the Sheriff to see. He leaned forward on his folding chair when he saw the Sheriff squinting.

It was a close-up image of the Sheriff's leather work. The collar on the dead coyote laying on a sidewalk.

"I guess the *not* funny part is, that young guy you had help you…" The interrogator pulled his tablet back and tapped around with his stylus more. "Bill Collins, they found his truck and trailer at the trail head when he went to check his trapline. Beacon survey records show that's about the same area you initially set that coyote loose with the tag about a week ago. Who would have thought the coyote would stick around like that? I thought they were smarter. Of course, I would have thought young Bill would be smarter than to try to outrun a helicopter with a skidoo. Guess he ran up a mountain side, triggered an avalanche. They found his machine half sticking out of the snow. They tell me once snow from an avalanche settles like that, it kind of sets up like concrete. Poor guy. They looked but couldn't find his body and it was a real bad spot for avalanches, kind of a chute it's described here. Guess they'll find the body in spring."

"So, that's one down anyway. Analysts assess he was one of the people who helped you, looking at the imagery of the vehicles parked at the trail head when they helped you with Tom Potter's escape. They have a picture match of his old dodge. Year, model, rust and dents, they know he was one. They'll start looking for who he associates with. Maybe they'll get the right guys, but who knows."

The Sheriff sighed reflexively and instantly regretted it. The interrogator didn't let on that he knew he'd hit a nerve, he was only getting started.

"And then there's your wife… I mean with the PERS thing and all it only made sense to monitor because of potential exposure."

When the Sheriff shifted on his thin mattress the interrogator looked up.

"Oh, don't worry, Taylor. She's not here. We have levels of these things, of course. She's set up in more reasonable accommodations, but she's really worried about you. Official word is you're still in a coma."

"And Craig, I'm really worried about him. He's younger, but not as strong as you, Taylor. And he's so worried about letting you down. He might die before he does that."

The interrogator continued to tap his stylus at his tablet.

"Could wind up being a long list of bodies piling up for one draft dodger. A whole county suffering so one kid can be… what? Free? Trying to survive in a frozen wilderness all alone, or living as a fugitive going from one hide out to another. Not sure that even qualifies as a life worth living, much less freedom. What do you think, Taylor? I'm just curious, you know, philosophically."

The interrogator looked the Sheriff in the eyes. If he found anything there, he didn't let on. Shaking his head, he looked down at his tablet again.

"Ya know, even in Afghanistan and Iraq when I was doing this, I always wanted to just deal with the right people. I mean from my end, it reduced the static, you know… I mean I wanted to focus on the real signal, not have to weed out the 'usual suspects' kind of thing. And back then, over there, seemed like we really tried hard to do that. Here, now, though… it's like they just want numbers. Like all that really matters is stats and surveys and they've got computers and programs all involved." He held up his tablet a little bit.

"See, my other big fear is, they're just gonna be bringing in whoever, ya' know. What I'm getting at here, Taylor... A lot of people are going to suffer unnecessarily. Just give me a list of ten names. Ten names is all I'm asking for and all this starts to go away, OK?"

The Sheriff shifted a little on the mattress.

"I'm not getting enough food to stay warm, much less think straight."

The man in the parka nodded as if with grave consideration. He stood up from his chair and walked to the door, which scraped open on his approach, it closed behind him and the Sheriff could hear talking on the other side. In his mind, he thought about rising, sweeping up the folding metal chair and planting it across the guy's face when he re-entered. But he knew that was pure fantasy. He wasn't strong enough, and they'd see it coming on the cameras, where ever they were.

The door scraped open again and the interrogator returned and resumed his position.

"I've got the guards working on that for you, Taylor. They're going to get something from their chow hall for you now, and I'll talk to the boss about upping your rations. It doesn't have to be this hard, ya' know."

*   *   *

Max did his best to ignore the helicopter slowing to land in front of his home as he parked the Sno-cat inside. Inside, he shut down and walked out the barn door as it closed behind him. The snow had started again and it came on gusting wind.

He saw it as a bad sign that the helicopter was shutting down soon after settling on its skids.

Max didn't recognize the men who got out and he took this as a bad sign, too.

His rich uncle, Max shook his head and could only laugh to himself.

As the men drew near to him, the one in the blue suit and the heavy overcoat spoke first.

"Max Valencour."

"Uncle Sam."

The man just looked at him with a blank stare.

"Old joke, never mind… they never issue you guys a sense of humor do they?"

The first man gave a fake smile while extending his hand, the other two were just muscle and a pilot.

"Regional Public Safety Administrator Booth. They've taken to calling the acronym RiPSAw, which I didn't like at first but it's kind of growing on me…"

Max didn't say anything but shook hands when they were extended.

"I'm formerly an FBI Special Agent, so I've read a lot about you, Mr. Valencour. We have a lot to talk about. May we come in?"

"Got a warrant?"

"Oh, it doesn't really need to be like that, Mr. Valencour. I'd like to reestablish what seems to be a very positive working relationship you've had with DOJ and… Other agencies."

"I'm retired, what is there to talk about?"

"There isn't really retirement from what you were doing. I mean you weren't any kind of official GS or government employee or anything. And it looks like your accounts are running low. Property taxes are pretty cheap around here, but this is a lot of property and I'm not sure how you're going to make it."

Max said nothing.

"The matter of a young man named Tom Potter is the most pressing. Our surveillance surveys indicate he was here."

Max just walked toward his front door and the men followed him.

"We know he was here."

Opening the door, Max entered and the men followed. He didn't protest as he walked to the kitchen. He motioned for them to take a seat as he sat at the table.

"I've been finding snowshoe tracks around the area, but nothing's been taken. Maybe that's your guy."

"Oh, he wouldn't need to take anything. He's well trained and well supplied. I have another team on the way here. They found a cache and a series of snow shelters in the area. They have a tactical tracker and a K-9. We'll see if those tracks stay on the perimeter or if they come right in your front door."

"I don't know what to tell you then, Booth. All I've seen are tracks overlooking my property here."

"Why would he come here, Max?"

"Maybe he likes bagpipes."

"Bagpipes?"

"I play them every day."

Booth looked at him a little puzzled.

"I find it soothing… not everyone does, but I'm out here in the middle of nowhere."

"Not entirely. Tom Potter found you. We found you."

"This should have been easy for you, I'm still registered, I'd imagine."

"Chris Harvey retired a few years ago, I called him. He was your last handler from what I read. They helped facilitate the move here."

Max shrugged.

The pilot was looking at his tablet. He grimaced a little and spoke up.

"Sir, this weather. It's IMC between us and base."

"English, please?"

"Instrument Meteorological Conditions."

"Like clouds?"

"More than that, Sir. Significantly reduced visibility. With the temps and moisture the way they are, when the bulk of it gets here we may not be able to get out of here because of icing. The S-92 with the tracking team has returned to base because of it."

Booth shook his head.

"The weather in this place, ugh. How do you handle it, Max? Why on earth would you pick here? Why didn't you go to Vegas or Miami like the rest of them?"

Max shrugged.

"Go figure."

"Alright, Max. Stand up, turn around and put your hands behind your back."

"What?"

The man who was Booth's bodyguard was up out of his chair.

"Cuff him, Jim. He's going with us." Booth had pulled a Glock and was pointing it casually at Max. "Honestly not the way I wanted this to go, but we need to have a long conversation. About what's going on in this county and how you can help. About your past, about your future. Once I'm confident I've secured your cooperation, I'll cut you loose again."

Max took a moment, he could take them. He could get to his SIG before Booth knew what was happening and shoot Jim while he was fumbling between the handcuffs he'd just pulled and the pistol that bulged in concealment at his right hip. The pilot wouldn't be a factor, he was still heads down in his iPad.

But then he'd be on the run again, and Max didn't feel much like running anymore.

*   *   *

Doug nodded to the sergeant standing beside the Humvee parked in front of the restaurant. The snow was coming down harder and the Sergeant had flipped the hood up on his parka.

"Stuck here by yourself, Sergeant?"

"I've got a squad on foot patrol. I'm just staying with the vehicle until they're done."

"You want to come in and warm up?"

The Sergeant looked around.

"Nobody's gonna mess with your ride. Not here for sure."

Even over the mask the man wore, Doug could see the smile in his eyes.

"Where ya' from, Sergeant?"

"We're ah… not really supposed to talk about… well, anything."

"Well, I get it. I spent twenty-one years in the Navy."

"Oh yeah?"

Doug let the Sergeant in and motioned for him to take a seat.

"I'd offer you some food, but I'm all shut down."

"Ah, no… this is really nice of you."

"Sergeant, I just wanted to apologize for my buddy the other day. He's a good guy. Everybody's a little uptight about everything going on."

The soldier nodded.

"They warned us about the people here. That we'd see a lot of that."

"A lot of what?"

"White supremacy, guess that's a big thing around here."

Doug laughed.

"I suppose there's some of that everywhere, and there was a larger movement here years ago but they pretty much got run out of town. That was before we moved here. And credit where credit is due, there's never been many of us here, it was the white folks who put their foot down and ran them out. My buddy isn't anything like that. In fact, he's old school Special Forces."

"Really?"

"Very old school, like Grenada, Panama."

"What did you do in the Navy?"

"I'm Doug, by the way." He extended his hand over the table and the Sergeant looked around a little before taking it.

"I'm Don, they warned us about getting friendly with the locals. That it could be a trap."

Doug smiled and shook his head.

"Relax, Don. So, my illustrious Navy career had me start out as a medic, I was a Corpsman in Ramadi and Fallujah back in 2004. I remember looking up one particularly busy day as a couple helos were flying over and thinking, man, that's gotta be better than this. I finally finished my degree and got a flying slot. I would have never made a career out of it if I hadn't made the change. Are you guard or active duty?"

The sergeant inhaled.

"We're not supposed to say, but I'm with the Guard in DC. I was active duty, I deployed to Iraq in '08. I was up at Spiecher. Always been an MP."

"Nothin' wrong with that, Don… Somebody has to hand out the speeding tickets and hassle people about PT belts on base." Doug laughed.

"Ah, it wasn't like that, man."

"I'm just givin' you a hard time. Hey, I've got a keg in back I tapped just before they closed everything down. I'll wheel it out here for you and your guys. You can load it up with your guys. No point in it goin' stale."

"Really? I mean we're *really* not supposed to do that…"

"Look, I know you guys are just doing your job and I hate that I had to come down here today and throw out some food that was going bad, but that was just some celery and lettuce." Doug shrugged and shook his head. "And I can't keep up with all these new laws and regs you guys keep throwing at us, but I have to believe wasting a keg of beer has got to be somewhere on your list. We can't really let that keg go to waste, can we?"

Doug could see the Sergeant's eyes smile again over his mask.

"How much longer are your guys gonna be?"

The Sergeant looked at his watch.

"Shouldn't be too long."

"Well, I don't want to have to kick you out, but I've got a ride coming in the next few minutes. Guess that heater in the old Humvee isn't really cutting it, huh?"

"Naw, not even that. We're having to conserve fuel."

"Thought they had a big fuel farm full of blivets they flew in and a bunch of Hemmet fuelers down on the south side of the airport."

"Guess getting the fuel to them has been a bigger challenge than they thought and they're having to fuel the snow plows and runnin' some kind of special missions that are burning through fuel too."

"Geez, well you can stay in here until my ride gets here and stay warm. I'll go get you that keg."

Doug walked back to the kitchen, grabbed the hand cart and the tapped keg. When he returned, Don was on his feet and saw his squad approaching.

"My guys are here now, thanks a lot, Doug." They got the handcart out the door and when the approaching men realized what was happening, there was a small cheer.

Doug saw Ski's truck approaching and pushed the hand cart inside the door, pulled out his keys and locked up. The soldiers had loaded the keg and hopped in the back of the Humvee giving a friendly wave to Doug, which he returned with a smile as he stepped into Ski's Chevy.

"That's playin' with fire, Doug." Ski said as Doug closed the door.

"That's developing intel, Ski. You know that."

*   *   *

"Public Safety Administrator Zites, I'd like to introduce you to Max Valencour."

"Can we dispense with the cuffs already, Booth? You made your point."

"Of course, how rude of me... Jim, please." Jim strode across the former office of Sheriff Taylor to the chair where he had unceremoniously planted Valencour. The tall man leaned forward in the seat to expose the cuffs and the bodyguard unlocked and pocketed them.

Max Valencour rubbed his wrists and looked around at the walls of the office. They were adorned with certificates of various types of accomplishments. Pictures of the man named Zites sitting in front of him with a variety of political and Hollywood personalities. It was very clear that Ted Zites was a man very impressed with his own accomplishments.

"Max Valencour is one of those very quietly famous individuals, Ted. Started out in the Navy, cryptographer that got caught up in some unpleasantness with the NCIS in the Philippines when stationed in Subic in 1990. A timely volcanic eruption covered most of that up from public view, but not from DOJ. He agreed to work off the charges of his horrific crimes by attempting to penetrate Abu Sayyaf. To everyone's amazement, he did it and survived. Turned out he was born for that kind of work. Became one of our... the FBI's... most successful Top Echelon informants. In that, unlike Bulger or Flemmi, to this day, no one has ever heard of Max Valencour. He went on to penetrate the Russian mob, a little organization in Syria and Iraq called IS, that was later known as ISIS.

"A really remarkable career really. Most Top Echelon informants were already on the inside when they approached the FBI for a deal. Not Max here, he could walk into any organization from street level and penetrate the very highest levels of leadership in less time than it would take you or I to apply and become Boy Scout Scoutmasters. Uncanny really. And very lucrative for Mr. Valencour, was it not?"

Max shrugged and looked bored.

"Of course, it was reasonable for Mr. Valencour to decide he'd had enough, so he moved here to the peaceful wilderness to get away from it all. Wound up smack in the middle of it."

"Smack in the middle of what, Booth? You're looking for this Tom Potter kid and near as I can tell this whole pandemic thing is BS. You're telling me one draft dodging kid is worth all this?"

Booth smiled and nodded, leaning against Zite's desk.

"Of course, I mean you have this all figured out, Max. I have a few things figured out too. You don't have nearly enough in any of your accounts combined to cover your upcoming property taxes. You're in trouble financially, Max. We could help with that."

"Or else?"

"Well obviously, if you can't pay your taxes, your property can be seized. Not that we need that with the WPA in affect, but, it's good to keep up appearances right now."

"What happened to the Sheriff? Is that what this is all about? Are the rumors true? Did he put together some kind of posse that got the kid away from you?"

Booth's smugness faded a bit and he had to force the smile.

"There are lots of people who think they can escape to a place like this in a time like now. They think if they are outside the cities they are safe, because the cities will demand the majority of resources to maintain control. Those in charge don't really care about the cities, Max. Surely you are smart enough to see that. What do cities produce? Cities only consume. You don't have to control the consumers, they're controlled by their consumption. You have to control the producers. This is all a proof of concept. Most of the cities can burn, and they are. It's to be expected. The government has the military running VIP extraction nightly to pull out people they do care about in the cities. But this, this here, is an experiment in complete surveillance and control in a rural setting, where no one expects it."

"Tom Potter is the figurehead. We have solid indications of movement as provided by our surveillance matrix. That's what led us to you, but of course, you haven't seen Tom, you're just some pied piper and he's only come to hear your music.

"I don't have any evidence to the contrary, but I do have complete access to your bank accounts, Max. We're going to crush this county. We are going to crush all resistance. Most people will fold in the first month, they'll be begging us for food and fuel. They don't fully realize it yet, but money doesn't even matter. We control everything and they can't buy their way out of this, except for a very fortunate few who have already left on chartered jets."

"I know it's your nature to choose the winning side, Max. I know you'll help us. I need you to infiltrate the brewing resistance, Max."

Max inhaled and slid down a little in his seat, a grin sliding across his face.

"I've already started."

Booth laughed and clapped his hands.

"Of course you have, Max. It's in your blood. It's why you're the best."

*   *   *

The man had relinquished his .44 as soon as Boggs and the Specialist arrived on scene. He dropped it, backed up quickly with his hands in the air. He'd seemed frozen, pointed in on the body and pool of blood in his living room when they first arrived. Now he looked exhausted.

"I thought he was gonna kill me and my family, I swear... I didn't want to kill no one, he broke down the door with that axe, he was saying something about the drugs. I've never done any kind of drugs in my life I swear, I don't know what he was talking about."

The body was long dead, the staged ambulance was pulling up as Boggs was pulling the middle-aged man aside. It had taken them a long time to respond, between being short of manning, the fuel situation and the snow.

The man said it had happened an hour ago and that seemed to match the call timeline.

"Why would he do this Deputy, what drugs was he talkin' about? Why here?"

"You don't recognize the man?"

"No, Sir." The man collapsed into a chair with his head in his hands and he was still shaking. "It was forever before you got here, I didn't know what to do but I didn't want him getting up, he still had the ax in his hands when he came in and he was just crazy like. Why would he do this?"

"This lockdown is affecting a lot of people in a lot of ways, the disruption in the supply chain is affecting people being able to get prescription and illicit drugs through normal channels. My bet is this guy was looking for the latter. We're also seeing a spike in mental illness related calls. Why don't we move back to the bedroom, Sir? You don't need to see this anymore."

Aside from the gunshot wounds, the half-dressed man looked like a meth head with sunken, gaunt eyes staring lifelessly at the ceiling. The trailer was small, they'd already gotten the wife and two little girls dressed warmly and off to the nearest neighbor after a quick interview. The man was shaking uncontrollably from the adrenalin dump. When they entered the messy bedroom, Boggs cleared a chair of laundry and checked under the cushion for any weapons.

"Sit here, sir. Try to relax. You've been through a lot and from everything I've seen and heard, you had no choice but to do what you did to protect your family. My report will have to go up to the prosecutor's office, and the scene is going to be processed as a homicide, but this is pretty clear-cut self-defense."

Boggs felt bad for the guy. He'd never killed anyone stateside and the few firefights he got into were fairly distant and fast-moving things. He was never one hundred percent certain he'd killed anyone. Some guys didn't even handle that well. Boggs had seen it. And it wasn't like he was some steely-eyed killer. The stress of kill or be killed regardless of outcomes had had its effect on Boggs and he hadn't always handled it well.

Boggs' Federal "Partner" had other priorities.

"Where are your other guns, sir?" The specialist asked harshly.

"Oh, I've got them all locked up back here in the closet."

"Open the safe for us and then step away."

Boggs looked sideways at the soldier as the man stood up to comply. He tried the safe combo a few times but his hand was shaking too much.

"I'm sorry… I…"

"Hey, what is this? We got the involved firearm." Boggs interrupted.

"We seize all guns in *any* call involving gun violence. If there are any bump-stocks or braces anything else illegal, he goes with us. Those are our directives."

Boggs shook his head. He'd already stopped initiating traffic stops, this was an in-progress call and the Federal response was making him ill. He wasn't sure how long he could do this.

"Tell me the combination and I'll open it." The Specialist demanded.

"Oh, come on!" Boggs exclaimed. "You can't be serious, this guy has rights."

"It's OK, Deputy, I don't want to cause any problems."

Boggs inhaled, poor bastard had no idea what a big problem that attitude really was. The Deputy took a step back, physically and mentally, as the man gave the soldier the combination.

Two pump shot guns and a beat-up old, bolt action hunting rifle.

The soldier slid the rifle over his shoulder with its sling and held the shotguns by the barrels.

"Any more?"

"No, sir. That's all, I keep everything locked up because of the girls."

The detective and coroner were pulling up outside. Boggs handed the man his card with the report number on it.

"I'm going to go outside to brief these guys, I've got everything I need here." He said.

"Me too." The soldier smiled as he held up the shotguns a little.

Boggs shook his head, he needed some fresh air.

*   *   *

The door scraping open woke the Sheriff. He rolled over as he heard the footsteps and the sound of something dragging.

The big men weren't your average guards, they were extraordinarily fit and very well equipped. They wore fresh multicams with no markings visible. Between them they dragged the suffering form of Deputy Craig Markdale. Laying him down gently, they exited wordlessly and the door scraped closed after they left.

The Deputy struggled to prop himself up to a sitting position on the cold ancient concrete floor.

The Sheriff threw off his scratchy wool blanket and rushed over.

"Craig, what have they done to you?"

"Nothing, I'm just not well. The cold and the food… It's all getting to me, Sheriff. I haven't talked, I haven't told them anything…"

The Sheriff pressed his index finger to his lips and pointed at the ceiling to indicate his certainty they were being observed.

"Have they started giving you more food?"

"Yeah, that has picked up a little, but I'm always so cold. Where are we, Sheriff?"

"Don't know, I'm thinking an old military base in Seattle or Vancouver… Maybe Whidbey Island. All I ever hear are the occasional jets and turboprops taking off and landing. I think this is some kind of old bunker, modified for… this."

"I don't know how long I can keep this up, Sheriff. But, I won't talk, I won't let you or the guys down."

The Sheriff was sitting down with the Deputy and he wrapped his arms around him and tried to give him some warmth.

"These bastards." The Sheriff said. The door scraped open, this time four soldiers entered. Two peeled the Sheriff from the Deputy and held him as the other two dragged Markdale out.

"How can you do this? How can you treat people like this? He needs proper food and he needs to not be kept in a damn meat locker on the verge of hypothermia." The one soldier was watching the other two. They were holding the Sheriff firmly and he realized then how much he had been weakened in his time here. He found the other soldiers eyes and he repeated himself sternly.

"How can you do this to Americans? You should be ashamed of yourselves."

The soldier held the Sheriffs glare and gave an almost imperceptible shake of the head and the Sheriff wondered what meaning that had.

*   *   *

Ski and Doug had picked up Roger at the park. No one had heard from Bill, the dead drop sites were cold.

The streets in town were unusually quiet for a Friday night. The driving snow was only a part of it. While many were trying to maintain a sense of normalcy and routine, others had given up on that.

Life was suspended, many had vanished.

"Do you think he was rolled up?" Ski asked as he navigated the streets in his big old Chevy crew cab.

Doug shrugged.

"Will he talk? Are we all compromised? Should we just stand down for a little while?"

"Lots of people are going missing." Roger said. "An elderly friend was symptomatic, she had her son take her to the hospital. She was released, they said it was just the flu. When she got out of the emergency room, he was gone. They told her he had been taken for treatment. Twenty-five years old, no symptoms, then gone. She hasn't heard anything from him."

"That's not reassuring, Roger."

"It's not meant to be, Ski."

They were headed to the north side of town to assess what they had seen on the only television channel and heard about on the only radio station now receivable. And, of course, the rumors that spread slow with the gathering restrictions now in place.

Such restrictions were waived at the grocery stores, they passed one on the way toward the mall. This was the most active part of town. Military Police directed all the traffic in an orderly fashion. There was no shopping anymore, but these were distribution points for family rations.

"Has anyone been yet? How much food do they give you?" Ski asked.

"I went yesterday," Roger said. "I guess they base it on census data. I got a small bag, a couple of MREs. Some canned food, some kind of famine ration things. Other people were getting more bags, families I think. They asked for my phone and I told them I didn't have one. They gave me a punch card but said that was temporary and they'd be issuing people who needed them some kind of smart phones for *more efficient food distribution*."

Passing the crowded grocery store parking lot, Ski stayed behind the only snow plow they had seen so far as it made a meager attempt to stay ahead of the snowfall.

"Holy cow!" Said Roger as they approached the mall parking lot.

Again, MPs were directing traffic. It wasn't as busy here as it was at the grocery store, but close. Two distinct lines came out of the main entrance.

"Prescription drug distribution and…"

"Weapons surrender." Doug finished Ski's thought.

"They're really doing it, voluntarily, no compensation." Roger was clearly incredulous.

"And it's just NFA items right now." Ski said.

"Registered National Firearms Act items. Registered, legally purchased machine guns, suppressors, short barreled rifles and shotguns. All legally obtained, all very pricey."

"And they paid a $200 tax on those things for their trouble." Said Ski.

"Now they're standing in a line out in the snow with those things to just surrender them, no compensation." Roger was shaking his head.

"People are scared." Said Doug. "They don't want any trouble and they see what's going on around them and people vanishing… I've heard some people are turning in non-NFA guns just to stay ahead of things."

"Alright, I think we've seen enough here." Ski wheeled around and made a series of right turns to head southbound on the highway without having to do a u-turn. Away from the distribution points, traffic was light and the roads were slick and slushy. The windshield wipers were barely keeping up.

On the south side of town it appeared that the airport was being slowly transformed into a fortress of sorts. ASVs and dirt-filled Hesco barriers blocked roads once open. They approached initially from the north. From a few blocks out, even through the snow and the falling darkness, they saw the entrance of FOB Prather, illuminated with portable tower lights. There were two ASVs there and men in dark uniforms.

"What do you think the guys in the black uniforms are, Ski?"

"I've seen a few around town. It's actually multicam black. I'm guessing it's Greenvale guys."

"Greenvale?"

Ski shrugged as he took a side street to avoid the entrance.

"Or whatever they're called now. OGA contractors. They change the names of some of those Private Military Companies as often as I change underwear, just to keep people guessing. They work for whatever "Other Government Agency" is paying. CIA, NSA, FBI, all of the above. They'll be all super experienced former tier one Special Ops guys. I don't want us getting stopped at a checkpoint, they may ID us all, then we get put together in whatever database they're compiling."

Weaving through the residential neighborhoods surrounding the airport, some roads were blocked by freshly stacked baskets of dirt that were Hesco barriers. Others were checkpoints manned by MPs or contractors. When they got to the south side of the field a large, formerly vacant area was blocked off with Hescos stacked three high and topped with razor wire. The main entrance was blocked by a pair of ASVs.

Just as they rounded the corner, they watched as the ASVs parted to allow a giant 8 wheeled HEMTT fuel truck out.

"Yeah, this is it, last week the Hescos weren't stacked as high and you could see them." Doug said.

"What exactly are we looking for, Doug?" Roger asked.

"We just found exactly what we're looking for, Roger… A target."

*   *   *

The fresh snow crunched crisp and soft beneath his feet. He'd driven his personally owned Subaru up the little back road he'd been on earlier and parked it a ways back, walking to the trailer. He was out of uniform and felt strangely liberated having instinctively left his cell phone at home. In his support hand he carried his badge wallet. In his weapon hand, he carried the shotgun.

He kept his flashlight pocketed, counting on the light of the trailer to adequately illuminate him. A dog at another trailer barked. His breath fogged in the falling snow and his resolve was fired by the injustice he'd witnessed earlier in the day.

He was going to correct that.

His fist closed around his badge wallet, he pounded on the front door of the trailer with his best cop knock. He stepped back, off line of the door and held the badge high, glinting it in the porch light.

"It's Deputy Boggs, I was here this morning, I need to speak with you for a moment." He said firmly as he heard foot falls on the other side of the door.

Dead bolts and chains were released on the other side of the flimsy replacement door that temporarily fixed the one damaged earlier by the ax.

The man he had met earlier peered meekly from behind the mostly closed door.

"Is everything OK?"

"I suppose that depends on how you look at things, sir. I'm not here in an official capacity, if that helps."

"Um… I'm not sure it does." The man's eyes were on the pump shotgun Boggs was holding muzzle down by the grip.

"It's OK." Boggs looked over each of his snow sprinkled shoulders, suddenly more nervous of being watched. "This is for you."

Presenting the old pump shotgun to the crack in the door, the man on the other side looked a bit confused and he shook his head a little.

"A good man shouldn't be left defenseless, that was wrong of that Fed to take your guns today, I'm sorry I didn't have the guts to stop him at the time. I'm still trying to figure out how to get through this. I hope this makes up for it. It's a Remington Model 10, the slide release is the little button on the side there. Feeds and ejects out the bottom. That gun has been in my family for seventy years, there's no paper work that ties it to me. If you say I gave it to you, I'll deny it."

"I don't have any money to…"

"I'm not asking for any, take it. This is to make up for my lack of spine earlier, use it wisely… I know you will. Use it to feed your family, to protect them if you have to. And remember. I wasn't here tonight."

The man opened the door wide to the cold and took the shotgun like something sacred. His lips parted as if to say thank you and Boggs merely nodded in silent acknowledgement. The Deputy turned and disappeared beyond the snow falling through the play of the light.

The feeling welling up from within Boggs' center was starting to displace the sense of disgrace he had felt leaving the scene earlier in the day. He was going to have to come up with a better way of handling things going forward, or he was gonna run out of guns pretty quick.

CHAPTER 6

"You're driving a hard bargain, Valencour. Frankly, I expected you to ask for more money."

"Money does me no good if surveillance burns me. It has in the past. In Syria I found myself hiding from Daesh *and* my guys overhead there to 'protect' me. I trust only *me* to keep me alive."

"Can you give me any names?" Zites asked.

"Not yet. A guy like me doesn't get where he is by providing a list of names of 'usual suspects'. I'm going to provide you with actionable intel, but I vet it all myself first. I penetrate the network and figure out the cell's structure, how they interact with other cells. It's early in this game of yours, a lot of what will become resistance is just starting to coalesce."

"There won't be any resistance. Layers of surveillance and aggressive Information Operations will see to that."

Max laughed.

"Don't kid yourself, Booth… not too long ago a large slow-moving Chinese intelligence balloon traversed this country, hovering over some critical nuclear sites along the way making this administration a laughing stock. Your experiment here is really doomed to failure if you go all in on your technology. Technology always fails at some point, often when you need it most. When technology makes war easy and clean, it's easy to rely on it too heavily. Eventually, they'll find gaps and exploit them. While your analysts are reviewing all the SIGINT data and overhead imagery, some crafty redneck is going to realize there is a bridge your patrols cross at a certain time of day, or maybe an Afghanistan veteran is going to find a mountain pass you need to traverse and he'll introduce you to proper command wire IED placement. They're back on their heels for now but they'll be coming for you in time. That's why you need someone like me. That's why I wasn't surprised when you showed up with your helicopter."

Booth gave a skeptical harrumph.

"Don't overestimate your importance to us, Valencour. We've got people turning in their guns already, we've only asked for the registered machine guns and suppressors. Right now they're turning things in just to make their lives easier, the motivation of fear hasn't even set in yet. Some people never imagined in a place like this we'd get so many AR-15's voluntarily surrendered. They are lining up in the cold to turn them in before we've even asked for them. And we're not too worried about the veterans either, we've been watching people like Jeff Potter under Operation Vigilant Eagle for years. These people have no idea how bad it is yet, we haven't even begun to really squeeze. They don't even officially know about the camps yet."

"Camps?" Max asked.

"It would be good for you to know about them, really. Just so you don't think about doing anything that might get you into one. Level one camp is a facility for more compliant internees who are of value to us, minimum security. They just built the camp on the west side of the airport in Moses Lake Washington. Level two is just north of Salt Lake, Brigham City airport I think it is. This is our high security 'quarantine' camp, suspects who are of grave concern but not available for military induction or they can provide ongoing intel. Nice facility, guess they've been quietly working on it for the past year. Finally, level three. That's where you'd wind up, Valencour. Maximum security in the Aleutians. It's for people who are a *fight* risk, not just a flight risk. While level one and two camps will be acknowledged with cover stories regarding the need for public health and order, no one will ever know about the level three camp. It's an old military base out there somewhere, a place people most likely will never return from. A place you would never want to wind up, Valencour."

*   *   *

It was warmer than the cache, because of the cows and the smell had started to become tolerable. The farmer was a strict man with a thick old Dutch style chin strap beard and dressed formally even when he helped Tom with his chores in the barn. Tom was glad for the work, it took his mind from being on the run. It gave him a sense of security and purpose.

The farmer wished to be addressed only as Johann, and when he first said it to Tom, it was in a hushed voice like it was his cover or something. This made Tom laugh a little to himself because even here, Johann would be a name that would stand out. Johann had introduced his daughter, Hannah, who had come out with him a few times to help in the barn. She wore a simple, undecorated hair covering and her dresses were always equally austere. Over the dresses she wore a weary, heavy Carhart jacket. Her hair was up, but that only high-lighted beautiful green eyes that Tom had never really noticed on a woman before. She was quiet and always had a bashful smile around him. Johann did not seem amused.

In the morning he was brought an ample breakfast and at night, a significant dinner. The accommodations amounted to a corner in the hay loft and a bucket, but the food was good, it was warm and he kept busy.

When Max dropped him off, it was unclear what the plan was, or if there was one, but Johann was clearly sympathetic and willing to help keep Tom out of the war. The farmer understood the risk involved to his family, but Tom realized there were limits to that and he didn't want to endanger anyone else.

Tom leaned on the shovel and took a break from mucking the stall for a moment. While there was a sense of contentment here, there was always the lingering guilt of those that had sacrificed for him. Starting with his father and sister, those brought him much sadness, but were somehow most reconcilable. Tougher for him was the Sheriff, a man he hardly knew and all the others that showed up that day at the tunnel, men he never even knew at all. They all risked everything for him, to buy him time, to give him a break so he could run.

Tom inhaled and shook his head. How could he ever repay that? Tom was unsure, but he knew it wouldn't involve running.

*   *   *

Ski watched the video monitor as the unfamiliar truck parked outside. Still in only sweat pants, he grabbed his braced AR pistol and made his way downstairs. His home was his little apartment within the pole barn so he navigated between his vehicles in the darkness to what was his front door, between the two large garage doors. He'd watched long enough to see the driver of the truck assist the man out of the passenger side and assumed this to be a ruse. A larger force probably waited somewhere beyond the video cameras and motion detectors on the long driveway.

Was this how it would end then? Sweat pants, unlaced boots, a chest rack of thirty round magazines and an AR pistol. Shaking his head, the AR wasn't even his first choice, just what he had on hand at the time.

Behind the corner of the cover of his truck, he had the AR pointed at the man door between the two bay doors as the banging began.

He knew he could shoot through this part of the structure and retreat to the reinforced interior as required. It was too late to get out, too late to run. Someone had come for him and this was how it was going down, he just had to accept that. His gut hanging out and a sub-par weapon to boot. It had a good light and an Aimpoint and was all ready to go with 29 rounds of green tips. At this close distance, even with the ten-inch barrel, he figured he'd be able to penetrate the body armor they'd be wearing.

His electronic hearing protection picked up a call from the other side of the door.

"Ski, Ski... I need help." The voice sounded desperate and familiar, then another voice chimed in, louder and stronger.

"Dude, you gotta let us in."

This had to be a trap. But somehow it didn't feel like that, and what was that first voice? Through the door, through the electronic amplification of the Peltors it wasn't quite sinking in.

In the darkness, Ski advanced, gun up, safety off. Quietly as he could, he unlocked the steel door, then scurried back to the corner cover of his truck.

The little red dot of the Aimpoint was at the center of the door and he was braced and covered well, this was as good as it was going get. If there was a chance that was someone he knew, he had to give them a chance. If this was the beginning of an assault, these first two were going to die at the very least.

"Slowly open the door and come in two steps." Ski yelled. The door opened and the two hesitated in the unexpected darkness. They were back lit by the motion sensing porch light, the silhouette of one man supporting the other, arm over the shoulder, painfully moving the two steps, then stopping.

"Hands up and turn away from me." As they turned, Ski illuminated them with his weapon mounted light, looking for weapons. There were only two hands up and he really needed to see four.

"Don't mess with me, I wanna see all your hands, now, or I'll kill you before the others get here."

"Ski, there's no others, it's me, Bill and I really need help."

"Turn around."

The two figures turned awkwardly squinting in the bright light of the pistol. Bill's face was nearly unrecognizable, drawn with pain and anguish. They were both trying to hold their hands up and the injured man collapsed to the floor.

"Hey, dude, he's really hurt. No joke, he's got some serious frost bite on his right foot and his fingers."

"Ski, please…"

The old man thought a moment, processing the information and sorting out options.

"You, pull up your jacket and turn around."

"Hey, I got a pistol in the small of my back."

"Very slowly, move only your left hand and throw it on the ground. You move fast or move any other part of your body, I shoot you first."

The man complied slowly and a pistol skittered across the concrete floor.

"Again, I want you to lift up your jacket and turn around."

The man complied revealing no more weapons.

"Now, lock that door."

Both men were bathed in the light of the weapon mounted light and when the man turned back from locking the door, he was partially shielding his eyes with his hand.

"Pick him up and move toward the sound of my voice."

"Can you kill that light, dude?"

"No."

The one man picked up the other and as the light played more on the injured man's face Ski could see that it was, in fact, Bill.

"Dude, come on. You don't have to make this any harder for us, he's really messed up. We weren't followed. But look at his fingers and his foot when we get in here, you'll see. I did what I could for him."

Ski was walking backward with the light up on them, using the familiarity of his place and the blinding light to his advantage just in case. Bill was unwrapping his loosely bandaged left hand. He could see the black finger tips just as his back was to the open door of the apartment.

"Geez, Bill… What happened?" Ski flipped the light switch for the living room of the apartment and lowered his braced pistol.

"They chased him with a helicopter into an avalanche, he tried to swim out of it." The other man said in a matter of fact way. "We do a lot of high marking together, it happens."

"Slab avalanche, bottom just dropped out on me…"

Ski let the pistol fall across his chest on its sling and helped guide Bill to the couch.

"Never got buried before. Opened a space out in front of my face, had to feel my spit to know which way was up, dug a space around me and worked my way to the surface, couldn't dig out 'til the helicopter was gone. Snow had carried me down to the tree line. Firmed up pretty good before I didn't hear the helicopter any more. Then I darn near couldn't get out. Got my way out, but my sled was buried but good. I tried to make my way back to my truck but they were already there. I was afraid to light a fire the first night but I got back in a half tree well and warmed up as best I could."

"He barely got to my place. I'm John." The man took his glove off and Ski shook his hand.

"Ski."

"It's getting really bad, worse than I know what to do with. If we went to the hospital, they'd disappear him, they must have run the plates on his truck so they must know who he is, right? I mean I couldn't take him to the hospital, right?"

"You done good, John." Ski said with a reassuring old man voice.

"He said you'd know what to do."

"Yeah, I got some ideas. You were right not to take him to the hospital. We'll take care of him. You're sure you weren't followed?"

"No sign of it, and I was payin' attention."

"Still snowing out?"

"Yeah."

"Are you warm enough, Bill?"

"Yeah, it just hurts so much, mostly my fingers. Never imagined fingers could hurt so much."

Ski just nodded and stepped back to the bed room. It took him a moment and he came out with a longer barreled AR-15 slung over his shoulder.

"You know how to run one of these things, John?" He presented the AR pistol to him.

"Sure."

Ski walked briskly out to the garage bay and came back with John's Beretta. He handed it over by the barrel.

"I'm going for help. *Don't shoot me or anyone I bring back when I return.* Shoot anyone else who shows up in the face."

*   *   *

The Sheriff's knee was killing him, but he was still kneeling in prayer beside the meager, thin mattress. The cold, cracked and broken concrete floor was merciless in so many ways. He had just scheduled the surgery to replace the thing and he wasn't really sure that mattered any more.

He prayed as long as he could, it sustained him, but the pain was always there and when it became too distracting, he would stop and stand stiffly and try to exercise a bit. When the door scraped open unexpectedly he turned, four of the soldiers were entering quickly. The Sheriff staggered a little on his feet. The two soldiers in back were dragging a figure and it took the Sheriff a moment to recognize him.

They lowered the body of Deputy Craig Markdale to the cold concrete, he was pale and looked deflated somehow, by the departure of life and spirit.

"No!" The Sheriff yelled and moved quickly against the pain, falling at the side of his friend. Instinctively he checked the neck for a pulse he knew wouldn't be there. There was no visible bruising or injuries.

"How in the name of all that is Holy could you allow this to happen? This is an absolute disgrace, he was a good man." The Sheriff was screaming and emotion was overtaking him. Two of the soldiers advanced quickly and scooped the Sheriff up by the arms, he screamed and kicked and struggled, but theirs was an iron grip and he was weak.

The other two soldiers were lifting the body to take it out.

"No, leave him here! Please, please don't take him, not yet, let me pray with him, please!"

The two soldiers pinned the Sheriff to the wall and as the body was removed, his eyes welled up and he sobbed uncontrollably.

"You bastards, how could you let this happen?" The Sheriff's voice faltered. One of the soldiers holding him, leaned into his ear and tried to calm him, speaking quickly and quietly.

"Sheriff Taylor, Sheriff Taylor." The Sheriff realized this was the first time someone called him that since he got here, he stopped screaming and tried to quell his sobbing. The soldier leaned in closer and spoke more quietly.

"Stay alive, give them nothing. We're going to get you out of here, but we need time to put it all together."

*   *   *

"Tom, Tom…"

There was, what he thought, was a sense of urgency in the girl's voice. He threw off the sleeping bag and quickly donned his BDU pants that had everything he needed, including his 1911 secured in the strap holster. He slung the HK-416 across his chest, donned and secured the NVG helmet and descended the ladder from the loft quickly.

Hannah was standing in the big door of the barn holding some kind of covered dish.

She looked a little alarmed, and Tom felt a little foolish. Snow had collected on her hair covering and on the shoulders of her Carhartt.

"I just brought you some cobbler, I'm sorry you aren't allowed to eat with the family."

"It's OK, your Dad is being careful. I'm thankful for everything he's doing for me, and you. It's risky for your family. I'm happy here."

"Why did you need all that?" She nodded at the guns and helmet.

"Sorry, you woke me up, I thought there was trouble." Tom took the peach cobbler she offered and sat down on a nearby hay bale.

"You impress my father, Tom. He said you are a believer and that you have spent your time in the wilderness. That you've survived things not many people could have."

"I've had help along the way... Good people. And... God. It certainly wasn't me."

Hannah sat on another hay bale looking at Tom. He opened the little container and there was only one fork.

"All for me?"

She nodded.

"My father said it has been terrible for you, that they killed your family."

Tom just nodded as he ate. He wasn't expecting this, any of this. The food, the conversation, the girl.

"I'm sorry this has all happened to you."

"I just wanted to be left alone, I didn't want to go to war. Then they brought war to me. I don't know what else I can do. I really appreciate the help your family is giving me."

"That's all we want, too, Tom. To be left alone." She had her hands in her lap and she smoothed out her dress a little. "I should go, it wouldn't do to have father looking for me. I hope you liked the cobbler."

"Thanks, Hannah, it's very good, all the food has been great. Thank you."

*   *   *

"Is that a road block? Damn."

"I don't think so, Doug. Relax."

There were two Humvees on the side of the road. The snow was coming down harder now and it was hard to see what was going on. As they drove by they saw one of the soldiers lifting a Jerry can with a spout up to the fuel filler on the lead Humvee.

"Ha, out of gas, Ski. Looks like that's a real problem for them."

"Yeah, some of the passes have been closed down by the weather, and they've re-routed all the trains. They underestimated what they would need here, especially in winter when they have to keep the roads clear."

"How are you sitting for fuel, Ski?"

"I got about three hundred gallons of treated diesel, about a hundred fifty of gas. You need some?"

"Nah, living in town makes that piece easier. We're good for now. But I think they'll be going after transportation next. There's no gas left to buy, only official vehicles can get any now. I think we'll start seeing roadblocks and them checking IDs and tracking who is associating with who."

"I imagine you're right, Doug. But we have to learn to navigate it, not be paralyzed by it."

"Don't suppose you have any cat food do you, Ski?"

Ski looked at him strangely.

"Not a cat person, didn't think so. That's one hole in our preps. But not something we long term planned for. Bianca got these cats, through the church. They were being fostered by some guy in Montana, guess some woman was at some kind of risk of violence and she didn't want her cats getting hurt… I don't know the whole story but Bianca says these cats are really important and we have to take good care of them. Like they're some kind of show cat or something, I can't figure it out, they look like mutts to me… or whatever you call cats that aren't purebred. Is there a word for that?"

Ski just shrugged, his headlights fell on the gate of his drive-way as he pulled off the road. He hit a button on his sun visor, but knew it wouldn't work.

"Haven't had enough sun for the solar to keep up. Just a minute."

Ski got out, opened the gate, drove through then hopped out to close the gate behind him. When he got back in the truck, he started talking again.

"I know we have to be careful about being seen together too much, but I really needed you for this."

"No, I get it, no problem."

The headlights fell on the big metal building and Ski hit another button on his visor. One of the big garage bay doors opened and he drove the truck in.

Inside the living area, Bill was laying on the couch, his hand up on a pillow.

Doug laid his bag on the chair and sat on the ottoman close to Bill.

"Pretty amazing, kid. Nobody knew what happened to you."

"I helped the Sheriff out a while back, we put a collar on a coyote. I think it was some kind of tracker…"

Doug was nodding as he listened along and pulled his trauma shears out of his kit and put on a pair of gloves.

"Keep talking, Bill. I'm going to cut these bandages off of you and get some fresh ones going."

"Well, I went out to pull that trap line, that same damn coyote got caught in the same damn trap, the coyote we collared with the tracker. They must have been waiting 'cause the helicopter showed up just after I stopped."

Doug was carefully cutting the bandages off of his hand and removing them.

"Well it took me a while to get out of there. It was supposed to be a real quick day, it was a close set and shouldn't have taken long. I should have been better prepared."

"Not sure how you prepare for a helicopter chasing you into an avalanche after finding a dumb coyote that you collared back in the same trap you first caught it. Really, Bill, that's some James Bond level stuff that you survived."

Bill smiled as Doug examined his fingers.

"We'll see what happens here, Bill. It looks bad, but there might be some viable tissue there, big thing is we gotta keep it dry. But, it's not as bad as I was expecting."

"They hurt like hell, Doug."

"Oh, I'm sure they do, Bill. Let's take a look at that foot."

Doug adjusted the ottoman and took Bill's booted foot in his lap, he didn't wince as much about the foot as he did the hand.

"Guys, I didn't bring my cell phone with me, but I need to know if I should go back and call in sick for work tonight or if I should just go in."

"What do you do, John?" Doug asked.

"Same as Bill, drive trucks for the county, I'm supposed to be plowing tonight."

"They know you're friends with Bill?" Ski asked.

"Yeah, that's no secret we ride together."

Ski nodded.

"Bill, can you get by without John?" Ski asked. "Might be best if he doesn't interrupt his expected routine."

"Yeah, I'll be... AHHH!" Bill yelled as Doug was carefully trying to remove the unlaced pack boot.

"Sorry, Bill." Doug said. "I'm going to need to cut this boot off."

Bill nodded as Doug reached for the shears again.

"Say, John." Ski said rubbing his chin. "Where do you get fuel for the county trucks now?"

"That big depot on the south side of the airport. Only place to get it now."

"Hmm." Ski folded his arms across his chest and nodded. "Pay attention next time you go there for fuel, John."

"To what?"

"To everything."

As the cut boot came painfully off the foot, the faint, but undeniable smell of something dead filled the air. Doug and Ski managed to keep stone faced, but John looked a little sick. John looked away as Doug cut off Bill's sock.

Doug reached for his trauma kit and pulled out a sterile towel. He opened the wrapper and carefully lifted the leg, setting the foot on the towel on the ottoman.

Doug nodded to Ski.

"Ski, I need to get some supplies from your kitchen here."

"Sure, Doug, whatever you need, I'll help you find stuff."

They walked quickly to the open kitchen on the other side of the room. Blocked by a wall, Doug spoke in a whisper.

"I told you in the truck, Ski. The right answer here is transport to the next level of care. I ain't it."

"You are, Doug. Like it or not. I can help you, I helped our 18 Delta's all the time."

"We are going to have to amputate half that foot, Ski."

"If we take him to the hospital, he disappears. Most likely a death sentence. But before he dies, he'll talk."

Doug shook his head.

*   *   *

Sheriff Grant Taylor couldn't control the stream of tears flowing down his cheeks and he was ashamed. He was ashamed not of the show of emotion and grief of losing a longtime friend, but of the show of it here, in front of this man. It was just what he wanted and he was going to exploit it for everything he could.

The normally, near jovial façade the interrogator presented, was gone. His face was now stern and he had a pensive tilt to his head as he stared above his tablet to the floor between them.

"Taylor," He said without moving his gaze. "I'm losing track… I mean I have it here as data. But that doesn't really matter when you're talking about lives. Lives of people you serve, lives of people you are responsible for, lives of people you love. It doesn't need to be this hard. No one wants it like this. Well, maybe you and Tom Potter do, I'm starting to think."

"Maybe you get off on people suffering. Maybe Tom feels important that people are dying for him. I can't wait to talk to him. What kind of Christian allows this to happen, Taylor?"

The Sheriff laid his head down on his forearms, he was curled up against the wall on the mattress.

"Render unto Caesar, that which is Caesar's, right? Caesar needs names. Give me ten names, I get your wife released. Give me the one hundred names we estimate to be in your posse, we start easing up on the county. See how easy this could be, Taylor?"

"You think those troops want to be there in the snow and the cold and so far away from home? No. Do you think the County would be happy to be going through this if they knew it was just about Tom Potter and your 100 redneck gunmen?"

The interrogator's question almost ended in a shout. Of course, the guy didn't give a damn about the life of Craig Markdale, or any of the others, Taylor knew that. The interrogator was losing his cool because he was being pressured. Whoever the boss was wanted more. If Taylor gave one name away, Markdale's death would be meaningless. If he gave away one name, he wouldn't be the man his wife married. If he gave away one name, he wouldn't be what God commanded.

The Sheriff smiled and laughed a little through his tears.

The interrogator stood up, put his tablet in the big front pocket of his parka, folded his chair and walked with it out of the door as it opened for him.

*   *   *

Max Valencour and the bushy haired operator in black camo eyed each other across the room while Zites and Booth fussed with the lap top and the powerpoint briefing they were trying to run on the new flat screen in Zites' office.

"I don't think it's the connection." Zites exclaimed.

"It has to be, it's showing up here." Booth was typing something on the laptop. "Call that number for the help desk."

The big, fit man was too busy measuring up Valencour to be as annoyed as he otherwise might be by the incompetence unfolding before him. They had been introduced, but the contractor and the informant were only introduced to each other by first names, Todd and Max. And Booth didn't bother with biographies or accomplishments for either man, there didn't seem to be time for it.

"There it is!" Yelled Zites. "Wait, go back, what did you do? It was on the screen."

Booth swore and hit a few more buttons until the PowerPoint came up as desired.

Max, Todd assessed, was in his mid to late sixties. Still in very good shape. His hair was a short fade and he was clean shaven. Not a military man by Todd's guess, maybe a cop.

"Alright, so we are making some progress here in our efforts to consolidate intel and identify networks." Booth spoke with a sudden calm, as if he everything was under control, now that the PowerPoint worked. "Weather has been the biggest impediment to collection. We have had a few days that our surveillance net has provided an absolute bounty in information. This imagery is a Gorgon Stare product, that is the pizza place on the south end of Main Street. These men have met together at this location multiple times. We've been able to positively identify the black male as Doug Worth, Navy veteran, owner of the restaurant. The man on the right here, through Gorgon Stare lookback, we traced back to the same truck you found at the trail head. Facial recognition gives us a partial ID but everything comes back to that individual being Bill Collins, the one you chased on the snow mobile, who died in the avalanche. We are still trying to develop ID's on these other two men."

"They are all surveillance savvy, we haven't been able to correlate these other two to vehicles or SIGINT signatures. They are being very careful. Our plan is to roll up Doug Worth tonight, get him talking and find the other two, this could be our big break, we…"

"Don't." Max said folding his arms across his chest.

"I'm sorry?"

"Don't roll that man up. Go back to the video of them standing on the street talking."

Booth skipped back a bit.

"Stop there. The older man with the beard is known as Ski. The man with his back to the camera is younger, mid-thirties and is known as Roger. This is the cell I'm trying to penetrate."

"Really?"

"Your collection hasn't shown me in that restaurant?"

"Weather has been a challenge."

Todd let a grin sneak out from beneath his thick mustache. So, Max was some kind of spook, or a high-end snitch.

"Give me another week, maybe two. I'll have those two fully identified and I'll be able to hand over most of the men they manage. You roll up Doug now, that sets everything back months as they all go to ground."

"OK, we've had the restaurant wired for sound and video surveillance the last two days, but with the lock down no one has shown up."

"I want someone inside." Todd said. "This weather sucks and our tech is failing. This guy is already way ahead of you and this massive surveillance matrix I keep hearing about. And I'm done with all the drone crap, I want manned ISR overhead my guys from now on."

"Well, Todd…" Booth smirked.

"Well, Todd nothin'. There's a reason my guys and I were brought in on this contract.
I get what I need one way or another, Booth."

Booth's smirk disappeared.

"I need a guy inside. I need guys whose asses are in the airplane looking at the whole picture, not some dude sippin' a latte in a shack back in Creech. I need people with skin in the game. That's how you win wars."

Booth shrugged almost submissively but the smirk appeared as if his body was exhibiting some kind of emotional rebellion.

"We're not at war, Todd." Booth managed a weak sounding laugh.

Todd stood up and half crossed the room, then pointed his finger accusingly at Booth's chest.

"And that attitude is how we lose wars in the first place." The operator shook his head in disgust. "Half the time we don't recognize we're in a war until it's too late and it makes it that much worse. Vet this guy, then get him inside and let him work his magic. Then we roll them *all* up. The sooner this is done, the better it is for everyone."

*   *   *

Tom descended the stairs with less urgency, but still as fully equipped just in case. It was habit at this point. The pistol and carbine were really a part of him, and he couldn't stand being outside after dark without the NVGs being at least within reach.

Hannah seemed more relaxed this time, smiling and presenting him with another covered dish.

"It's apple pie, I made it myself. It's the last of the fresh apples."

"Hannah, you don't need to…"

206

"I want to."

He was surprised because she cut him off rather assertively. She was a beautiful girl, really. She just didn't try to be. It was their way to dress simply and he respected that. In the glow of the light that always came on at darkness in the front of the barn, he could only just see the green of her eyes. And now there was a persistent smile, instead of the bashful one that so often disappeared.

"I mean, your family has done so much, I don't want to impose any other hardships like getting into your food supplies."

"You milk the cows, you muck the stalls, you earn your keep here, Tom. My father is impressed with how hard you work, for an outsider."

Tom shrugged, now the bashful one.

"We are well set for food. My father has always said there will come a time when we just need to accept the old ways. Like food being seasonal. We have apple trees we harvest in the fall. Those are store bought, but you can't get them from the store now. You can't *buy* anything. It's all allotted, the government is giving out rations."

"I heard something about that, Hannah. That the grocery stores are just government food distribution points now. Have you been there? How does it work."

"Father won't let me go anymore. The last time he went he said a huge fight broke out over something small. People are all on edge."

"A fight? Like the food riots they talk about in the cities?"

"I don't think it was that bad here, Tom."

"But still, I didn't think anything like that could happen here."

"Between the virus and all the government controls, people are afraid and they're angry. And even here most aren't prepared, not the way they should be. We are, but even for us it won't be easy or pleasant. No apples until fall. We may never see oranges or bananas again, my father said. No good cuts of meat again unless…" Hannah pointed to the three Holsteins in their stalls.

"Hannah, do you think the virus is real?"

"I don't know, Tom. My father doesn't. He thinks it's a distraction."

"A distraction from what?"

"I don't know… The war, the… everything falling apart. All the accidents." Hannah suddenly looked overwhelmed.

"It's OK. Your father, your family are well prepared. Don't get too wrapped up in things you can't control. That's all for God, right?"

The gloom her face had assumed in the shadows was replaced by a warm smile.

"You are so certain of things, Tom."

"Really?" It wasn't the response he expected, or even wanted. He only wanted Hannah to not worry as much as he did. He was afraid of saying what came next, but he felt strangely compelled to.

"What if all that is happening now, all the lockdowns all the suffering, is because they are looking for me? What if… What if turning myself in turned all this off, Hannah?"

"What do you mean, Tom?"

"I mean… so many people have sacrificed for me… your family included. What if there was no virus and they were playing all this up just to find me and all the people that helped me?"

"Tom…" Hannah wasn't sure what to say. "Tom, they have shut everything down, everything is dependent on the government now, do you really believe it's because of you?"

"I don't know, but I don't believe it's because of a virus. If it is because of me, should I just turn myself in?"

"No. Don't even think that, ever… Then all those that have suffered, did so for nothing. You always have to stay alive. That is your burden. You have to stay alive and free and that way *they* lose. If that is what this is really all about. If they are lying about the virus even more so… You have to stand and we have to fight this. That's what my father believes."

"What do you believe, Hannah?"

"Before I met you, I believed my father was… Overreacting, to say the least. Now, I wonder. What if my father is right?"

She saw Tom's smile in the darkness. She knew it wasn't a smile of happiness, but rather one of regret.

"I remember once, my father said that he so much wanted to have grandchildren so that he could give his grandkids what he failed to give his kids…"

Tom's lip quivered and he almost didn't complete the sentence as it impacted him more than the memory ever had before.

"Hannah, your father is a very good man, and my father tried to be…"

"Your father was too, Tom. I know that just from what I know of you."

"He tried so hard to not make this all happen. He was trying to surrender when they murdered him."

"Oh, Tom... I'm so sorry."

"I hate them, Hannah... I never knew hate in my life, but those men that killed my father with his hands up, and that hunted me and my sister and killed her... I hate them!"

Tears erupted unexpectedly from his eyes.

"I'm sorry, Hannah."

"Don't be, Tom." She had a handkerchief out and was delicately wiping the tears away.

"So many people have it worse than me, Hannah. So many people have sacrificed for me, I'm in no place to complain. I'm sorry."

"I can't even begin to imagine what all you've gone through, Tom. Have you used those things?" She seemed to nod to the totality of his kit.

"Yes."

"Have you had to kill?"

"I've... tried. I don't know if I killed anyone or not. I know my sister did, I saw it. She was always a better shot than me."

"Will you... kill, Tom?"

"If I have to, yes. I just wanted to be left alone but they can't do that now. And I've had a long while to think about it. I'm trying not to let the hate grow in my heart, I pray for some kind of deliverance from that or some help in dealing with it. But those that come for me, are the same kind that killed my father and my sister and... I'll do what I have to do."

She looked down at her boots and Tom realized there was an edge to his tone.

"I'm sorry, Hannah, if that makes you feel less about me somehow. It's the truth. I'm hunted and I can't run and I can't hide forever. I have to be ready. In here especially." He pointed to his head.

Hannah forced a smile.

"That makes sense, Tom. I just wish it didn't have to be so." She tilted her head looking at the helmet on his head. "Are those the things that let you see at night?"

Tom beamed.

"NODs, Night Observation Devices, I think. Or NVGs, Night Vision Goggles… Hey, you want to see something?" His darker tone was suddenly excited and even a little like the teenager he should have been.

"OK?"

"We have to go out back, that light will ruin the affect out here."

Walking through the darkness along the side of the barn, Tom took Hannah's gloved hand to guide her. Because of the glove, he felt no warmth, no softness and it hadn't been any kind of romantic gesture, he just didn't want her to get hurt. But, Tom felt a sudden human connection that he hadn't felt for so, so long.

He'd lowered the goggles and they had turned on automatically, with the security light at the front of the barn it seemed nearly a pale green day light. As they rounded the corner of the back of the barn it was darker and here it would be better.

"Here, Hannah." Tom handed her the helmet and she put it on awkwardly. "Look up, look further away from the barn because they're still picking up the ambient light out front."

She held the ill-fitting helmet awkwardly.

"Oh, my word, Tom... There are so many stars... I had no idea!"

"Pretty amazing isn't it?"

"It's so beautiful... Those flashing lights, an airplane?"

"Yes."

"Oh, should we worry, is it looking for you?"

"No, I can see the lights too, the ones we have to worry about won't be running visible lights, that's an airliner."

"This is so amazing, Tom. I could look through these for hours."

"I used to do that with my Dad. If you see a streak across the sky, it's a meteor. If you see a steady un-flashing light it's a satellite."

"Oh! I just saw a shooting star, Wow!"

A harsh voice erupted from behind them, as Tom spun, he was met by a flashlight beam.

"Hannah, Tom."

"Father!" Hannah handed the helmet to Tom.

"I'm sorry, Sir. It was my fault, it was my idea. I didn't think it would be bad for her to see through the goggles."

"It's not, Tom. I don't care about that. Both of you get back inside the barn."

Tom had a terrible sinking feeling and Hannah had her face half buried in the collar of her coat. Once back inside the barn, Johann began talking again.

"I don't care about your technology, or even your weapons. What I care about is reckless behavior that can get you and my family caught. You are a young man, she is a young woman and it appears you are a bad influence upon one another… in these times that is particularly hazardous. Hannah, go back to the house."

"Father!"

"Go." Johann turned back to Tom. "I appreciate the difficulty of your circumstances and I wish you well. This is not working out here, have your things packed in the morning. As soon as I have found other, safe arrangements for you, Tom, you will be gone."

"No father, no!"

"To the house, Hannah."

*   *   *

They had delayed the procedure for the next day, to follow a "shopping" trip in town. The first step was to pick up Roger, then a stop to visit Ski's ex-girlfriend, a vet with a veterinary clinic just on the edge of town. With those first tasks successfully completed, Doug wanted to stop by the restaurant. They parked in the alley out back.

It didn't take Doug long, he knew right where they were in the kitchen. The pounding at the front door seemed to start as soon as he had turned the light on in the back room. He grabbed what he needed, then turned the light off. Peering carefully around the door jam, the figure pounding at the front door was back lit by the nearby streetlight.

Doug shook his head when he recognized the tall older man. He thought about going out the back and just ignoring him. Instead he walked to the front door and opened it to the cold.

"You."

Max held his finger to his lips and nodded to the back of the restaurant. A few times Doug tried to talk and Max's index finger went up again. Doug finally figured it out and walked him out the back of the store. When Max deemed it safe, he began talking.

"I'm glad you're here, I need to talk to you and the others. I didn't want to go to your home. What brought you here, Doug?"

He held up the bone saw and cleaver without any further explanation.

Max gave a little shake of his head.

"I need to talk to you and the others, as soon as possible."

"We have some pressing matters. Ski is waiting in his truck across the street there, we just grabbed Roger, let's go talk to them." Doug locked the back door and started across the street. "So, how are your field medicine skills, Max?"

CHAPTER 7

They had carefully moved Bill to the spare bedroom where he was made as comfortable as possible. They had front loaded Tylenol 1000 mg and an ample dosage of Woodford Reserve.

Doug looked at his watch, waiting for the ketamine to take effect.

He looked at Bill's infected foot, laid out on a sterile sheet on top of lots of towels. There was a plastic garbage bag held open in a basket at the foot of the bed. Also, a sterile sheet draped across a stool with all the tools Doug thought he might need. He'd start with the tourniquet, and a check of the distal pulse.

Roger, Ski and Max stood in the background as Doug leafed through a book gravely titled Emergency War Surgery. Max was strangely unsettled but everyone, even Ski assumed it was just the gore of the foot and what was about to happen.

"Look, I really need to tell you all something." Max blurted.

Doug had his head in the book.

"Look, you guys go out to the living room and talk, I need some time here and I kinda need to be focused, ya' know? I'll call when I need help."

Ski nodded Roger and Max left to move out to the living room.

"What is it?" Ski had his arms across his chest.

"They know who you all are."

"Who's they?" Ski asked.

"The Feds."

"How do they know?" Asked Roger.

"I told them."

"What?" Ski exclaimed. Then he looked back toward the spare bedroom. He continued, trying not to yell. "What do you mean, *you told them?*"

"They brought me in, I had to give them something. Just first names, they have Doug and Bill fully identified. They were talking about bringing Doug in for questioning."

"I knew we couldn't trust you."

"But you can."

"How?" Roger asked.

"I wouldn't have told you if I was working for them. Think it through. They have surveillance footage of *all* of you. They are piecing it together with facial recognition. Doug needs to go to ground, he can't go home from here. They think Bill is dead of course."

"What about us?" Roger asked.

"They don't know you beyond first names yet."

"Thanks to you." Ski growled.

"They were going to figure it out."

"And now they've tracked us all here, how convenient. Maybe you're just buying time for the team to get into position."

"That makes no sense, Ski. I am on your side and I'm trying to help you."

"Why, Valencour? Why help us?"

"You know a little about me, Ski?"

"Enough."

"I've been labeled lots of things in my life, Ski. A snitch, a mercenary, a felon... I've seen enough wrong in my life to want to do right. I'd like to just be left alone, but I knew that wouldn't happen when all this came down. When Tom showed up at my place... I don't know if it's his innocence or maybe he's still naïve after all he's been through. Something about him had a calming effect. Something compelled me to watch over him, and to try to help get us through this the best way I know how."

"Anyhow, you should be safe. I waited to try to make contact until it was another low overcast night. Of course, it had to be the night this was happening... The weather has been playing hell with their surveillance. I will tell you everything I know about their operation when all this is done." Max motioned back to the back room.

Ski shook his head and just then heard Doug call his name from the spare room. He took just a moment to cast one last accusatory glare at Max. Roger stared pensively after Ski and spoke quietly after he left.

"I guess I don't really know who, or what you are, Max."

"Past tense. I worked for a variety of three letter agencies providing information and intelligence."

"Were you a spy?"

"Nothing nearly so noble. I was a paid informant, that's all. Started it all working off charges. Turns out getting people to trust me, then betraying them came so natural for me, it was a career… and worse. It became a kind of habit. So, I locked myself away from everyone. Women, town. No more wives to betray. No one on the street to lie to just because I couldn't help myself. And as everything was spiraling out of control, I was even more happy to be alone in my wilderness."

"And then?"

"Then this kid shows up. Drawn to me… I play bagpipes. He heard them and I saw him…"

"You said something about feeling compelled to help him. What was it?"

"I mean, he looked hungry and cold, he'd been out a long time."

"No, I mean what compelled you?"

"I ah…" Valencour paused for a moment, then, unexpectedly, his eyes filled with tears. "I'm… not sure."

Max rubbed his eyes and dropped to sit on the sofa behind him. Roger stepped over and patted him on the shoulder, then silently walked to the kitchen where he drew Max a glass of water. He set it on a coaster on the coffee table in front of Max and sat down in the chair across from him.

"Thanks." Max gestured to his face. "Been pretty stressful, guess I don't handle it the way I used to."

"Who, in this country, has ever handled what we've been going through the past few weeks before? I mean in our lifetimes, Max?" Roger laughed a little.

"True."

They sat quietly in their own thoughts for a while.

Roger wasn't sure how much time had passed, but it was sooner than he expected that Doug and Ski emerged from the spare room. Neither man looked as grim as they had before. Doug washed his hands again in the kitchen sink and Roger and Max walked up to him.

"How did it go?" Roger asked.

Doug shrugged.

"We'll see. I took a third of the foot, hopefully that was enough. It's a procedure called a guillotine amputation. We're going to have to keep up with the dressing changes, keep everything clean, keep him on some antibiotics. Hope there's no sepsis or infection, hope I don't have to cut any more off."

Drying his hands Doug looked at Ski, Roger then finally to Max.

"So, what did I miss?"

*   *   *

The old Toyota truck smelled like cigarettes and had an interior that looked nearly as beat up and life worn as its driver.

"My place is on the other side of town. It's not nearly as nice as that Mennonite farm, sorry. And I don't have a daughter, so that'll keep you out of trouble. Can't believe you fell for the classic *farmer's daughter*."

"I didn't fall for her, we didn't do anything, I didn't do anything." Tom was defensive and uncomfortable.

"Sure, sure… Just cause ol' Johann was on his game. I get it kid."

"We were just friends." Tom stammered, and he immediately regretted saying anything further as the man with the long jet-black hair pulled into a pony tail laughed. He lit another cigarette and it gave Tom a chance to change the subject.

"What's with all the cars on the sides of the road?"

"Ah, mostly people run outa' gas. Some broke down and there's no parts. And they don't have the fuel to tow and impound 'em. People aren't traveling much. This is the first time I've been out in weeks and I won't go out again anytime soon."

The snow was a fine mist that melded into an obscure, but bright overcast.

"Is it safe to travel during the day like this?"

"Don't know, haven't been out, kid. I didn't have any problems or see any roadblocks when I came to get you. 'Course I tend to not travel to places where they'll have troops set up. I got enough food stashed to last us a while so we don't need to go to the circus those food distribution sites have become. Heard a guy pulled a gun when the crowd surged around him. Just panicked. He got shot and killed by feds and they wounded a couple of bystanders too. People are getting scared and desperate, and I don't think it's going the way the feds want either. You sitting in my truck for example." The man trailed off to a laugh as he puffed the cigarette.

"What do you do for a living, Randy?"

"I don't do anything for a *living,* I just do whatever I want. I'm on disability 'cause I broke my back in a logging accident years ago. Just as well because right now, no one is doing anything for a living in this county. Most are out of work because of the lockdown unless they work for the county. I've done some "unregistered pharmaceutical sales" before, too, may go back to that. Now, I just don't really care anymore. My place is paid for. I get enough to pay for beer, cigarettes and groceries and I cover my taxes."

"Will you have work for me around your property?"

"Nah, I just live in a trailer. Just a place to lay low, then I pass you on to some of my Lakota bros on the rez. Kind of my specialty. That's how I know Mr. Valencour. I helped him years ago the first time he came through here on a job."

"But that's outside the county."

"Us Indians are sneaky like that. You watch, we'll get you out."

"I don't want out, I think I need to stay."

"Those are my instructions, Tom. If you get to me, I'm to get you out of the Enclave."

Randy took the exit for the bypass that took them around town. Tom strained to see the grocery store on the north side of town. The parking lot was crowded, equally with cars and people. He could see Humvees and 5-ton trucks and the uniforms of all the troops there to distribute the food and attempt to maintain order.

Town had always been such an inviting, warm place and now he shivered and was glad Randy was taking the bypass. He didn't want to get too close to what it seemed to have become.

"Jobs, money, guess none of that matters anymore. Did you hear they've gotten rid of money?"

"What?"

"Yeah, kid. Bunch of people went to the bank to pull cash, 'course it was more than the bank had on hand, darn near had a riot. That was just last week, so now the FCE is on an *economic freeze*. Hardly anybody gettin' paid anyway. And they sell it by talkin' how taxes are suspended. BS. Everything is suspended. Frozen alright. They figure they're providin' food an' tryin' to provide heating fuel for everyone. So, that's all anyone gets. No more greenbacks."

"Wait, what is FCE?"

"Ah, yeah, you been out playin' in the woods a while. Federal Cooperative Enclave. That's what they're calling the county now, I figure it sounds better than quarantine zone or something like that."

"And no money? Is that like, everywhere? Or just the... *Enclave*."

"Well, no one really knows... No one that's talkin' at least. The feds won't say. But they're saying they'll replace it with written scrips until the whole digital thing is set up and everyone has phones. That's another thing they're doing, everyone is getting issued a phone if they don't have one. That way they can track rations better."

"That's not all they're gonna track, Randy."

"Bingo, kid... Guess you of all people sees where all this is going, huh?"

Tom just nodded, a little in awe of all that he was learning and how much the world had changed.

"They're just getting things set up now, though, kid. Lots of holes in the system right now. We gotta take advantage of them in every way we can."

*　　*　　*

Doug had his face in his hands sitting on the sofa next to Ski.

"There is no way I'm not going back to get my family, Max."

"You would put yourself, us *and* your family at more risk, Doug."

"You've got to be kidding, Max! You're the one who put all of us at risk with all of this."

"They came to me, I had to give them something believable if not verifiable..." Max paused, in thought, for a moment, then continued. "I'll get your family, Doug. I have a place I can take them, and I'll get Tom and bring him back. I'll need to use one of your vehicles, Ski. Something that won't show up associated with me if I'm caught in surveillance."

Ski glared at Max, then looked to Doug.

"He's going to take one of my trucks and run back to the feds and then we get raided, Doug."

"I'll go with him."

"No, Doug. No offense, but I work alone."

"Not on this one, Max. My family wouldn't just hop in a vehicle with you. I go with you, that's the only way this happens."

"I got forty-five acres here, Max. Doug goin' with you is the only way you don't wind up buried somewhere in that forty-five acres."

Max returned Ski's glare then relented with a nod of his head.

"Now, what about this thing about bringing Tom here. What is that about, Max?"

"He wants us all in one place for the take down, Doug. I don't trust this son of a bitch a single bit."

"You're right not to trust me, Ski. I've done a lot of bad things. But this won't be one of them. Tom Potter needs to be a part of this fight. A man can't run forever."

Ski's stern face softened a little.

"That's what I'm talkin' about." said John. He'd come over after his shift to check on Bill. And at that moment, the sound of Bill vomiting came from the back room. Doug jumped up.

"It's one of the effects of him coming down from the ketamine, I'll go check on him, I put a garbage can there for him."

Trotting to the room, he stopped at the door way.

"He's OK, but he missed the can."

"At least he didn't hit that nice throw rug in there, right?" Ski said as they were all getting to their feet.

Doug gave a little frown and shook his head.

"Afraid he got that pretty good. You guys stay there, let him get his gyros re-caged and I'll take care of him and the mess."

"So, Max." Ski sat back down. "Tell me what this fight looks like to you."

"We start out small. Small victories count and we can build on them. Harassment and misdirection operations."

"Well, shoot." John laughed. "Bill and our guys have already started that."

*   *   *

From the air something seemed off to Chambers, but he couldn't quite place it. They had been tasked with checking out fresh tracks detected by Synthetic Aperture Radar and spotted during a break in the weather. The tracks corresponded with the edge of the radius the analysts determined Tom Potter might have reached on foot. The trackway arced through the snow from one large outcropping of rocks to another.

The team departed the S-92 with guns up and scanning the mountain above where someone may have taken cover to set an ambush.

Chambers just shook his head and didn't bother getting his measuring tape out. Before he could say anything, Paulsen exclaimed excitedly.

"This guy's not wearing shoes... Those are bare foot tracks... and they're *huge!*" Paulsen was looking back at Chambers wide eyed.

"No, Paulsen, it's not Bigfoot."

"What do you mean, look at them, Chambers. Those are twice the size of my feet. That is the definition of a bigfoot, that's a freekin' Sasquatch track."

"That is a fake, Paulsen. And not even a very good one. That is someone with some ply wood cutout strapped to their feet. That is some local yokel screwing with us."

"Look at this terrain, Chambers... and the toes."

"Paulsen, that is not a Sasquatch track. They are all identical." The tracker crouched down examining the track a little closer. "A real foot bends and flexes with the terrain... and look, you can even see the imprint of the strap that's holding the wood cutout to his boots. This is some climber or some redneck with just enough beer on board to think this is a good idea. It's somebody who has a good knowledge of the area, but it's not Tom Potter. These people are starting to mess with us."

"You said *that's* not a Sasquatch track, Chambers... you've seen them, haven't you?"

Chambers just looked to his team leader.

"This is a waste of our time, Gary."

"Yeah, I'll recall the helo and we're out of here."

"So, have you seen them, Chambers?"

"Shut up, Paulsen."

Gary was talking on the radio and the S-92 was in the turn instantly, headed back to them.

"I knew it... You've spent enough time in the woods, you would see one."

"Just shut up, Paulsen."

The helicopter flew in to flare to a landing, making conversation impossible, even as Paulsen continued.

*   *   *

The operator's muscular arms were across his chest and he leaned back in the chair across from Booth and Zites in a casual way that made the two administrators even more uncomfortable. He cracked a frustrated smile a few moments before he finally spoke.

"Gentlemen, you guys are in charge of this Enclave, correct?"

"Administratively, yes." Zites said.

"And militarily?"

"Well, Todd, we administrate order through the military, so we are ultimately responsible for all military in the enclave."

"And then there is us." Todd pointed to himself. "We alleviate any messy Posse Comitatus stickiness I assume, right?"

"Well," Booth smiled confidently. "It's not like that is any kind of impediment to our operations now. You and your teams are responsible for seizing High Value Targets that are developed by our intelligence section and you are given the latitude to use whatever means of interdiction you see fit."

"But ultimately, you're in charge, right, Booth?"

Sensing some kind of trap being laid, Booth stammered a bit as he went.

"Well… ah, yes… absolutely."

"You are in charge of me and my guys, you are in charge of all established local authority, the military… and most importantly, to me, the people who provide us with intelligence."

"Yes, of course."

"And this whole fuel thing…"

"You and your teams will continue to have priority…"

"Maybe a better solution would be getting more fuel in here and finally getting serious about finding some quality intel. We just burned up over 600 gallons of fuel chasing fake Bigfoot prints." The operator laughed a little. "See, I talked to the intel section. I guess their imagery analysts got all excited because this big computer program they're running that collates all the disparate intel into a usable product ran whatever algorithm it had and came up with this hit on human-shaped foot prints. What the computer seemed to miss was that these tracks were over twenty inches long and obviously fake Bigfoot tracks."

"Isn't that just what you call the cost of doing business, Todd?"

"No." The operator smiled and leaned forward. "That's what we call a wild goose chase and a waste of valuable resources. So, what are *you* going to do about the fuel and intel situations, Booth?"

"Well, actually we are looking at opening up the rail lines again. This winter has hit particularly hard and beyond the shortages caused by the war we're also seeing some passes closed that are usually over road fuel routes. We are looking at opening up rail in the enclave again and diverting some of what they call 'gas local' trains that specifically deliver fuel."

"And the reason those rail lines were closed?"

"Just another avenue for contraband to come into the enclave. We had to shut down things tight initially just to get everything under control." Zites said.

"And you think things are under control now?" The contractor laughed and stood up.
"How about the intel piece, where is your boy Max on things right now?"

Booth and Zites just looked at each other.

"He's been out of contact. He's used to working deep cover."

"He is well vetted, right? No chance he's working for them..."

"Not a chance, I'll show you his file. He's done amazing work for the FBI, CIA and DEA. He knows we pay him handsomely and more importantly, he knows what happens if he betrays us."

The operator started walking toward the door and Booth was feeling bullied.

"What about the Sheriff's wife, Todd? Have you done any follow up?"

Todd stopped and turned.

"Initial follow up proved negative. And frankly, she's about the bottom of my list of priorities."

"She's on the list of HVTs we provided you that we want caught. She could provide leverage for the ongoing interrogation of Taylor."

"Where they have a man like Taylor, having his wife isn't really important. They'll just tell him she's in custody and he'll never know the difference. And for a man like Taylor, it won't really matter either way. He knows he's going to die there, and he knows there's not a thing he can do for his wife."

"We need her brought in, Todd." Zites suddenly asserted.

"Either of you married?"

Zites kind of raised his hand.

"It's one thing to take these draft dodgers in. People kind of expect that, these folks around here are torn. Everyone's expected to do their duty and all, right? And these are law abiding, God fearing folks, so part of them still thinks going off to this mess overseas must be the right thing to do... but we start going after people's families... Well, gentlemen, that's gonna be a whole different kind of war."

*   *   *

Boggs woke to the luscious smell of bacon, eggs and fresh ground coffee. He had the early shift and she knew that. His wife, in bed beside him slept soundly, she didn't need to be up for school for another few hours.

Boggs shook his head with a little smile. Barney, the golden retriever, was at the foot of the bed resting his head there, wagging his tail as he always did just before the alarm went off. But the smell of the food woke him up 15 minutes early.

"This woman's throwing us all off, isn't she, Barney?"

Barney's only response was to wag faster.

Boggs threw on some sweat pants and a hoodie. His uniform would be hanging up in the kitchen, ironed crisply.

He walked into the kitchen with Barney in close trail.

"Good morning... Don't let Barney con you, I already fed him."

"Good morning, Mrs. Taylor." Boggs closed the kitchen window shade. "It smells great, but you really have to keep the shades or curtains closed in any room you're in, please."

"Oh, Frank… First off, you need to quit calling me that. It makes me feel old."

"I've told you it's either that or Mrs. Sheriff."

"Oh, heavens no… I'll try to remember the curtains better, but I swear, if it were up to you, I'd be up in the attic like Anne Frank."

"Well, it is kind of up to me, we just don't have an attic." He laughed a little as he sat down behind the prepared place setting.

"Ha! Grant would say the same thing. We always let you men think you have more control than you really have in the household, you realize that don't you?"

"Shhh… Don't give Carol any ideas."

"Oh, she already knows, we've talked."

"Great, you guys are talking. I don't stand a chance."

She laughed as she brought the plate of eggs and bacon over and sat it in front of him.

Frank Boggs bowed his head in prayer for a moment. It was a new thing to him, this religion and prayer thing. He was still trying to sort it all out. But with the way things were, he prayed to give thanks for his food, and for the health and safety of his family and he prayed for the Sheriff. And he prayed for proper words for the inevitable conversation that was about to happen.

"I hope he's eating enough. He never does when he's sick."

Boggs nodded.

"I'm the same way."

"You men… Of course, they always say, starve a cold, feed a fever. I wonder which one this one is? If it's even real."

She didn't know the details of the take down that had been observed on the road. The nearest country house to where the Sheriff had been taken was owned by a retired cop who knew what a well-executed PIT maneuver looked like. When the Sheriff was extracted and 'treated' and thrown in the sprinter van, the man saw the whole thing from his porch. They even had a tow truck to take the Sheriff's vehicle away immediately. When the dust settled, the retired cop called for a deputy and was deliberately vague in describing a 'suspicious circumstance' over an open 911 call. He'd used words like men with guns and in fear for his life and that got folks rolling, but when the two deputies arrived, Boggs being one of them, all that was left was skid marks and torn grass and dirt.

The retired cop knew the Sheriff and knew his Tahoe. Boggs knew it was no good, he left the other Deputy to handle the paperwork and ran code directly to the Sheriff's house to get her. He tried not to alarm her at the time, said there had been some kind of accident and they were still trying to get the whole story, but that she needed to grab clothes and come stay with his family. She saw the urgency in his eyes and probably saw something there he wasn't telling her too.

She made quick arrangements to have a neighbor take care of their animals and the neighbor was the kind to not ask questions when he heard her voice cracking on the phone, saying something had happened to Grant.

Mrs. Taylor had instantly assumed a soft matriarchal role in the Boggs household and she had a certain calm and wisdom that came with her age and devotion to God and her husband that was really a positive in the house, but Boggs worried.

"Do you think it's real, Frank? I don't think I do, I don't care what the Telescreen says."

Everyone called it the Telescreen now, the one approved channel that was the only one they could receive, just like Orwell's 1984. Turned out he was just a little premature. The Telescreen was where she saw the video of Grant and Craig on ventilators being wheeled into the big grey medivac planes at the airport. That was the last image she had of her husband.

Boggs privately wondered if the Sheriff was even still alive. Boggs' first instinct was validated a few days after taking her in when a BOLO, Be On the Look Out, for one Marjorie Taylor came down from the feds. He'd even been careful not to tell too many people at the department about his new house guest, but several knew. They weren't talking.

His instinct was telling him they would never see the Sheriff again.

He smiled and shrugged a little. It was so uncomfortable. Ordinarily, if he was dealing with relatives of crimes or accidents he found it best to just relate the truth as best he knew it as compassionately as he could... but, now... what was truth?

That was where he sought guidance. Was it better for her to have some hope, did that sustain her?

For the past week he had been trying to develop the courage to carefully broach the possibilities of his thoughts with her.

"I wish he had got that new knee done before all this. It's gotten to where it just always hurts him, he's not even comfortable sleeping and has to take some ibuprofen before bed. He had just scheduled the surgery too."

"Mrs. Taylor, how can you be so calm and cheerful through all this?"

"You mean, am I deluding myself?" She grinned a little mischievously and sat down across the table from him. She was a subtly attractive woman, farm fit but with a few more curves than she liked. Her hair was mostly white now with a few streaks of black that were remnants of her youth. She figured she'd earned each wrinkle that creased her face and didn't bother trying to cover or alter them with makeup. She talked a lot, and when it really mattered she always spoke her mind.

Boggs nodded a little, almost submissively.

"Let me tell you something about Grant Taylor. Long before he was Sheriff, he was the man I loved. When he was a cop in L.A. and I was doing outreach work there, he was the same man he is today. He didn't want to be there though, he wanted to be someplace like this. But, after the Army, he wound up there. And he needed to be there, and so did I. We did some good things for good people stuck in bad places in their lives. One of the things I love most about my man is that he has always stayed where he felt he needed to be, whether he wanted to be there or not. He knew the Lord would put him where he would be of the best service… even if it wasn't really the best place to be!" She pounded the table with her fist and gave a little laugh.

"I know, where ever Grant is right now… for whatever reason, it's where the Lord wants him to be, and he's given him the strength to endure it."

*   *   *

Sheriff Grant Taylor wept.

He knew God had not abandoned him, he knew God was providing all he *truly* needed. He knew his faith in God was unshaken. The Sheriff, however, feared he was missing something.

What if God was speaking to him and he wasn't hearing?

Despite the grueling pain of the crippled knee, the Sheriff was on his knees in prayer. What if it was all his failure? He asked for forgiveness for not having acted sooner to prevent the shootout at Potter's cabin and wondered if his lack of preemptive action was a kind of cowardice that was a kind of lack of faith that he didn't recognize in himself.

He prayed for Craig Markdale and wherever he had failed him, he prayed for forgiveness for ever thinking his ever-faithful friend might be the mole in his department. And now Craig was dead. Grant shook his head. He thought if he acted too soon, too many would die, but look at where they were now. Was this all, ultimately *his* fault?

Lord, dear Jesus, help me I tried to do the right thing as I saw it… and so many died…

The door scraped open behind him and he turned and looked.

Two soldiers, fully equipped, with carbines even. He looked long enough to recognize the eyes over the mask, the one soldier's eyes he had seen before. The one who suggested they were going to get him out. He knew that as just another one of the mind games they would use to manipulate his psyche to get him to talk. As much as he wanted to believe, he wouldn't let himself.

The other soldier tossed him a large parka that hit him with enough force to almost knock him over.

"Put it on." The soldier said sharply.

Grant wrestled himself into it. The pockets had all been crudely sewn closed and the soldier whose eyes he recognized tossed him a pair of arctic overmittens, then motioned the Sheriff out of the cell.

The other soldier threw the coyote ruffed hood far over his head so he couldn't really see and they led him by the arms down the halls of the facility until they finally came to a series of doors that ultimately led to the outside.

The Sheriff didn't remember the last time he had been outside and seen the sun. But there was no warmth. A cold sea wind blew in off the sound of light surf and smelled salty and bit cold, deep into exposed skin.

He walked toward the rocky beach and the one soldier he recognized walked close to his shoulder, almost yelling against the wind;

"It's safe to talk here, Sheriff, but don't... Just listen."

A low surf roiled into the sand and rocks of the beach. The sky was tremendous blue and there were no clouds. The Sheriff's view was constrained by the hood, but he suddenly realized this was a place much more severe than anywhere in Washington.

"First off, Sheriff," He recognized the voice as the one that whispered in his ear and matched the eyes over the mask. "You need to know, they don't have your wife, that was just a bluff. Your wife went to ground and no one has turned her over. I think it's safe to assume she's with a neighbor or friend."

"Second, you need to understand the worst is yet to come. Now, listen closely to what I say next, this is what I've been instructed to say; *Be on your guard, stand firm in the faith, be courageous, be strong…*"

"Corinthians… 16:12 no 16:11… I can't remember… who told you to say that?"

"Again. Just listen, don't talk, Sheriff. The worst is yet to come. You've given them nothing, continue with that." The soldier spoke firmly against the wind and the low sound of surf.

"How do I know I can trust you?"

"You can't trust me, Sheriff. You can't trust anyone here. I'm just trying to tell you. We don't all believe in what is happening and some of us know what is coming next. There are triggers, that, when tripped, will hopefully bring more on our side. We will have more support as more see what is really going on. You are not alone here, there are others in captivity resisting. Craig Markdale didn't die alone, the Governor of Alaska died here too. This is bigger than you may imagine."

"Where is this place?" The Sheriff took the chance of pulling the parka hood back and they didn't stop him.

He looked out across the black gravelly beach and into the thick ice fog that hung just off of it, obscuring any notion of a world beyond.

They surprised him with an answer.

"This, Sheriff, is a forgotten corner of Eareckson Air Station, Shemya, Alaska… The ultimate black site. There is no trail, paper or digital that leads to you here. They don't care if you live or die, you are just here on the off chance that you will break, because everyone does, one way or another."

The Sheriff fell to his knees, took off the mittens and ran his fingers through the fine gravel.

"How many can we count on?"

"Right now, besides other detainees? You're pretty much lookin' at it, Sheriff. There are a few others, some outside. There's no getting out of this without help from the outside. I may not understand or share your religious beliefs, but what is coming is damn near Biblical, and I know you're willing to die for your beliefs, aren't you?"

The Sheriff nodded solemnly.

"Well, don't… That would be easier for certain, but we need people like you for the fight that's coming."

*   *   *

The crucible was small and sat deep in the coals. Ski tended to it with tongs and when the assorted scrap wires and short pipe lengths were sufficiently molten, he pulled it out with the tongs. Bill watched as Ski carefully poured it into what appeared to be a small whiskey jug.

"Ski, I have to say your ways confound me." Bill had come out on his crutches to get some fresh air. Instead he walked out into the smoke and fumes.

"Yeah, it would be better to have a forge but I don't have one. Fire is barely hot enough, but it'll get the job done."

"No, Ski." Bill shook his head "I mean, first of all, why are you melting copper, second why are you pouring it into an old whiskey jug?"

"Just an old hobby of mine, something I picked up in the military a long time ago. Fun to keep up with from time to time. And this little jug has just the convex shape in the bottom I need. When it's cool and hard, I'll just hammer the jug off from around it. Easy."

Ski was concentrating on the pour as he started and he spoke as if that should explain everything to Bill. When he was done pouring, he looked into the mouth of the jug with a pen light, satisfied with the level, he put the excess scrap away and just poked at the coals a little.

At this point Bill had ascertained he might not get a straight answer from Ski. He had some ideas but thought he might need to approach it from another angle.

"Do you think it's all worth it, Ski?"

"What?"

"What we're doing, what we're going to need to do."

Ski nodded reflectively and stirred the coals a little more before he spoke.

"How old are you, Bill?" Ski asked as he pushed the coals around the crucible the way he wanted them.

"Twenty-eight."

"No military, right?"

"No, went to work for the county when I was eighteen."

Ski nodded and watched the mesmerizing glow of the coals in the night.

"Yeah, you're just a youngster. Probably doesn't feel like it to you, but you are. When I was a kid, I knew all the World War Two vets in the neighborhood and they were my grandfathers and their friends and I knew all the Vietnam and Korea vets and they were my uncles and cousins. Some of those folks were the kind of guys in the neighborhood you might need to think twice about chasing a ball in their yard and I didn't really understand that as a kid. Then it was my time and I went to work on the hot side of the Cold War. And now there's guys like Doug and Roger who went to fight in the GWOT.

"Well the World War Two guys are mostly dead and gone now, same as the Korean War guys and now it's the Vietnam War guys that are getting harder to find and most people just forget about them. The things my guys and I did, well, none of that made the history books. And no one remembers Grenada or Panama and no one knows half the stuff that went on along the DMZ. And all that GWOT stuff, well, it was all streamed or you can find a 15 minute video on Youtube of it if you want. But it doesn't get remembered the same way as a book, does it?"

"Guess not." Bill shook his head.

"One common thread, when you're able to get close enough to any of those guys to get them to talk sincerely about it is *was it all worth it*. After five years or so of the Global War On Terror, I know people were asking that question. And they sure as hell were asking it about some of the stuff we did in the cold war era and Vietnam. Even Korea and World War Two, I heard some of those vets asking that. I imagine a lot asked it of the Civil War, the way folks suffered and endured back then."

"I don't know, Bill, if any of that was ever worth it. But this, this is something different. This is our home, this is every essence of our freedom. Took me a long time to put this place together. I may lose it all if I fight for it. I'll definitely lose it all if I don't."

"Now, if everything we've all been through in our lives, everything we've all learned along the way, every path we took has led us all here together to help preserve the freedom of our community, our county, hell, maybe the freedom of our nation... then, yeah, it's all been worth it."

Bill let that all sink in a respectable time before getting back to his original question.

"Does it have anything to do with the 55-gallon drum of gasoline in there?"

"That's more than just gasoline, but, yeah, it has to do with that."

"You're making a bomb aren't you, Ski."

"A bomb? No... what kind of person do you think I am, Bill?"

*   *   *

Bianca carefully answered the door with the cocked Colt .45 replica hidden behind her leg. No one came knocking these days, but Doug had been gone much longer than she expected and she hoped this was news from him.

The tall, fit older man who had been knocking had a pleasant and reliable face and she instantly didn't trust him.

"Mrs. Worth, I'm here on behalf of Doug. He is with your Uncle Alfonso and it is an emergency, are your children all here?"

Bianca backed into the house leveling the revolver at the man, but allowing him to enter as she processed what was the family code word. It was something Doug had brought up from time to time. For the purposes of authentication, or for the children to have an out if they were ever in an uncomfortable place. If Uncle Alfonso's health came up, it meant the family should listen carefully to whatever was going on.

Uncle Alfonso was the only relative of Bianca's that Doug got along with well and he had died when the children were very young. Alfonso was a jovial, rotund man who loved a good intrigue or conspiracy, so the invocation of his name in such a way would have met with great approval by him.

"Doug said to grab your go-bags. It could be a while."

"Are we in danger?" Bianca's words were stern but carried on a slight Italian accent that, any other time, Max would have found time to consider delightful.

"Who isn't these days? Yes, madam, we must go, there isn't a lot of time."

She stood glaring at him a moment, he didn't seem fazed by the presence of the large Uberti revolver, but he didn't seem to doubt she would use it.

She shook her head with a strange kind of growl and called out to the girls in Italian, issuing what had to be rapid fire orders.

Valencour looked out the windows across the street to Ski's old Suburban he had parked a few houses down. He looked up and down the quiet residential street that was glazed with ice from the falling sleet and freezing rain.

There was no tail and tonight there would be no effective surveillance.

There was a frustrated bustle behind him and he turned to see Bianca and the girls burdened by backpacks and two small animal crates.

"What is that?"

"Cats." The older girl said with much attitude.

Bianca snapped at her in Italian.

"I'm allergic to cats." Said Valencour.

"I…," Bianca snarled. "Am allergic to strange men showing up at my door at night and speaking of Uncle Alfonso. These cats are important. They go with us."

Valencour looked at her. Beside the back pack she wore over her back, she had a smaller one strapped across her chest. She still carried the .45 but he noted that now it was uncocked.

He nodded and tried to smile.

"It all goes in the very back of the truck, *do not react to what you find there.* You will be happy but ignore what you see and sit in the seats behind me, make like everything is normal. Understood?"

Bianca and the girls looked concerned but nodded.

"Let's go, *quickly.* It's the blue, older Suburban on the other side of the street, a few houses up."

They scurried through the darkness, taking care on the slick spots across the road. They moved with a quiet desperation and a fear they dared not show. This was a time of grave uncertainty and a good world gone by and they knew, as they had discussed, that they might have to adapt quickly.

Valencour motioned to the handle of the old swing open barn doors of the '89 suburban and Bianca opened it. The younger girl handed the older girl the crates, which were now meowing, and she went to set them inside. The pile of blankets on the floor moved and startled the girl, so she jumped and she had to suppress a squeak as Doug peaked out from underneath with his index finger to his lips.

Her fear quickly melted to a smile and she rapidly closed the doors.

"What is it?" The younger girl asked.

"It's good, it's all good." She smiled and made sure to flash the smile to her anxious mother as well.

Valencour shook his head.

"Alright, load up. We need to be out of here quickly."

The mother said something to the older daughter in Italian and the teenager dutifully took the passenger seat beside Valencour. Bianca sat directly behind the driver seat.

When the last door slammed and the big V-8 started with a sustained grumble, Valencour spoke again.

"As your daughter discovered, Doug is under the blankets in the back. He has been compromised and they are looking for him. I'm taking you someplace where you can be safe and where they won't find you to take you to use as leverage against him."

Bianca looked back over the seat quickly and Doug flashed a quick smile and a wave and covered himself again.

"Compromised... By what... why are they looking for him?"

"Compromised by me, and for suspected resistance activity... they'll call it insurgent activity."

"What do you mean by *you?*" Bianca hissed. Valencour even thought he heard the pistol cock again, but that might have been his imagination.

Valencour sighed before launching into his explanation.

CHAPTER 8

Boggs didn't like Zites before, he always seemed like a schemer. Now he liked him less and he really had to watch himself as the man sat behind what had once been the Sheriff's desk. Of course, that old beat up desk wasn't good enough and had been replaced by some glass top, expensive and modern looking thing that held multiple computer screens and no paper.

Boggs had done his best to stay below the radar and not even have to deal with Zites directly, but that had apparently ended today and he figured it had to do with the MP who sat quietly in the corner. That and the fact that his regular federal *partner* hadn't shown up for shift.

"Deputy Boggs, this is Sergeant Don Peters, U.S Army. He is your new federal partner." Zites looked at one of his screens. "Your previous partner filed a complaint, said you weren't aggressive enough in enforcement activity. Sergeant Peters is going to evaluate you."

Boggs looked at the man, who wouldn't make eye contact and Zites was now clicking his mouse and looking at another screen.

"I've been going back over your stats for the previous twelve months. Looks like you were never a particularly hard charger, but your stats have dropped off significantly since the Enclave went up. Why is that, Deputy? Do you suddenly have a problem enforcing the law?"

Boggs shifted a little, uncertain there was a right answer. He kept his mouth shut.

"If you no longer wish to be employed with this new department because of the changes, just let me know. This is a chance to be part of something new and better, you should be glad for the opportunity. You should be happy just to have a job given the circumstances."

"Well, I suppose I'd get by with the economic freeze and all." As soon as he'd said it he regretted it.

"I think you're smart enough to know that those with jobs, those still making money, will do better than those without."

"I thought money was no good now?"

"See," Zites looked to the Sergeant. "I thought it was an attitude problem."

Boggs inhaled, frustrated. There was no winning this argument, so there was no point talking but he just couldn't help himself.

"Tonight, at midnight, the curfew officially goes into effect. As of tomorrow, anyone caught driving after dark will have their vehicles confiscated and they will be detained pending investigation and charges. You have seen the paperwork for essential personnel?"

Boggs nodded.

"So, this is their grace period. It's been announced on radio and television and the electronic information boards all over the county. There is no excuse for people to not know at this point. I want you pulling over every vehicle you see tonight, log a warning for your stats and let them know of the consequences for lack of compliance. While you're doing that, think of the consequences you'll face if you don't get with the program, Boggs. Dismissed."

Deputy Boggs just nodded, then turned to the MP and pointed toward the door with his chin. The MP stood and followed Boggs out the door, he didn't bother looking back at Zites either. The MP upped his pace to catch the Deputy as they plunged into the crisp evening air beyond the glass doors.

They had replaced the Specialist with a Sergeant because they were beginning to doubt Boggs' commitment. This Sergeant would likely say anything to get the goods on him and prove his own loyalty to the new cause. What would he expect if Boggs made a stop? How far was he willing to go to prove himself to Zites and the new *rulers* of the Enclave?

*   *   *

Valencour had recounted the story and the plan the best he could, but Bianca sat silently behind him and he couldn't see her in the mirror. He had just assumed she had the revolver pointed at the middle of his spine.

"Hey, babe, we just have to go with this right now." Doug called out from the back.

"So, he takes us to some farm to hide out and you do what, Doug?"

It was quiet a moment and Valencour searched the mirror for some sign of Doug or the angry woman sitting directly behind him.

"Bianca," Doug had sat up in the back and wrapped his arm around his wife, snuggling tenderly against her head with his. "You brought me to the Lord, Bianca. He commands us to be strong and courageous. And not just on Sunday morning when it's easy, he commands us to be strong and courageous when it really matters, right?"

Bianca's hand had gone to his arm and she was nodding and fighting the tears that were forming.

"I have to go where God needs me most, Bianca. I have to help work against all this craziness that is going on and I need to know you and the girls are safe. And you have to take care of yourself and protect the girls. That's how we've always done it, it's just a little more difficult and uncertain now."

Valencour could see her head now as she kind of leaned into Doug's head and he could see that she had both hands gripping his fore arm so at least he knew she had dropped the damn revolver.

"You'll have some time to catch up at the farm, stay out of sight for now. We may run into fed patrols or checkpoints."

Doug disappeared from view just as headlights merged from the ramp in town. They grew larger. The vehicle was moving fast despite the weather and road conditions.

Then the blue and red lights lit the rear-view mirror.

*   *   *

Randy crushed another empty Rainier can and tossed it toward the big bag of crushed empties. It missed just like the last one had.

"Do you believe that stuff, kid?"

Tom was starting to feel that he just belonged in the woods. He couldn't seem to get along with anyone who was trying to help him. Randy seemed like an annoying older brother, or perhaps a jealous cousin.

In response to Randy's query, he lifted the open Bible off his lap.

"This?" He asked, but he knew.

"Yeah."

Tom just nodded.

The man popped open another beer, slurped at it and continued.

"Probably nice to believe in something, I suppose." He said it with more sincerity than Tom expected. Randy took another drink from the can and set it on the cheap table in the shabby and dirty kitchen.

"They came for our Gods a long time ago kid, now they're coming for yours. You see that don't you?"

Tom nodded.

"What tribe are you, Randy?"

The man laughed a little and picked up his beer again.

"One of more than three hundred tribes unrecognized by the federal government, it doesn't matter."

"It matters to me, Randy."

"Thanks, kid." Randy just shook his head. "My Mom gave me up for adoption when I was real young and it was kind of shady. And there were a lot of foster homes. I don't know if what she said was even true. My genealogy is lost. I got plenty of Native blood quantum, but the tribes don't care about that. Haven't been able to find my Mom or any original family. I don't have a tribe because I can't find family, the feds won't take our petition to the BIA 'cause there ain't enough of us or something and white people don't take us seriously because we don't have a casino."

"Seems like we can't trust the white man." Tom said, a little grin curling subtly at the corners of his mouth.

"You bet we can't." Randy pointed his beer can toward Tom, then his expression went kind of cold with a certain stern bemusement. "Did we just quote The Outlaw Josey Wales?"

Tom's grin just turned to a full smile and Randy broke out laughing.

"You're alright kid."

"It was kind of required viewing with my Dad." Tom said.

"Yeah, I imagine. That kind of makes a lot of sense." Randy was laughing more and shaking his head. Then Randy stood up and raised his hand.

"I am Ten Bears... No, wait." He held up the Rainier can. "I am Ten Beers!"

Tom laughed and closed his Bible, setting it aside.

"You know Tom, these Lakota guys, they'll be here in a day or two. Once that gets set in motion, they can't turn it off. They're not telling anyone how they get in and out and it takes them two or three days to get here, there's no way to tell them to stop now. They're the real serious type. I know you said you don't want to go, but…"

"I appreciate everything everyone is doing for me, all the risks being taken on my behalf. Randy… I have to stay. I have to do my part, I can't keep running."

"What good does your being here do anyone? Look, Tom, these Lakota guys are serious dudes, man. They call themselves warriors and see themselves as rising to the occasion. They see this as a place where the white man is turning against the white father, the federal government. They see getting you out of here and safely to the rez as a way of sticking it to the man. Like it or not, you're a symbol, Tom."

*   *   *

Boggs called in the location of the stop and the plate and vehicle description. He figured he'd call in the ID of whoever looked least likely to be eligible for the draft and leave everyone else out of it, so he was relieved when his flashlight fell across the grey hair of the driver.

"License and registration, sir."

The man produced the documents without saying anything.

"I just need to let you know that the new curfew goes into effect tonight at midnight." The driver had his hands on the steering wheel and he sat cold and unshaken. Behind him was a beautiful woman that Boggs thought seemed familiar but he couldn't quite place her or her teenage daughters. They were locals, he knew he'd seen them before, but she looked at him with a scornful and irritated expression. Flashing the Streamlight to the back of the Suburban, he saw a pile of blankets that clearly covered the form of a human body. The MP was approaching the truck from the back with his flashlight up.

The girls looked frightened, the mother looked full of hate, the driver looked cool and hard. The hair on the back of Boggs neck was up and he shifted the driver's paperwork to his flashlight hand to free up his gun hand. Something wasn't right, or something was about to go horribly wrong.

The MP at the back of the truck had grabbed the handle of the 'barn door' and depressed the thumb button. Something had caught his eye, there was something under the blanket in the back he needed to see. Swinging the door open to its stop, his flashlight illuminating the interior, the Sergeant reached to lift the blanket. Before he could, he saw, emerging with movement below, the muzzle of a 9mm Beretta.

As Boggs saw the MP lift the blanket in the back, he was back pedaling to cross beyond the C pillar of the back door. Drawing his pistol he wondered who he was going to have to shoot first. Would it be the man so casually cold behind the wheel? Would it be the woman who glared at him with a beautiful face of hate? Or would it be the federal partner he knew he couldn't trust?

"Whoa, whoa…" The Military Police Sergeant was backing up with both hands raised. "Be cool, be cool, we're outa' here, OK?"

Boggs was flashing the Streamlight deliberately in the eyes of the woman, as she was the only one glaring at him. Turning the high intensity light at the driver a moment, he saw him sitting there like stone, eyes forward, no movement, no motion. He put the light back on the woman who seemed suddenly more of a threat.

"Driver." Boggs said loudly. "I'm gonna drop your documents in your window, no one in the vehicle moves until we are back in our vehicle. You go your way, we go ours. Nothing going on here is worth anyone dying for tonight, understood?"

"Yes, Deputy." The reply was firm, but without fear or threat.

Boggs stepped forward to drop the paperwork in the window, then backed toward the open back door of the Suburban. Flashing the light in, all he saw was the blanket move a little as whoever was under it settled back in.

Boggs shut the back door awkwardly with his flashlight hand and continued backing toward his Tahoe, losing himself in the overpowering back light of the spotlight on the driver's rear-view mirror.

Back behind the spot light, where the red and white overheads reflected more off the falling snow, he looked across to the Sergeant. He was wiping his face and the Suburban was in drive and pulling away.

With a hand shaking from the surge of adrenalin, Boggs carefully re-holstered. He didn't remember drawing.

"I almost shot someone, and I don't know who or why… This is a damn mess." Boggs shook his head as he felt the pistol lock into retention.

"Hey, Boggs, let's uh…" The MP was holding up his cell phone and pointing toward the patrol vehicle. Boggs didn't understand for a moment, until the MP made a show of throwing the device into the passenger seat and closing the door again.

Grasping what was happening, the Deputy threw his on his driver seat and closed the door again.

"They monitor us with those things, Boggs."

"No kidding."

"Look, I didn't want this… none of us did, we didn't want any of this."

"And yet you're here."

"They told us this was an exercise, they told us a lot of things…"

"So, how does this work, Peters?"

"I don't know, I don't know that anything works right now."

"I don't trust you."

"I know. There's a lot of that going around right now. They took us from the city, they brought us here for an exercise. Then this new pandemic went hot and they told us we were trying to contain a bunch of white supremacist rednecks who would lynch us first chance they got us alone."

Boggs squinted at the MP a little, his skepticism trying to process the apparent reality.

"I stopped doing traffic stops when I pulled a guy over for a minor infraction and they showed up with armored vehicles and yanked the kid through the window to fly him off to who knows where for who knows what. I have a tough time with that on my conscience."

"Yeah, I get it, Boggs."

The deputy opened the door, pocketed his cell phone and buckled up behind the wheel. He keyed his microphone, then released, thinking a moment. He'd already given the plates to dispatch, they'd be expecting at least driver information to run him for warrants. Boggs shook his head, keyed the mic and spoke with authority.

"November Twelve, 10-8. Elderly driver, sole occupant given verbal warning of approaching curfew as instructed."

"Roger, November Twelve... We are getting multiple calls from Three Cross Mountain of shots fired and possible multiple shooters and subjects down. Need you to start that way, next available back up is forty-five minutes behind you, a city unit is all we have right now."

"November Twelve's 76."

Boggs looked at the Sergeant and shook his head. "Three Cross Mountain?"

The deputy just put it in drive, checked his mirror and hit the siren with the overheads still turning. Hauling the Tahoe into an immediate U-turn, he accelerated quickly northbound.

*   *   *

"What do you mean he's not here, Johann?"

"It wasn't working out here, Valencour. I handed him off to the Indian. That was the plan if things went badly here."

"What went badly here?"

Johann looked to his daughter who was helping Bianca and the girls with their bags.

"Are you kidding me?"

"To be honest, Valencour, I think it was mostly the girl's fault. I couldn't have that here either way."

Max Valencour shook his bowed head. Hands on his hips he looked quickly to his watch as Doug was walking up to him.

Doug was smiling at his family but that faded as he saw Max's distress.

"What's wrong, Max?"

"Tom has been passed to the next safe house, the curfew will go into effect by the time we can get there. That part of the plan has other people coming to get him from the outside. We've already been stopped once with this vehicle, we can't risk moving until the curfew lifts in the morning."

"What do you mean you were stopped in this, you said nothing about that, Max." Johann spoke quickly, nervously.

"What do you mean 'people from the outside', Max? Who is getting in from the outside?" Doug seemed flummoxed.

Max held his hands up to quiet them both and addressed Johann's concern first.

"We weren't followed and the Deputy didn't have the stomach for any follow up or we'd all be dead. That vehicle is best considered burned for now. Is the vehicle I staged here still in running order?"

"Of course."

"Good, I'll trade you. Park this one in your barn for a while, put a set of those extra tags I left you with on it if you need it."

"I have certain networks I've had in place for a long time, Doug. People well paid to be available to get me out of situations in which I might find myself. One of those networks seems to have found a way through the containment. My plan was originally to get Tom out if it was going badly in the enclave. The triggers have been met and people will be on their way to get Tom out. We need him here."

*　　*　　*

The illuminated sign next to the secured gate across the driveway caught Peter's attention.

"Calvary Ranch, huh?" The MP inquired.

"Yeah, like horse soldiers, I guess."

"No, Boggs, that's cavalry. This is like Golgotha… Like the hill where Jesus was crucified."

"Oh, that makes more sense, then. It's a, uh… religious community. We don't get a lot of calls up here, they keep to themselves. Just let me do all the talking, maybe stay in the truck."

The sergeant set his jaw and looked at the deputy a little sideways as the gate was opening automatically. Driving up the unplowed road, Boggs saw two fresh pairs of foot prints in the snow. He'd turned the siren off a few miles back but left the overheads on for identification. At the top of the hill, where the cabins were, he saw a pair of headlights flash.

"Dispatch, November Twelve, how far out is back up?"

"Stand by, November Twelve…"

Boggs looked a little disgusted as he looked at the radio and slowed the Tahoe.

"Sorry November Twelve, just getting a call back from one of the RP's, he's identifying himself as 'Pastor Dave.' He says he has two intruders down and he is armed. He says he sees you and is flashing his headlights at the top of the hill. He says it seems secure for now."

"10-4."

Boggs drove up the hill carefully, sweeping his spotlight back and forth across the sides of the little road. All there was were the two pairs of foot prints. Beside the old Chevy Blazer at the top of the hill, an older man with a long white beard stood. He had a camouflage painted AR-15 strapped across the chest of his denim jacket. He squinted against the high beams and spotlight of the Tahoe. The old man kept his hands up.

Boggs stopped, put it in park and was a little perturbed to see Peters stepping out of the other side of the Tahoe.

"Gentleman…" The older man extended a nod of equal respect to the deputy and the MP. Boggs knew Pastor Dave only a little from a few casual encounters in town. "I'll keep my hands up all you want, but I won't disarm, and you'll understand when I show you."

Peters looked at Boggs who nodded.

"OK, Pastor Dave, we got reports of a shooting? What's going on? Who was doing the shooting?"

"I was. And given the current climate, if this were anything else we would have handled this in house."

"Do we need an ambulance, Pastor Dave?"

"No, I shoot better than that. Gonna need two slabs in the morgue though."

Boggs inhaled.

"This way gentlemen." The older man was leading them to the open door of the large central cabin. Two crumpled forms lay there, one half in the door slouched unnaturally against the door jam, looking lifelessly up in to dark sky, the other face down with a pistol kicked from his hand according to how the snow was disturbed.

"They were both armed, the shotgun fell inside on the floor. I fired from that cabin over there." Boggs flash light followed where the man pointed, then came back to the bodies where he looked closer at the injuries.

"Two to the chest, one to the head, eh, Pastor?"

"Mozambique… fight as you train I suppose. Didn't give it much thought really, they were kicking in the door and it was a ladies' Torah study in there tonight. I ordered them to stop, and the one with a pistol fired at me. But look closer at them, the face and neck. That's why I called, you need to be aware of this."

"Those tattoos…" Peters said.

"Cartel." Boggs said as the light splashed across the now bloody neck and face ink.

Pastor Dave nodded.

"Here?" The MP asked.

"Yeah, we have a few of them. They help run things north to Canada."

The flashlight glinted off the pistol brass in the snow.

Boggs stepped back from the conversation a moment and hit the number for dispatch on his cell phone.

"Dispatch, November Twelve. Start me a supervisor and detectives. We have two subjects 10-7, no medical required. Thanks."

Boggs pocketed the phone and stepped back into the conversation.

"Ever seen them before? Do you think they knew about your community here, Pastor?"

"No, and I don't think they knew the women folk were in there tonight. I don't believe that was what this was about. I think they knew about us in a general fashion and knew we're prepared to take care of ourselves for the long haul. I think they just came for food. They're cut off from their logistical chain just like everyone else. They knew by our reputation we are amply stocked. The isolation of the county and further, the war with China really has them cut off. They're hungry and scared."

"The sad thing in it really, even for such as these… we've prepared to help where we can. We've been helping some neighbors, believers or not, all they have to do is ask and we'll do what we can."

"My concern is that there may be more; there may be retaliation. Against our community, against the county as a whole perhaps. I'm not real clear on the current state of the Constitution or rule of law in the county now, Deputy. What happens next?"

"The detectives will be here soon to conduct a homicide investigation. We've been getting a lot of this lately, Pastor. Desperate people acting violently, violent people acting desperately. Good people doing what they have to in order to protect themselves and others… it's just where we are." Boggs looked at the MP suspiciously, then continued.

"Honestly, the feds are kind of overwhelmed right now. Now is the time to set a precedent of determination, not victimization."

"That's good to hear, Deputy." The pastor turned to Peters. "And I guess you are the federal representative. What is your take on it?"

The MP shivered a little, looking at the bodies and at the AR.

"Looks like clear cut self-defense to me… But Pastor, I can't begin to tell you what direction this is going to go. We've all been lied to and all we have left now is survival I think."

*　　*　　*

"You need to get your shit together, Randy."

The man with the short black crew cut looked around at the condition of the trailer with disdain and then the other one spoke.

"This is a time for men to stand, not cower. You are like a caricature of us, the *drunken* Indian." The lip of the man with the shaved head curled with disgust. They looked to Tom, or maybe looked through him, with a certain intensity.

"Are you packed, Tom? We leave immediately."

The sun had been up for maybe a half an hour and Randy wasn't quite to the point where he was really hung over, he was just ill. He really didn't want to be awake.

Tom was a little afraid, but more inspired by their intensity.

"I… uh…" He paused a moment to find his strength. "I'm not going, I'm staying here. I'm done running."

The shorter man with the crewcut sighed, the taller man with the shaved head smiled.

"I'm afraid you don't understand, Tom. We are here to get you out, that is the plan, we are sticking with the plan especially after what we've gone through to get here. You're going with us."

Tom thought a moment. He thought about his father and all he had told him and he tried to cultivate that wisdom that he may not have fully understood or appreciated at the time. The young man flipped back his BDU coat revealing the 1911 at his hip and he summoned his inner Clint Eastwood again and growled a little as he spoke.

"That's not *my* plan. I'm staying. You said this is a time for a man to stand not cower. Well, that's what I'm doin'. I appreciate what you men have done and what you have risked and I mean no disrespect, but I've been through too much myself and have too much more to do than to tuck my tail and leave this county. This is my home, and they may try to rule it and they may win in the end, but I'm not going to give up without a fight. If they want this county, they are going to pay for every inch of it. We all have a role in this, all of us who seek freedom. Those of us who know the true benefits and burdens of it. Everyone in this trailer understands that."

Tom looked at Randy who had his aching head in his hands.

"We all know what we have to do whether it's what we want to do or not. The time has come to be what we need to be, not what we want to be, not what we've allowed ourselves to be."

Randy leaned back in his chair and folded his arms across his chest. He shook his head, he just really wanted to sleep this off.

The sound of car doors closing stopped the conversation. The Lakota with the crew cut went to the nearby window and discreetly pulled the blind aside enough to see.

"Two guys in an old Chevy. Black guy and an older white guy, I think. He's wearing a hooded jacket." He reported. "They're coming to the door."

The two warriors drew Glocks from their waists and went to the low ready. Tom's 1911 slid from its holster and tucked alongside his leg with his thumb on safety as he concealed himself half behind a nearby door jam.

There was a soft knock at the front door.

"Answer it, Randy." Snarled the shaved head one.

Randy stood, slumping his shoulders. He looked through the peep hole first.

"Relax, it's Valencour and some other guy."

Valencour and Doug entered as Randy wordlessly gestured them in. They immediately felt the tension in the room.

The Lakota's Glocks went back to leather as they recognized Max taking his hood down. Tom smiled as he re-holstered.

"We have a problem, Valencour. Your boy doesn't want to come with us."

"That's not a problem. There's been a change in plan. He stays."

"Then we went through all that for nothing." Said the one with the crewcut.

"Not for nothing." Max smiled. "We know it works. And you may have news from the outside. We are completely cut off in the Enclave. What are they saying out there? They have ended money here, is that a nationwide thing, or just here?"

The two men looked at each other and the shaven headed man spoke.

"I don't know what you're talking about money wise. I mean they are talking about going digital but that hasn't happened yet. There is no news outside about the Enclave; it's disappeared from the headlines. It's all about the war, all about selling it to do your duty. Support the draft, or better yet, go and volunteer to fight Chinese and Russian aggression."

"There's another thing you should know, Mr. Valencour." The man with the crewcut interjected. "We expect our unit to be getting activated soon, all the signs are there. They're getting all the paper work and qualifications up to date, wills, records, vaccinations. We just don't have a date or a direction."

Valencour nodded, like it was something he was expecting.

"And what will you do if you get orders?" He asked.

"We'll be AWOL. We'll vanish from the Res. They won't find us."

Valencour nodded again and the shaved head man spoke.

"The problem is, this may not work when we're under charges."

"I can get you new badges and credentials, under different names. It will be up to you to find a new route."

"They'll use facial recognition, it may not be as easy as the old dead babies routine."

"We cross that bridge when we get to it. And you know if it comes to that, we can hide you here in the Enclave."

"We've talked about that. It will depend on the circumstances."

"What else can you tell us about what's going on outside?" Doug asked.

"What is there to say? It's all propaganda and lies. Maybe you're better off without it." The shaven headed man said.

Doug didn't seem satisfied with that answer but let it go.

*　　*　　*

Sheriff Grant Taylor felt mind numbed to everything but the pain in his knee. The cold and the damp, the hard floor and meager mattress all conspired against him. When sleep came, it was brief and from pure exhaustion. All his time was spent in prayer or in pain or mostly in both. He was ready for it to end, because now he knew it would, somehow and not the way he wanted.

The interrogator sat before him, wordlessly tapping at his tablet screen.

He knew this would be another calculated tactic. The silence and asking no questions. He knew this was a tactic just like the illusion of hope they were playing on him about some mysterious element positioning to get him out. It was all, he knew, ultimately designed to get him to talk, to provide the names they needed to crush what they knew could be the foundation of resistance. The list of names of men who had already taken a stand and would now be ready to take action.

The Sheriff brooded and he knew they would take note of that, too. There was no winning this, there was probably no surviving this. Now, for him all that was left was his own resistance. His own intellectual struggle against *them* and maintaining his own sense of honor, integrity and connection to God. Those were things they would never take from him.

"When I first moved from L.A. up to the county, the first year I was eligible to hunt elk as a resident, we didn't have horses yet and I had a tag for a unit on forest service land." They wanted him to talk, and all the isolation even gave the Sheriff a certain need to talk. "It was public land and lots of pressure so I knew my chances of even seeing a bull elk were pretty slim. The trail in was covered with fresh early snow at that altitude, and the tracks of other hunters and folks just enjoying the trail."

"Right in the parking lot of the trailhead was a set of moose tracks and I was just overnighting. I was going to be happy if I just saw that moose. Wasn't far from the trailhead that I came across a really big dog track." The Sheriff held up his hand and smiled at the memory. "I wanna say it was as big as my hand, and that may be a bit of exaggeration, but not much."

"Then I saw another set of extraordinarily large dog tracks, then I saw another and I realized, pretty quick, they were bracketing that moose. There were these big dog tracks up hill and downhill of the moose and, of course, a couple sets right on its trail."

"You don't have to be an expert tracker to see a story unfold in the sign you're following and the story I was seeing unfold was dramatic and timeless, really. I was starting to realize that when I came across the first tuft of moose hair in the tracks."

"Then it was a few drops of blood staining the snow, then more hair now with a little hide. Then there was more blood and more hide. It was very apparent this wolf pack was taking down this moose on the run as the strides stretched out. You could see the desperation in these tracks, see a running fight for survival."

The interrogator said nothing, just looked up from time to time from his tablet.

"There's only so much fight a moose can offer. He's not getting out alive, but he's not quitting, not in his nature. Not in the nature of anything free, really. Soon the blood and hair and hide turned to chunks of meat and it wasn't long after that I came across the carcass of the moose. What was left of it."

"In their own way, they're really majestic animals but there's really never any majesty in death, even after heroic struggle or brave defiance. The moose was only half eaten. It was an easily accessed trail and there were lots of other foot prints, so, I imagine, someone came along and scared the pack off before they could finish their meal."

"A lot of folks assign certain mystical qualities to the wolf and there's no doubt they are amazing predators and they have their place in nature, but we get so out of balance these days. Elevating one animal over others or thinking of predators without thinking about their prey and what they do to it. They ate that big moose alive and took him down on the run. The moose didn't have any choice in the matter but he couldn't just quit, he fought as best he could as long as he could with what he could. 'Course the wolves didn't have any choice either. Those animals were brought together in that same time and same place. The wolves needed to eat and they won."

The interrogator looked up from his tablet and finally spoke.

"Are you the wolf or the moose, Taylor?"

The Sheriff forced a smile and spoke through tears he couldn't explain or stop.

"I guess we'll see."

*   *   *

Tom had gone from being so alone, to now being the center of attention in the garage bay of Ski's metal building. Max and Doug had brought him in and Ski, John, Bill and Roger were all there helping him with his few bags, his carbine drawing a lot of attention. Beyond trophy status, it was a symbol in itself.

Bill was on crutches and clearly in a lot of pain and they soon moved into the living area where he could sit down and elevate his bandaged foot. It wasn't clear to Tom yet what had happened to him.

It was a lighter mood than a lot of people had felt for a long time and a sense of camaraderie that Tom had never really felt before.

They ushered him in with a certain sense of celebrity that Tom didn't feel entirely comfortable with. Ski guided him to a seat in a comfortable looking recliner while Doug got a pillow to elevate Bill's foot on an ottoman on the couch next to him.

"Can I get you something to drink, Tom?" Ski asked.

"Could I have a mug of hot water please?"

Ski had taken the 416, made sure it was clear and safe and was admiring as he spoke. He smiled widely.

"Hot water? I've got anything you want, Tom. We're well supplied here, so don't be bashful."

"I kind of got used to just hot water, I guess."

"I've got tea, I've got hot chocolate, I've got coffee, I've got Bailey's, I've got a couple different whiskeys, vodka and beer."

"I'm only 18." Tom smiled, remembering his bout with whiskey while dealing with the sprained ankle.

"I think all that's kind of out the window at this point, Tom." Doug offered with a smile.

"Just hot water, please."

"You got it, Tom. I'll go put it on for you. Gonna be some time to readjust, I imagine." Ski was still looking at the carbine as he walked to the kitchen and spoke over his shoulder. "HK, this is a fine piece, Tom. Got it off a fed, didn't you?"

"Yes."

Doug spoke up while Ski was getting water heated.

"How are you feeling, Tom? We heard you'd twisted your ankle pretty good."

"It's a lot better now. I took time to keep the weight off and keep it elevated, then when it was better, exercised and stretched it as best I could. It gets a little stiff once in a while, but it's good I think."

Ski had come back with a mug of hot water in one hand and the 416 in the other. He passed the carbine on to Bill.

"I got this too." Tom said as he reached into his coat and pulled the 1911 from its strap holster. Tom dropped the magazine, then thumbed the safety off to eject the chambered round. Locking the slide back, he handed it grip first to Ski who was smiling again.

"Springfield Professional, weapon mounted light and RMR. They stopped issuing this to HRT guys years ago, went to Glocks. Allowed guys already qualified on them to carry their own if they wanted." Ski laughed and continued. "Bet that was particularly painful for that dude to hand this over to you."

Tom just smiled and sipped from the mug. The pistol and carbine eventually found their way back to Tom. He reloaded the pistol and re-holstered then leaned the HK against the chair where he was sitting.

Ski noticed how naturally the young man handled the weapons. Not any kind of show or display, not any kind of awkwardness. They were very much a part of him.

"So," Tom said over his mug. "What's the plan?"

"Plan?" Doug asked.

"We're going to start fighting back, right? We need a plan. You guys must have a plan. What is it?"

Ski smiled and held up his finger.

"Just a minute, I have to run out to the freezer."

Doug looked at the others a moment and shook his head. When Ski returned he was carrying a fairly small object wrapped in butcher paper and a zip lock bag.

Laying it on the table in front of Doug, he nodded toward it.

"Go ahead, open it up."

Doug hesitantly opened the zip lock and dragged whatever it was out and left it on the table.

"Back in World War II, British intelligence came up with this plan called Operation Mincemeat. They planted a body with false documents and information on it to wash ashore somewhere and throw the Nazis off the intended invasion of Sicily. Since we don't have any dead bodies yet, I've got this."

"Oh, geez, Ski…" Doug recoiled a little. "What is it?"

"Go ahead open it, it won't hurt you, Doug."

Looking at Ski sideways he tugged at the paper, then unrolled it, revealing a dead pigeon.

"Why do you have a dead pigeon in your freezer, Ski?"

"They roost out in the garage bay in the spring, shoot 'em with a BB gun. Got him last year."

"So, that doesn't really answer the question, Ski."

Ski ignored Doug.

"I'm going to write up some kind of simple shift code, it will give a fake target that will draw the feds in the wrong direction. Put it in a little plastic bag and tie it around his ankle, leave it in a parking lot downtown somewhere."

Tom couldn't help but laugh.

"That's your plan?"

"And this has been in your freezer for a year, Ski? Why would you put a dead pigeon in your freezer?" Doug was exasperated.

"We're going to need more than a dead pigeon if we want to take our county back guys." Tom suggested.

Ski nodded and a serious expression melted his smile.

"We have some other plans, Tom." He looked around at the others and they nodded, as if with approval. "Come with me, Tom."

Tom stood up, subconsciously slinging the HK over his shoulder, a behavior noted by the others. He followed behind Ski, back into the darkened garage bay. Ski hit the lights and spoke, leading him to a corner behind the vehicles and equipment.

"I was an 18 Charlie in the Army. Special Forces Engineer. Got to do a lot of demolitions stuff. We're still developing the target, recon, intel gathering. But we have a target selected that will cripple the feds and we have this…"

Ski pulled a heavy tarp off of it as Tom walked around it and realized the others had followed in behind him. It was a 55-gallon drum on its side, cradled and buttressed in plywood and heavy gauge steel plating on three sides. At the end of the drum was something the size of a coffee can with what appeared to some kind of convex copper end.

"A bomb?" Tom asked.

"No, Tom, classic fougasse. With a little upgrade of my own."

CHAPTER 9

Grace was a new event in the Boggs family home. She hadn't really insisted on it, but Marj had first offered it. Then after some initial protest and with some coaching, Frank Boggs took over the task and each night it was getting a little better and a little more natural. The two young children were getting better at behaving through it and through dinner in general and Marjorie Taylor was the impetus of a lot of good in the household.

Marj most often cooked and the family cleared the table and cleaned afterward. Boggs brought her a mug of coffee after the children were done and his wife was finishing up. He took a seat across from her.

"That was really nice tonight, Frank. You said the part about Grant a little differently tonight though."

"I ah… Thought I said it the same as I always do."

"The words were the same, the inflection was different."

"Was it?"

She nodded and looked down, fidgeting with the napkin on the table.

"Um… Sorry?"

She smiled.

"It's alright, Frank. You've done so much for us."

He shook his head, not liking where the conversation was going. So many uncomfortable conversations he'd had to have with families on various scenes in his career. It was different when it was so close to home, so hard to distance himself.

"You don't think we'll ever see him again, do you, Frank?"

He so wished he had a cup of coffee or something to look at other than the freshly cleaned table which seemed a shallow diversion, but was better than looking into her eyes right now.

Frank Boggs couldn't help but shake his head a little. It had to come out, she had to be ready for it.

Looking up through his own watering eyes, he saw her tears forming above an inexplicable smile.

"It's OK, Frank. Where ever he is, the Lord is with him. We've always known this was a possibility with the job. That God might put him in a place where his service was contrary to what we might want out of life. The only difference now is that then, when the world was different... normal... I always knew I would have the comfort of knowing where, how and why. That's the challenge now. I know he's not sick. You know that too, don't you, Frank?"

"Yes, Ma'am."

"That will hurt a lot. But I'm sure the Lord will let me know when he's gone. I'll just never be able to see his face again. Closure they call it. He'll just be among the disappeared. That will be hard. Do you think it's all about the Potter boy?"

"I believe so."

"Is it because they are still after him?"

Frank nodded.

"But they haven't caught him still?"

"Not as far as anyone knows."

"Good. We've been seeing for a while now what some people are capable of. Some of it the very good and too much of it the downright evil. There is more evil coming, I think, Frank and we all need to be getting ready for it, in every way possible."

*   *   *

The operator stood with his arms across his chest, trying not to shake his head.

"So, you're pulling us off the search for HVTs to conduct Protective Service Details on yourselves and all the other high-ranking officers and administrators?"

"That's right, you saw the briefing?"

"This is about the pigeon?"

"Yes, that's how they're circumventing our surveillance, carrier pigeons."

That Booth was able to say it with such a straight face was the thing that sparked Todd's spontaneous laugh.

"You have got to be freakin' kidding me... The briefing itself said the bird had a small caliber BB wound in its neck."

"I don't care what killed it, I care about what that deciphered message said strapped to its leg."

"Somebody took a page from British intelligence in World War II, they just didn't have a human body handy. They used an old Caesar shift code so it would be easy to break. This is a ruse, you're making us all look like idiots and easing up on the pressure we have on the High Value Targets. We'll find them when they wear down and make a mistake. Right now, we're the only ones making mistakes."

"You have your orders."

"Yeah, you keep pulling that, I'm not military anymore. You keep making dumb decisions and I have the option of taking my toys and going home. There are only two words that keep me here."

"Duty and honor?" Asked Zites.

The tall man laughed again.

"Not even close... *Direct deposit*. When the stupid outweighs the deposit my guys and I are out of here and I recommend you not forget that."

"What ah..." Zites seemed to stumble over his words with a kind of contrition. "What would you, ah, recommend we do here, Todd?"

The operator looked at Booth whose arrogance was a twisted smile. He looked to Zites and saw at least some humility there.

"Look, they've seen the ASVs pulled over out of fuel. These people have horses and farms with their own fuel storage. They know about our fuel shortages. You are better off bolstering defenses around that big fuel depot here at the airport. If I was them, that's exactly what I'd hit."

"Well, Todd, you just don't really see the big picture. The manpower we have is stretched thin enough already." Booth was shaking his head as he spoke. "Now we have to reinforce security around all headquarters nodes and those high-level officials who live in the Enclave. That leaves you and your men the only ones available and qualified to provide PSDs."

"Yeah, whatever." He looked at Zites. "Give me a list of what you need, we'll do what we can."

Todd left the room in disgust.

*　　*　　*

Ski put the cell phone in the ammo can, its two wires running out of a small hole. They had been hastily soldered to the little igniter that was inserted into the model rocket motor.

"I've insulated this box pretty well. No signal can get into or out of it just so it's not popping up on surveillance while we're doing our tests here. I've got the igniter rigged up to the burner phone's speaker circuit and, with the real thing, we'll have an arming switch to keep it from going off with a stray call when we are getting into position. Right now, it's just set for the alarm to go off in... four more minutes." Ski was looking at his watch and setting it all down inside the circle of men standing outside.

Tom, John, Bill, Doug, Roger and Max were all staring at it for what seemed like a lot more than four minutes while Ski was looking at his watch. He initiated the countdown at the five second mark.

"Five, four, three, two, one."

The model rocket motor torched a hot flame for a few moments then popped and smoke came out of the cardboard tube.

"Well, that was kind of anticlimactic, Ski." Doug said with a laugh.

"Oh, that's plenty to set it off."

"Wait..." John interrupted. "You mean this is going to set off the bomb?"

"The fougasse." Ski corrected.

"Well, that's not going to work." John spoke up as if startled a bit.

"What do you mean?" Asked Max.

"You know, I guess I forgot to mention this." John said sheepishly. "This is probably important... um, well, my phone never works when I get within half a mile of that fuel depot. Can't call out, can't receive calls, can't even get a display."

Ski's expression flattened as he looked at Max, who sighed loudly.

"Yeah, that's kind of important." Doug said.

"They're jamming there." Ski said.

"Of course." Max said, trying to smile.

"That fougasse is pretty big, and it's going to set off all the fuel in the depot?" Tom asked.

"Sure will, Tom." Ski said in a matter of fact way as his mind was on other detonating triggers.

Tom turned to John.

"How many soldiers are in the depot, John?"

"Well, that depends, during the day as many as ten guys or more running around doing stuff. At night I've seen just one or two plus the gate guard. Like I said, they just have a simple gate now, not those armored cars like they used in the beginning."

"We should do it at night." Tom said. "And we should have a way of trying to scare those few soldiers away."

"Well, Tom." Ski giggled a little. "The plan *is* to do it at night just for the dramatic effect, everyone will see it better, all over the county. But you know we're going to have to start killing people. That's kind of how all this works."

"I know some people need killin', Ski." Tom suddenly sounded older, and more serious than anyone had heard before. "But a couple of guys whose job it is to fuel trucks… they don't deserve this. And I'm not too keen on killing soldiers anyway. They've not been as big a problem as the feds."

"Tom, you know as well as anyone at this point… this is a kind of war and killing is a part of war. They are here occupying this county. Some of them are going to have to die and you're gonna need to be able to face that." Ski was suddenly serious, too, and everyone else went quiet.

"I get what you're saying, Tom. And I agree with you." Doug interrupted as he looked at the smoking rocket motor. Then he looked at Ski. "Ski, those soldiers don't want to be here."

"Doesn't matter whether they want to be or not. They're here, they are occupiers, this is an invasion, this is war. You don't win a war by *not* killing people."

"No, but you win the peace by treating people right. We do this wrong and we're the bad guys and we turn the whole county against us as well. That Sergeant who pulled us over, the one who found me in the back of the Suburban. I told you, he's the one I'd run into at the restaurant. These guys have been fed lies and they're starting to see it. We blow up some trucks, we make life miserable for them because they have no fuel, that's all the more reason for them to be further demoralized. We start killing them when we don't need to and they have something to rally around. We need to obviously be trying to minimize casualties when we can. A toe to toe firefight is different, but this kind of strategic bushwhacking, we don't need a body count out of this."

Ski looked around at the consensus of nodding heads around the circle. He shrugged a little.

"OK, we need a new trigger and low body count, got it."

*   *   *

This early in the morning, his knee was stiff and he really couldn't walk on it. They gave him nothing for the pain. When the soldier whose eyes he recognized showed up and the other one passed him a parka he shook his head.

"No, I can't walk… my knee is a mess, I'm tired, I'm weak and, honestly, I'm not in the mood for games this…"

Before the Sheriff could finish his sentence, the soldier with the familiar eyes belted him across the face and followed him to the ground.

"We're under orders to get you exercise and sunshine, you're coming with us." The two men scooped him up under the arms and when they had him out of his cell the one with familiar eyes whispered in his ear.

"Count your paces, note your turns."

"What?" He couldn't really walk and they had his arms over their shoulders and were dragging him.

"One, two, three…" The other man was counting out the paces and noting the turns for the Sheriff. *"eighteen, nineteen, right turn."* They were going somewhere different from the beach this time. They had to go through more of the building. The beach was just two left turns and he had no idea how many paces or why such a thing would matter. This illusion of escape was really getting old and he wasn't allowing himself to be lured into it anyway. *"Thirty-five, thirty-six, left turn."*

They continued dragging him and keeping up the nonsense of the count and turns until they were finally in the open air. Someone flopped his hood back so he could see, it was a cloudy morning and the air was fresh and he appeared to be on a large ramp of the airfield. They continued dragging him around the perimeter of the ramp and he looked out to see the taxi and runway lights on little yellow stanchions.

"What is all this?" The Sheriff gasped with an exhausted kind of disgust.

"How many turns and how many paces to the beach exit, Sheriff?"

When he said nothing, the man spoke gruffly.

"How many?"

"Two left turns, I have no idea how many paces."

"Ninety-two. This is one hundred seventy-three. Remember right, left, right, right. Now say it."

"Oh, come on."

"Say it, Sheriff."

"One hundred seventy-three, right, left, right, right."

"And the beach exit?"

"Ninety-two, left, left." The Sheriff sighed heavily and just shook his head as they continued dragging him.

"You need to be able to navigate this in the dark, in smoke, in fog, under fire."

"How will I know it's time?" The Sheriff said with a skeptical shake.

"It will be fairly obvious."

"How will I know which way to go?"

"There will be more instructions to follow. Now, keep reciting the turns and pace counts. Burn it into your head, and work that knee and work the strength of your good leg, we may not be there to drag you out."

*   *   *

"Look Zites, I don't care if he was a SEAL or a Ranger or whatever he was. In the end he's just another knuckle dragger who can't see the big picture here. This isn't about a couple of High Value Targets. We'll get them someday. This is about total control, this is the new way forward and some people don't have the depth to understand that. For the new way to be established, we have to isolate and dominate resistance. You and I are on the very leading edge of this proof of concept."

"We don't have the manpower to lock down the entire nation like this, but we don't need it. We find the pockets of the most extreme resistance and we isolate them with laser focus. When people realize what's going on, they'll all fall in line because they'll see what can happen to them if they don't."

"You've seen all the briefings on this. I'm not telling you anything you don't know here, Zites."

"It just seems like with his background, he might be onto something and it might be worthwhile considering tightening security at the fuel depot."

"And he bases that on what? There is no evidence of that, no tips or leads giving us any indication that's a target. Look at all the people already turning in their neighbors and sometimes even their relatives in the daily roll ups. People aren't even really hungry yet. They're turning on each other just to try to get some political favor or positioning themselves for some creature comforts. These people around here aren't as tough as they're made out to be. All that self-reliance goes out the window when they don't have fuel for their vehicles. If someone was planning to hit that fuel depot, we'd be hearing about it."

"And we do have proof they are going to start targeting officials like us. We broke their code after someone shot one of their carrier pigeons in the parking lot of the county courthouse. That was a lucky break for us, but I'll take it. That's really the kind of cowardly resistance I most expect, really. And with all the guns these people have, they certainly have the means to pull it off."

"In the next few weeks they expect the weather to be clearing and our surveillance will really start to pay off then. The new restrictions and seizures will be announced and I fully expect we will see great increases in both enforcement actions and overall compliance. People want easy, even in a place like this. Hell, especially in a place like this. I'm really starting to believe, after seeing what we've seen here that all these *patriots* are nothing but talk. It was all just a big show. It was easy to talk big when you had freedoms and protection of the constitution."

Booth shook his head with derision.

"I've been seeing the same thing during my church visits. They say participation is down and, of course, the Pastors try to attribute it to the fuel shortages, but that's not it, Zites. It's a lot easier to believe in God when all your needs are met. Things get a little hard and people see how it really is. I mean sure, there are going to be some zealots, but for the most part, everyone will learn that the state will really provide for them. Soon they'll all come to the realization that, really, the state is their new god."

Zites didn't seem entirely sold on this and Booth could see it in his eyes.

"What? You don't see that happening?"

"I guess I've just spent a little more time in this area and around these people. I think you're underestimating them, and Todd too. He seems like someone we should listen to on this. I know there are people here, in this very department, that hate my guts. I see it in their faces. I spent enough time as a street cop to have certain Spidey senses. As much as these people resent me and what I'm doing here, I don't believe they're out to kill me."

"Ah, so that's it, Zites? A little Stockholm syndrome? Don't kid yourself. Anyone of these gun nuts around here would love to put a bullet in our skulls if we gave them the chance. We're not going to give them the chance. We're going to announce the pistol and semi-auto rifle bans in the next few weeks. In the end we'll be going after all rifles too. I argued we should go after all large caliber hunting rifles too, but they want to save that, keep it incremental. They'll get to keep their shotguns if they really feel the need to kill what they eat."

"See, Zites… I think you're kind of failing to see how we are on the very cutting edge of social change here. This is about so much more than Jeff Potter or his draft dodging kid. This is about the social mechanisms of change and control and we're proving how it can all work, right here in front of us."

Booth seemed strangely giddy. Zites leaned back in his chair and put his hands behind his head.

"What if we just haven't seen the real resistance yet, Booth? What if they're waiting, planning, prepping for something really big."

Booth shook his head with a confident smile.

"Oh, I wish I could fill you in on some of those briefings I've been in, Zites. If they're stupid enough try something like that, they'll see. They'll learn who their god is then."

CHAPTER 10

Tom, Ski and Doug stood around the chalk drawing on the floor of the garage bay. For the past few evenings they had done walk-throughs of the plan based on John's sketches of the fuel depot, the surrounding streets and roadblock placement.

Bill sat in a chair they brought out for him. He was in obvious pain and Doug had given him a new antibiotic. He'd quietly confided to Ski that he was afraid there was still some infection and that he might need to take the whole foot. Doug was giving the Z-Pak a few days to work its magic and then he'd let Bill know how it was looking.

In the meantime, Bill wanted to be part of the planning, especially since the most crucial part of the plan was going to be John getting the County plow truck, loading the fougasse in the back, then using it to deliver it to the depot under the auspices of needing fuel.

John had also provided a set of the papers the county had issued to "Essential Personnel" that would allow the bearer passage on the roads after curfew. Ski had used an offline computer and printer and photo shop to give everyone a set of the paperwork in different names. Bill leafed through the papers as the others set up the walk through.

They had a couple of different sized wood blocks that represented the county plow dump truck, the getaway truck that Ski and Max would drive and the backup getaway vehicle Roger, Doug and Tom would be driving.

Ski had a mechanical timer for the fougasse and had it rigged so they could wire it into the cab of the Plow truck. It would give John two minutes to run clear while yelling fire and getting the soldiers to run from the depot. Just enough time to hopefully escape the blast envelope, but not to give anyone any time to go investigate what was really happening.

They were still waiting for Roger to get back with John for the final walk through, the next night it would be snowing and they decided that would be the day. Roger was running late so they were working through their parts of the plan.

Without John there, Tom pushed the big block representing the plow down the streets, through the check point and into the depot. The two getaway vehicles followed the plow at a distance in case there was a problem. Ski and Doug were noting all the known road blocks and considering what was visible from where.

The driveway alarm went off and Ski grabbed an AR and went to the monitor to make sure it was just Roger. He then went and opened the door for a harried looking Roger.

"Where's John?" Doug asked.

"Nobody knows, his wife, the guys at the bar I know he hangs out. He seems to have disappeared sometime this afternoon."

"Damnit." Doug said.

Roger looked at Bill.

"If he's been disappeared, do you think he'll talk, Bill?"

"No, no way."

"People always talk, it's just a matter of time." Ski said looking back to the fougasse covered by the tarp.

"Then we go tonight." Bill said.

"How?" Snickered Ski. "We're dead in the water. What we need to be doing is getting the hell out of here and getting everyone to one of Max's safe houses. John never knew details on any of that."

"No, we can still do this." Bill insisted. "Everyone thinks I'm dead, no one is looking for me. I know how to get the truck, I know how to drive it, I know how to get into the depot."

"Yeah, nice try there, Bill." Doug crossed his arms skeptically. "This whole thing is predicated on having two good feet. Do you really think you can drive like that? Can you even get up into the cab? Let's say you can manage all that. There's a two-minute timer, we can't extend that any, or someone may try to get in to see what's going on while you're trying to run away yelling 'fire'. I know for a fact you aren't going to be able to get far enough away in two minutes. If you go, this has become a suicide mission and that was never in the cards. Ski is right, this one just didn't work out and we need to worry about compromise and security right now."

"I can go with him." Max said. "I can get him out of there in the two minutes."

"There it is." Ski said. "That's the final piece of the puzzle for you. For all we know, you're the reason John got rolled up, Valencour." Ski was nearly yelling.

"If I was still working for them, what would be the point of letting it get this far, Ski? It's not like they care about evidence or building a case. The law, the Constitution doesn't exist here anymore. If I was working for them, you all would have disappeared weeks ago."

Doug looked at the men around the room. He thought a moment, then spoke.

"If he does talk, it probably won't be immediately. If this goes tonight, the chaos it causes might help us get out of here and before compromise sets in on us. Max are you sure you can get him far enough away in two minutes?

"Yeah, I do Crossfit."

"That's a lie." Ski said bluntly. Everyone looked at him. "If he did Crossfit, he'd have told us by now... They can't help themselves, they're as bad as vegetarians and fighter pilots."

Doug gave Ski a quick scowl and continued.

"Bill, I have to tell you I'm worried about infection in that foot, can you really drive that thing?"

"I've driven hurt before, once with a broken ankle... well I didn't know it was broken at the time, but that hurt a lot too. Look, I know the codes to access the trucks and the keys, John said they still haven't changed any of that stuff. If somebody sees me, they may not even give it a whole lot of thought. The feds thought I was dead so it's not like my face was ever up on a wanted poster or anything. Heck, people are afraid of even talking about people who've disappeared. If someone does see me, I'll just tell them I had an accident. We get the truck and we're out of there. I'll tell them Max is a new guy I'm training. They won't have time to look into it. We blow the depot and we head for a safe house. Totally doable."

*   *   *

He couldn't kneel any longer.

It hurt too much.

But, Sheriff Grant Taylor still prayed. He had no tears left, they gave him just barely enough water.

He felt his strength diminishing with his limited rations.

He knew, they knew, at this point he wouldn't provide any valuable information. He knew, at some point, if they really wanted to commit the resources and the energy, he would have to give them something. He knew, they knew, it would either be made up names or the names of criminals who had played the system and won. He had given thought to those names, the ones who had navigated the "justice" system and walked away with little or no price paid. He had been thinking of that list of names.

What they didn't know, was that when he prayed upon it, the Sheriff couldn't give those names either. That would fall into the purview of vengeance. As a lawman, the Sheriff had been tempted by that on occasion, when he saw the system faltering or outright failing. As a Christian, he knew better. As an American he wanted better. He took comfort in knowing God would take care of that... eventually.

Taylor shook his head and prayed for strength and patience. Sometimes God took a long time, but the Sheriff understood upon whose timeline he really had to work.

The saddest part was that he felt done here, that this cold, dark, damp quiet place would be where it would end. It wasn't his place to know what purpose he served the Lord here. He thought maybe it took resources from somewhere else. Maybe even diverted evil long enough that maybe it couldn't take firm root in the County.

That thought brought the beginnings of a smile to his pained face.

Maybe that was it. His place in the Plan. It's just the ending wasn't as he imagined.

It sure wasn't down to his last magazine in blazing firefight with an overwhelming force of outlaws with no back up nearby. It wasn't holding a baby up just long enough in a rain swollen river.

He almost even laughed at all that.

It would be here, now, then. He looked around at the dank surroundings. It would be here and no one would know and all he had left to give them would be lies. That was, perhaps, what he was most disappointed in. That his life would end with a lie. He imagined them getting more creative with the interrogations and in imagining it, he saw himself giving them a final piece of his mind before it finally became too much for his body and spirit to hold out. That at least he could go out with a fiery defiance.

But, that wasn't the way these sorts of things really ended.

There was no point dwelling on that. Being a Christian wasn't about pearly gates and beautiful angels. Sometimes it was about suffering and enduring until the very end. That was where he was now. He could feel it. Like something creeping into him.

"One hundred seventy-three, right, left, right, right"
He heard it more as the soldier's voice in his head than as his own. *"Ninety-two, left, left."*

No, that was a lie too.

Some kind of psychological manipulation of the variety of false firing squads and such. Just a mind game to try to make him hopeful that there would be a rescue and that when it never came it would be soul crushing.

No, not his soul. He knew their games, and his soul was girded with the armor of God.

For some reason though, he just kept thinking it.

"Beach, ninety-two, left, left... Ramp, "One hundred seventy-three, right, left, right, right"

*   *   *

Everyone was waiting for Max and Bill to get back with the truck, to load up the fougasse and get things started. Roger and Doug busied themselves making sandwiches in the kitchen. Ski noticed Tom had quietly disappeared.

He found Tom sitting on the tractor seat reading his Bible.

"Everything OK, Tom?"

Tom nodded.

"It's OK to be nervous before something like this, Tom." Ski noticed Tom had his HK leaned against the wheel fairing of the Kubota.

Tom closed his Bible.

"I'm sorry, Tom. I didn't mean to disturb you, just checkin'."

"Are you nervous, Ski?"

"Little bit."

"Worried the fougasse won't go off?"

Ski shook his head.

"No, that'll go off, of that I'm sure. Just need to get it in position, that's the tricky part."

"What is that thing on the front of the drum of the fougasse?"

"That's an EFP, Tom. Explosively Formed Penetrator. In the sequence of the explosion, the way it's configured, you get a molten copper slug coming out ahead of the fire ball. That'll penetrate the thick rubber fuel blivet. The fougasse itself is a huge incendiary device. One blivet goes, vapor, heat, fragmentation sets most of the others off as well. Should be quite a show."

"Did you do the same stuff my Dad did in the Army, Ski?"

Ski smiled and shook his head a little.

"Oh, it's safe to say your Dad was next level stuff to me. Heck, I knew some of the original folks who went into that unit when they first started it, back in the day. That's how far back I go."

"This is going to start a war isn't it, Ski?"

"War already started, Tom. This is just us letting them know we're fighting back, that somebody is out there finally making a stand."

Tom nodded thoughtfully.

"I wonder what it will be like after."

"Hard to say, Tom. This isn't like any other war this country has been involved in."

"I don't think it will be like the Civil War, Ski. Maybe the Revolutionary War."

"Well, it sure won't be the blue and the grey clearly defined, that's for certain. But the American Revolution was different too. They got a lot of help from the outside, Tom. I don't think anyone's coming to help us."

"We'll have help." Tom said with a surprisingly confident smile.

The driveway alarm went off and they each grabbed their carbines as they went to make sure it was Bill and Max in the plow truck. Assured it was them, Ski turned on all the lights as Bill was expertly backing the truck around in the confined space of the driveway. Backing up to the bay, Ski mounted the tractor. He had already scooped the fork lift on the front loader under the fougasse assembly and as soon as the diesel was up to speed, he was lifting it into the dump of the yellow county truck. Roger and Doug were standing by to strap it in place.

Tom went to the cab, where Bill seemed to be forcing a smile through a whole lot of pain. He opened the door.

"I'm not getting out now, Tom, getting in was the worst part. But could you go get me an empty Gatorade bottle?"

"Empty Gatorade bottle?"

"For... You know."

"Oh, right."

Max had hopped out to watch the loading and securing of the fougasse and then quickly returned to the cab. Bill noticed he seemed to have an interest in operating heavy equipment and Bill enjoyed sharing his knowledge.

"It's sitting kind of high back there. You'll need to tilt the dump several degrees to make sure that EFP hits the blivet directly. How will you do that?"

"Oh, that's easy, just this lever here."

Max took his place in the passenger seat again and watched in the mirror as Doug and Roger had scampered into the dump. Even over the idling diesels of the truck and the tractor, he could hear the big ratchet straps tightening on the incendiary device.

In the mirror, Max saw Ski walking up to his door with something in his hand.

Max opened the door and Ski handed the little wired box to him. It was two switches, roughly labeled with tape and Sharpie. *Safe* and *Arm*.

"Hitting safe gives you continuity, that red light will come on. Hit arm and the timer is started and the red light will start blinking, you'll have two minutes. May want to make sure you have him out of the vehicle and in a position to move before you hit arm."

"Will do." Max half yelled over all the noise.

"And Max, don't do anything that will make me have to hunt you down and kill you."

"I assure you, that won't be necessary."

"You guys get to the end of the driveway and we'll follow you then to give you a reasonable lead. How were the roads? Any new road blocks?"

"No. Roads are quiet tonight."

"Alright. Good luck, Max." Ski adjusted the AR on its sling over his shoulder as he helped close the big passenger side door.

On the other side, Doug was checking on Bill.

"It was easy, there was nobody at the shop."

"That's not what I meant Bill, how are *you* feeling?"

"I'm good, Doug. Really. I can do this. I took some more of the meds you gave me."

Tom broke into the conversation, passing the empty Gatorade bottle to Bill.

"Thanks, Tom."

"We'll be just behind you guys. We'll see you about when all the fireworks start."

Bill smiled at Tom's optimism, gave a final wordless nod to Doug and swung his door shut.

"Well, Max, this is it."

Max nodded.

"Do you want to take care of that first." He said half pointing at the Gatorade bottle.

"Ya' know, now that we got that bomb loaded a few feet behind us, I suddenly don't really feel like I need to go. I just want to get this done now."

Putting the truck in gear, he used his good foot on the accelerator, it was awkward but he was making it work. It was well after midnight and a dark, dark night. The headlights swept across the empty highway as they turned from Ski's driveway. It was mostly cloudy with a half moon that attempted to poke through the clouds at times.

Both men were silent until just before the edge of town when Max spoke with a commanding voice.

"Pull over and stop, Bill."

"What do you mean?" Bill looked over to see Valencour leveling a pistol at him.

*　　*　　*

"Why are they stopping?" Roger was sitting beside Ski in the old Chevy Duramax. He had replaced Max in the primary getaway vehicle. He was subconsciously gripping the AR that sat beside his leg, thumb resting on the safety.

"Damnit Valencour!" Ski slammed on his steering wheel as he drove slowly past the plow truck. Bill was facing Valencour and they had no idea what was happening. "I knew it! I knew we couldn't trust that sonofabitch!"

Ski took his foot off the accelerator but didn't hit the brakes, the slow deceleration of the vehicle would attract less attention than sudden brake light flare would. Ski scanned the highway and nearby intersecting crossroads for headlights, or any sign of feds or military.

"What do we do?" Roger asked.

"Bracket 'em… is all I can think. We're lead now, Doug and Tom will fall in tail end Charlie. Then we just see what happens next." Ski was shaking his head and trying to suppress the anger that he knew would cloud his thoughts.

*   *   *

"What do you mean get out?"

"I mean get out or I'll kill you." Max spoke in a firm even tone and he held the SIG pistol like he meant it. "Look kid, I've done a lot of bad in my life, this wouldn't come close to the worst and wouldn't bother me a bit. I'll waste you and slide your carcass out of that seat on to the cold road below."

"I don't believe you'll kill me, Max. You're a better man than that, a better man than you think. I don't know what you did in your past but the man you are now won't kill me."

In the glow of the instrument lights Bill saw Max smirk a little.

"OK. Actually, I don't need to kill you, kid, just wound you enough to distract you so I can shove your big cornfed ass out from behind the wheel."

"Well, I confess, I do believe you're still mean enough to do that."

"You know it. We both know you aren't doing well enough to get to safety in two minutes. Forget the foot, you're sweating and feverish. The infection is back. Now get out of this truck before you have to worry about more than just how much foot you have left. You still have a chance in this life, kid. You get out of here and save what's left of that foot. Let me go and try to save what's left of my soul."

*   *   *

"What the…" Doug exclaimed as they saw Bill's figure fall out of the driver's side of the truck into a crumple on the ground. A fraction of a moment later the big truck was under way again. Around Bill's body, it swerved into the travel lane obscuring the tail lights of Ski's pickup truck further ahead.

Before he could really process it all, Tom was out of the Blazer beside him and running to Bill. Doug drove slowly up to the scene and hopped out to help Tom drag Bill back to the seat. They got the man wedged in behind the front seat and the door frame and he was groaning. Doug looked up and down the road for other traffic, all he saw were the two trucks ahead departing. He ran around to the driver's side again, got in the back seat himself and pulled from under Bill's arms.

"You're a bigger guy than I realized, Bill, give us a little help here."

It was a struggle, but they got Bill into the back seat as he growled with pain.

Doug hopped back to the driver's seat and threw it in gear, following the plow truck.

"What is going on, Bill, what happened?" Tom asked.

"Max took my ID and kicked me out… it's like a suicide mission for him. He wanted me to have a chance."

*   *   *

The sentry half looked at the ID and didn't bother telling the old man that his finger was half covering it. Max had counted on the peril of complacency and the power of a warm confident smile on a cold night when a soldier really wanted to be just about anywhere else.

He drove the truck slowly through the serpentine of T-walls, Hescos and razor wire. Something like this was only going to work once. The feds hadn't encountered any real resistance yet and they were short on manpower and long on bad decisions.

Once fully into the depot, he drove past the fueling station to a blivet that would be easy to back into. As he did so, he raised the dump, aiming the deadly, fiery IED at the big rubber fuel bladder. He hit the safety button and the red light came on, he quickly hit the arm button and the red light flashed.

Outside the truck, he could hear someone yelling. He jumped down with SIG in hand to address the soldier running at him from the fueling station.

"Fire! Fire! It's gonna blow! RUN!!!" Max yelled with a fearful voice as loud as he could so anyone might hear. He had his pistol hidden behind his leg, but as the young soldier continued running as if he was trying to help, he raised it toward his face.

"Turn around and run as quickly away from here as you can, this isn't worth you dying over, tell everyone to run."

The soldier's hands went up reflexively and he looked confused as he started backpedaling before turning to break into a run.

Max looked around. Another soldier rounded the corner near the entrance, but the panicked kid yelling at him got him turned around quickly. Max sighed as he walked to the back of the truck and posted there. He hoped no one else came, at this point they might not have time to escape.

He lowered his head and clasped his hands around the Sig.

"God... I don't even know how to do this. Forgive me, I don't know where to start..."

*   *   *

It seemed to Ski, to be a long time from when he watched the truck enter the control point from his rear-view mirror, to the time he saw the first soldiers running away. Then an even longer two minutes before the first flash. Then, his trained ear was barely able to discern the crack of the initiating charges of the fougausse and the EFP followed by the WHOOMF sound and the deep in the chest concussion of the blast wave. No doubt they would feel the heat if they were outside as the wave rocked the three-quarter ton truck a little on its suspension. The light filled the mirror and the fireballs quickly expanded more than he could see from within the vehicle. But there was no need to get out and gawk.

In fact, as Doug and the Blazer pulled up beside him and waved for him to drive on, he already had the truck in gear and knew that Max Valencour was never coming out of that alive and that he had misjudged the man. A lot of people had misjudged Max Valencour really, but none so much as Valencour had himself.

*   *   *

Because he would never ask his men to do anything he wouldn't do himself, Todd was scheduled for the first week of night duty on Booth's PSD. He couldn't help but smile when the towering fireballs went up a few miles away, outside the windshield of his up-armored Suburban.

When the sound and concussion reached them, it gave everything a resounding shake and left dogs barking and car alarms going off in a ripple through the area. Todd walked casually to the front door of the house Booth had secured for himself as the sound of the explosions began echoing off the mountains.

Booth opened the door with significant bed head, wearing a wooly robe and carrying a Glock like a vestigial appendage.

"What was that?" He asked, suddenly awake.

"That would be your fuel depot, I imagine."

"What? How... wha..."

Todd just laughed at his stammering.

"There's nothing funny about this, Todd. Your time is short here, I can tell you."

"You have no idea. I'm pulling my guys first thing in the morning. The stupid has officially outweighed the deposit. You might as well have lit that match yourself, Booth. You handed this to them. They *had* to do this."

Booth stammered again, just watching the roiling fireballs climb skyward and turning the area nearly into day.

"Yeah, you demanded to have some of the highest trained guys you have babysit you day and night. Four guys a shift. Four shifts a day with a couple guys off. Plus, all the uniformed soldiers you pulled to protect your office. At least twenty-five guys a day to protect you from a pigeon. This..." He waved back to a now illuminated mushroom cloud. "This is all you bud. They had to pull resources from everywhere else. You got sentries falling asleep standing up 'cause you're not managing your manpower. You are pushing these people into a corner and you leave a target like that wide open. Great job Regional Public Safety Administrator... *RIPSAW*, yeah."

Booth steamed and nearly screamed as he spoke.

"These idiots have no idea the hell they've unleashed, this is insane!"

"You know, I bet they're saying the same thing about you, the ones who are out there that just got away with this. They're going back and thinking about what an idiot you are and what hell *they're* gonna unleash now... and I think *they're* right, Booth."

"Where are you going, Todd?"

"Me? I told you, me and my guys are going home in the morning, we gotta go pack. I wouldn't bother packing if I were you though, Booth. You're probably headed to one of those camps you're so fond of. That's how it works in this mess we've allowed to happen. Hell, you might be cell mates with that Sheriff you put there." Todd shook his head and smiled. "Nah, I imagine that guy would eat you alive."

*　　*　　*

Frank Boggs followed Barney as the dog ran barking toward the door. The dog started barking not at the flash, but with the shake of the house. His wife and daughters met him on the porch as they watched the fireballs rising from the distant horizon.

"Nukes, Dad?" The ten-year old sounded a little terrified as she said it.

"Nah, Kate." Boggs managed a reassuring laugh, but it wasn't helping a lot. "Nothing around here anyone wants to nuke, that's down by the airport."

"Plane crash?" His wife asked.

"Don't know, I just probably need to go get ready. They'll be calling soon."

As he turned to go in the door, Marjorie Taylor was coming out. He saw the reflection of the distant, still rising fireballs in the window beside the door and could see the flicker of it in Marj's eyes.

"It's bad, Frank, isn't it?"

"It's going to be, yeah."

*   *   *

The Sheriff hardly rolled over when the door scraped open. It was the interrogator's usual routine and the sound of the metal chair squeaking open and being set down on the cold floor. But then there was a second chair set down and he heard, or just kind of sensed the movement of two people.

Grant half rolled over just enough and saw another man seated next to the interrogator. The new man wore a green wool great coat and uniform. Squinting, the Sheriff wasn't really sure what he was seeing. And it was earlier than usual.

Too early to expect much of the knee. He rolled back over facing the wall and ignored the new development.

"We have a guest this morning, Taylor."

The Sheriff said nothing.

"You won't talk to me, but I think you might be talking to our guest."

"I've been talking." The Sheriff offered.

"You have been playing games." The other voice spoke with a thick accent and a harsh tone. "Playing the country bumpkin with your rural anecdotes and cowboy philosophy. I have watched the tapes, you are just filling the air with diversion. The time for that is over, Taylor. Your *posse* has started killing people and destroying infrastructure that threatens the whole county. Your government has no choice now. Your continued silence means more will die, more of the people you were sworn to protect. You *will* tell me what I need to know, Taylor. My methods are different from those used here previously."

The Sheriff rolled over. The knee wouldn't support him so he kind of crawled with his wool blanket to sit with his back against the wall.

"This can't be." The Sheriff shook his head as he saw the man's uniform better, saw the man's facial features. "This is all just another mind game, it has to be." He dropped his face in his palms and sobbed.

"No, Taylor. I told you. Time for games is past. This is your new reality and the sooner you embrace it, the less people have to die."

*　　*　　*

The trail was steep with lots of switch backs, but as it leveled off they found what they were looking for just inside the tree line. A rocky outcropping that provided good cover and concealment but was open to the east with a tremendous, near aerial, view of town. Tom had led them there. It was a trail his family had hiked when he was much younger when they lived in town.

Doug and Ski were pretty well winded and they lay prone behind their packs. Doug had a big pair of binoculars and Ski had a powerful spotting scope. Something was still smoking significantly at the fuel depot even hours later and there was lots of activity at homes immediately surrounding it. People were being herded out of their homes and directly walked to the airport ramp and waiting C-130s.

"What are they doing, Ski?"

"Well, they're kicking those folks out of their homes."

"I don't see any blast damage." Doug said.

"Expanding their security perimeter, I imagine."

"So, do you think those people are being disappeared?"

"Probably and worse than that, Doug... Look up at that northmost house. Those crates they're carrying in..."

"What is it, Ski?"

314

"Explosives. They're gonna blow all those houses, go full on false flag on this. Those people disappear, they have images of all those houses blasted, we're on the hook for a bunch of civilian casualties. All over the Telescreen, all over the news outside the enclave."

"Damn."

"It's gonna get a whole lot worse before it gets any better."

Doug was scanning the area around the northern house that was being set for demolition.

"Hey, Ski. What are those weird armored cars one street north of that house? That doesn't look like ours, that looks like something foreign."

Tom watched as Ski repositioned and noticed he kind of looked startled.

"WZ-551s, Type 92s specifically."

Doug lowered his binoculars and looked sideways at Ski.

"Is that Canadian?"

"Guess again, Doug."

"That sounds like… No, way, Ski. Are you sure?"

"I was a First Group guy. That was our area of responsibility. Armor recognition was part of that; I've kind of just kept up with it as a hobby. That is no doubt a Type 92. Look closer, you can see the markings."

"That makes zero sense, Ski."

"What is it?" Tom asked, noting Doug's concern.

"It makes sense if you are familiar with General Smedley Butler, guys." Ski just shook his head and pulled away from the spotting scope. *"War is a racket."*

"But we're at war with *them!*" Doug said loudly, pointing down at what he didn't want to believe.

"*Some* of us are at war with *some* of them, Doug. *Some* of us and *some* of them profit greatly from this. We're being played."

"What is going on? What are you guys talking about?"

Doug and Ski looked back at Tom, Doug didn't even want to verbalize the conclusion they had just formed. Ski filled in the blanks.

"PLA, Tom. People's Liberation Army. It's the Communist Chinese army, Tom. It appears they are assisting the feds."

CHAPTER 11

It was more food than he'd seen all at once since he'd arrived in this place. The first time he'd sat in a chair too. But he was strangely without appetite and for some reason, the folding metal chair was terribly uncomfortable. He attributed that to loss of fat and muscle mass.

This time the Chinese officer was without the interpreter, but behind him, stood an assistant, another Chinese officer of some kind, but Taylor didn't know anything about the PLA rank structure.

The food on the table between them *looked* good, it certainly *smelled* good. But Sheriff Grant Taylor had no appetite. The Chinese man sat with arms folded and a smile across his face.

Taylor sat slumped, his lame knee as straight as he could get it. He wasn't yet defeated, but he was ready for it all to be done.

"It makes no difference if you eat this meal or not." The Chinese officer said. "It makes no difference to me if you live or you die. Tomorrow everything changes for you. Nourishment might be good now. But, really, to me, you are not as important as some here seem to think you are. To me, your former position, your title, even your name matter none. To me, you are just prisoner number six I must deal with. This mythos of the *Western* Sheriff, the *Constitutional* Sheriff. These are archaic absurdities in the coming world order. And really if they *ever* existed the way you see them, they are a thing that has been dead a hundred years. Your whole culture, your values, really, they are all a lie. You will see."

The officer pulled out a tablet from within the inner pocket of his great coat. It was the same type the interrogator always had.

He tapped around with the stylus and turned it around for him to watch a video compilation being played. A massive explosion, some kind of terrible conflagration and when the daylight images of the destruction appeared, he recognized it as being somewhere near the airport, but much had been changed. Then the photos of badly charred bodies appeared, some tragically small.

The officer spoke without emotion in a smooth voice with English that rarely faltered. He was well educated, well trained and very disciplined.

"This is the handiwork of your *posse* now. This is what they do, they are terrorist mongrels. Last count I heard was 130 dead, but they are still finding bodies and some may never be found. I won't bore you with the ah… breakdown. Numbers of women and children. I really don't think you care. You *Christians* have a history of slaughter, don't you? You and the Muslims both. You all conspired to murder, to massacre over 200 million of my countrymen when you took down that dam. If a full count is ever made it could be the death toll is equivalent to the population of your entire *country*. My wife and daughters among them."

"Yet, you genuflect in your zealotry to your God many hours of the day, I have watched the tapes. You Christians claim to be all about love and forgiveness and redemption. I don't believe you even have it for each other."

The officer paused finally, just long enough to shake his head in disgust.

"So, the 130 and counting of your county don't matter to me, but the terrible secret is, that I know, *they don't matter to you.* You let these religious terrorists loose, you let them run rampant without consequence. I have no doubt you cheered when you heard the news of the Three Gorges Dam destruction."

Taylor just looked at the creamy chicken alfredo and broccoli before him. A good nourishing meal. It could give him energy to resist. It could give him energy to prolong whatever torture the man on the other side of table had in mind for him. It could be poisoned or drugged.

It would look great planted all over the PLA officer's face. He smiled inwardly at that thought. Not sure he had the energy to smile visibly, much less the energy for one last act of defiance.

No, he wouldn't eat. And he wouldn't respond. And as best he could, he wouldn't even listen to all the things this man was saying. While it was hard to always tell what the truth was in this world, Taylor still knew lies when he heard them.

*   *   *

Roger had been tending to Bill and loading the ¾ ton Chevy while Ski, Doug and Tom went on the scouting trip. When they arrived, there was an urgent vigor applied to loading the vehicles and getting ready to move out.

"I don't get it, we're at war with China." Roger said with loaded ammo cans in each hand as he headed to the truck.

"Here, Roger." Ski was showing him pictures they had taken with the digital camera. The telephoto lens wasn't great, but it was clear to Roger the armor wasn't anything he recognized as belonging to the US military. He shook his head as he continued loading. Doug was loading cases of MREs and Ski put the camera away in the Blazer to grab water.

"I've got some additional rifles to grab and somebody needs to fill those jerry cans with fuel from the tank outside, diesel, these trucks are both diesels."

"I'll get that, how many do we want filled?" Tom was finishing loading some of the boxes he'd been directed to load.

"As many as we have or where ever you're at in a half hour, we need to get rolling." Doug said. Tom heard the level of concern in his voice. It hadn't been there before.

"Does anyone have any idea where we are going?" Ski asked.

Doug paused a moment before answering.

"I know right where to go, but we don't want to show up empty-handed anywhere."

*   *   *

The Chinese officer looked down at the untouched plate.

"We will be moving you to the new facility tomorrow. Your conditions will remain relatively unchanged, but I will have a more… professional environment for my work."

Taylor looked at the plate and then finally at the man's face, into his dark eyes. The man smiled and the Sheriff looked down at his straight and pain filled knee. How much energy would it really take? What he wanted most was to launch off the chair with blinding speed and enough power that he could send the whole little table skyward, humiliate the man and really hurt him all at once.

But, that was sheer fantasy and he knew it.

Taylor looked down at the plate. If he played it right however...

"You Americans are so wasteful. I was told, when you would have been young, your parents would have admonished you for leaving a plate full of food to go to waste when children in my country were starving... In those days it was true, we had little. But our people had more appreciation and respect for those that provided. And now as we begin to take our rightful place of proper leadership in the world, you try to starve us again with this treacherous dam attack and your support of the separatists in Taipei. Now, your rich country is in disarray. Your men are infantile and weak, your women are confused and presumptuous. Half of you don't even know what bathroom to use! Ha! The world laughs at you. This illusion of American leadership and superiority is finally unveiled for what it is, what it truly has been all along. Another myth, a Hollywood screenplay. Now we have to come to your country to properly manage your resources, to establish social and cultural morality, to show you how to control your spoiled population."

The Sheriff sighed. He pulled the flimsy little table closer. There was no silverware, just a plastic spork. He inhaled the aroma of the meal.

"For what it's worth, I'm sorry about your family, and the suffering of the innocent, it's a terrible thing." The Sheriff pulled the plate a little closer, trying to conceal the fact that, as best he could, he was coiling energy like a spring. "You're right, it would be wrong to let this go to waste."

Diminished muscles, unnourished and dehydrated core almost resisted him, but Sheriff Grant Taylor's spirit fired off like a priming charge. Summoning the very last bit of physical defiance he could, he rose quickly out of the chair and launched the plate at the officer's face.

It wasn't enough.

The officer was quick, and Taylor hadn't the energy to get the plate high enough. Still, it glanced off the shoulder of his great coat leaving a mess.

The officer's feckless assistant, or whatever he was, seemed to clutch at the officer from behind, but it wasn't clear to Taylor whether the man was trying to pull the officer out of the way or hide behind him. For a soldier, the assistant seemed shocked by the American's violence.

Taylor stayed painfully on his feet but he wanted to collapse, the pained knee wanting to buckle.

The officer looked at the mess on his shoulder and looked up grinning.

"Good, you will have plenty of energy for our first session tomorrow." He called over his shoulder but the door was already scraping open. "Guards!"

The four American soldiers charged in, two peeling off to escort the PLA soldiers out, two predictably grabbing Taylor under the arms and pinning him to the wall. He found the familiar eyes over their masks. The soldiers looked back over their shoulders and the one leaned in close to the Sheriff's ear as he made a show of slugging him in the gut.

"It will happen soon and it will happen fast, remember *one if by air, two if by sea.*"

Taylor absorbed the blow to the stomach as if hurt more than what it really did, but he wasn't sure what the guy was saying.

"What, what do you mean?"

"*One if by air, two if by sea…* You'll understand as it happens."

*   *   *

The Mennonite held a Remington 7600 across his chest as the two vehicles pulled into the drive in front of his house.

"You must leave immediately, none of you are welcome here." Johann was yelling before Doug and the others even had their doors open enough to step out. "Go, you are not welcome here, none of you."

"Whoa, whoa." Doug had his hands up, leaving his carbine on the floor of the Chevy and his Beretta concealed under his insulated shirt. "Hey, man. I want to see my family and we have an injured man."

"No, after what you and your militia have done, absolutely not... I will not expect your wife and daughters to vacate, I see them as widow and orphans, for they will be soon."

"Aw, come on..." Doug shook his head and Ski took over, his hands raised also with no visible weapons.

"Sir, what have you heard?"

"Your reckless and unnecessary bombing of the fuel depot has killed hundreds and more will perish because there won't be fuel to provide food and heat to people who are already approaching desperation."

"Sir, I don't know where you heard that, but it's untrue, completely false."

"Word is all over the county about this, you and all of your militia are wanted and I should turn you in for all you have killed."

"Only one man died as a result of our action. It was Max Valencour and he died so no one else would."

The bearded man lowered the muzzle of the pump action rifle.

"And we're not a militia." Ski added.

"What are you?"

"We're the resistance, just like you."

"Valencour is dead?"

"Yes. We were very careful about how and when we carried out that attack, specifically to minimize casualties. They are lying about it, we did a post strike battle damage assessment. The feds were blowing up houses the next morning, all we hit was the fuel."

"Fuel that people needed as another storm approaches."

"Do the people need the government to take care of them, Sir? Or do they just need each other?"

Johann cradled his rifle as he pondered Ski's words and Tom stepped out of the back of the Chevy.

"Sir," Said Tom. "For what it's worth, I was there for the BDA and all the planning and you should also know, after the fuel depot went up, there were Chinese military vehicles on scene. It's not just about *our* government tyranny any more, it's way deeper than that."

"Chinese?"

"He's right, Johann." Doug offered. "We weren't close enough to see what kind of strength or have any idea of the depth of their involvement, but they are in the county."

"But, we're at war with the Chinese?"

"Unless they already won." Ski suggested. "We're only getting information we're being fed, maybe we lost a long time ago and all the news we've been fed has been a lie. It's more important now than ever to work together and see past their lies."

Johann nodded more and slung his rifle.

Hannah appeared on the front porch and stepped tentatively down the steps. Johann saw Tom notice and he smiled a little and turned a little to the girl.

"Oh, come on." He waved her toward Tom.

"Hi." Tom waved and she waved back from a more than respectable distance.

"Doug, you could stay here with your family. They have been very helpful, even those cats. I do not understand this idea of keeping cats in a house, but the cats have been catching mice in the guest house. I do not have room for anyone else and the increased activity might raise suspicion."

Ski looked at Doug, then back to Bill who was asleep in the passenger seat of the Blazer, where Roger stood with the driver's door open.

"Where else can we go?" Ski asked Johann.

"You can go to the Indian."

"Well, I appreciate your offer, Johann. I think I better stay with these guys for now, I'll spend a few minutes with Bianca and the girls and we'll be on our way. Is there any other place we can go? Randy was pretty rough."

"It'll be OK." Tom asserted. "We can go there. Randy's a good man, he just doesn't know it yet."

*　　*　　*

Todd and his team were packing up their Suburbans. The S-92s were technically on a different contract and try as he might, they weren't able to catch a ride out on them. He'd had to make a few vehicle manning changes, mostly because Chambers was trying to get away from Paulsen and his incessant talking.

Booth was in Zites' office again. He ignored the contractors when he walked into the building, very specifically evading Todd's gaze.

The armor of the Suburbans took up a little extra space and they were only just able to fit all their gear and personal equipment in, which was good because Todd didn't want to go to Booth or Zites to request transport of anything.

He was just closing the rear hatch when he heard the armored vehicles approaching. Todd turned to watch them roll by. It was a type with which he was unfamiliar, but he knew what the prominent gold bordered red star meant. The vehicles parked in line in front of the building and Zites and Booth came out beaming to meet their new guests.

Todd couldn't help himself as the Chinese men in modern body armor dismounted with slung Type 95 bullpup rifles and approached Zites and Booth.

Todd walked up as they were all shaking hands.

"You got a minute, Booth?" It wasn't really a question as Todd's unshakeable grip wrapped around the bureaucrat's bicep. He dragged him not so discreetly away while Zites entertained the Chinese.

Inside the glass doors, Todd leaned in close.

"You, ah, wanna explain this? Last intel report I read, like yesterday, we, as in United States military forces are engaged in combat with the PLA."

Booth looked down at his bicep, aching still after Todd released it, and spoke with unhidden contempt.

"Not PLA, Todd. PAP, People's Armed Police. I guess I could see where you might miss the distinction."

"Um, all under CCP, right? Chinese Communists assuming a position of authority of some kind here?"

"Perhaps it's a little complicated, Todd. You're not read in on the whole picture and really you just need to stay in your lane."

"Oh, really." Todd nodded looking out at the crowd of foreign uniforms. "Huh."

Todd didn't say another word, he opened the door and stepped smartly back to his men. They were gathered looking at the line of the six wheeled Chinese military vehicles and Todd stood in the middle of them.

"Guys, let's go someplace private where we can talk. I may have been a little premature in my thinking, there may still be some work here for us…"

*   *   *

The sky cracked as though the heavens were torn, he felt tossed on the floor with the thin mattress. The reverberation brought concrete dust and pebbles down from the ceiling. The sound trailed off with a tearing roar, an unzippering of the atmosphere, the thunder of a single jet in full afterburner.

Sheriff Grant Taylor rolled off the mattress, trying to get up and make sense of whatever just woke him up and shook his world. His mind was fogged with fatigue and the torments that had so reduced him over the last few weeks, *months*? He didn't know.

It was a jet, flying low and fast… and it was a sonic boom.

A single sonic boom.

One if by air…

As the pieces were coming together, the gunfire started. Some distant, then some very near until some was right outside the door. He heard the crumple of a body there, then the scraping of the door opening.

The Sheriff saw the familiar eyes, now without the mask.

"One if by air… we go to the ramp?"

"That's it, Sheriff. Remember the paces and turns," The soldier was sliding under the Sheriff's arm to help him out of his cell. "I may not be able to stay with you, you know your way to the ramp."

Stepping over the body of a guard he had just killed in the hallway, he helped the Sheriff get his feet under him.

They didn't get far when there was movement at the far end of the hallway. The soldier braced his carbine against his shoulder with one hand and fired a burst, still supporting the Sheriff. The sound of the full auto burst battered the Sheriff's unprotected ears and gunpowder burned in his nostrils. A shower of expended brass bounced off the wall beside them and tinkled to the floor. One man dropped at the other end, but he was followed by more movement.

"Go, Sheriff, Go!"

Staggering with the pain but sustained by an unexpected surge of adrenaline, the Sheriff counted his paces and made his turns. The gun fire continued behind him, and it was elsewhere on the base, too. And there was a sound of jets and then the unmistakable growl of a Vulcan gun spewing 20mm fire on a target.

The soldier caught up with the Sheriff again, grabbing him and dragging him along as he led with his carbine. When they got to the door, other soldiers had just opened it to make entry and somehow, the man who broke the Sheriff out, recognized them as his. That was when the Sheriff saw the red engineering tape they all wore on their arms and headgear.

The Sheriff was passed off and hauled out the door into the cold morning air, it was just after dawn and the Sheriff saw an F-16 arcing around initiating a strafing run as its Vulcan unleashed again.

The morning sky was a cold grey and the soldiers were pointing to something off the darker side of the field, what must be the west. A large four engine airplane loomed in the distance, something a little out of time and place, or maybe not.

"There's our ride." One of the men shouted. "We got the others out?"

"They're coming, I'll go make sure."

A second F-16 rolled in on a gun run and the Sheriff got the sense they were laying down containment fire. More soldiers came out of what now appeared to be an old ammunition bunker or something. They were dragging others who had to be prisoners. They all looked underfed and a little disoriented.

Bullets cracked the air and impacted the concrete beside the Sheriff and he dropped to the ground.

"Contact left!" Someone yelled as they returned fire. Two soldiers advanced aggressively toward the direction of the incoming rounds and fired when they had targets.

"Come on you old bird!" Someone yelled and the Sheriff looked out to see the four engine propeller driven airplane, looking like a World War II bomber, closer to the end of the old runway, but still not there yet.

F-16s criss-crossed overhead. No wonder this all took so long to put together, the Sheriff thought. He allowed himself a smile. For now, at least, he was free. This was no trick, this was rebellion against tyranny. There was no faking the dead men falling. Lines had been crossed, too many had been pushed too far.

Smoke rolled off the wheels of the four-engine airplane as it touched down at the far end of the old runway. The roar of the big radials could begin to be heard over the gunfire that was becoming more sporadic.

The timeworn DC-6 taxied up to the ramp, which the Sheriff now realized was more of a turnaround at one end of the unmaintained runway. With the four engines running, belching exhaust, the airplane spun in the turn around as the cargo door opened. The propwash made it difficult to get to his feet, someone helped the Sheriff up, and then he and the others were dragged through the exhaust and the cyclone of propwash. At least half a dozen men in military tactical gear dropped from the airplane and took up defensive positions. The liberated men were handed, nearly tossed, up to others waiting to receive them.

Roughly dragged aboard, the men were placed in litters and each attended to by pairs of men.

"Are you Sheriff Taylor?"

The Sheriff nodded to the young man kneeling over him and yelling in his ear over the engines.

"I'm Jimmy, we're gonna start some IVs to get you guys hydrated and get you some energy, alright?"

The Sheriff nodded again. Men piled in the cargo door with help from those already aboard, the airplane was moving again and cargo door being hefted closed.

There was a prick in his arm and an IV bag hanging over him. The engines revved up and the airplane accelerated, rotating after what seemed too much time on the ground. Free of the ground, Taylor could feel and hear the pumps and motors driving the landing gear into their wells.

A cheer went up in the dark, austere, tube of the fuselage and a smile broke across the Sheriff's face.

Jimmy gave him a confident nod.

"This thing must be as old as I am, Jimmy."

"They said it was 50's vintage."

"Well, so am I."

Jimmy returned the Sheriff's smile as he checked his blood pressure and slipped an oximeter on his finger.

"How ya' feelin', Sheriff?"

"Better. Lots better."

"I'd imagine."

An older man in a flight suit walked down the aisle and looked down at each of the men, smiling and introducing himself to each of them in turn.

"Sheriff Taylor." He said.

"Yes."

"I'm Colonel Jack Crane, welcome to the revolution."

AUTHOR'S NOTE

In 1946, a small group of veterans rose up to fight against corrupt law enforcement and political officials in what was known by some as the McMinn County War. Fresh off of WWII battlefields the men stood up to corruption that had run unchecked for a decade.

They had fought against tyranny abroad and they weren't going to stand for it at home. First, they attempted to work within the law, putting forth their own candidates to restore order. When they saw the election being stolen out from under them by an entrenched political machine, the veterans took up arms. Twenty men stood against 200 hired guns in badges and the ensuing firefight left some injured but none dead and the kingpin and his henchmen on the run.

Also known as the Battle of Athens, Tennessee, I would recommend the book *The Fighting Bunch: The Battle of Athens And How WWII Veterans Won The Only Successful Armed Rebellion Since The Revolution* by Chris DeRose.

Made in the USA
Coppell, TX
23 May 2023

17201902R00184